W9-CQZ-339

There was no grandfather

and grandson now.

All boundaries had dissolved—

time, place, family.

They were simply two rune readers.

And they were going to shape

the wyrd of the world.

The Runestone Saga

Book III

POSSESSION

CHRIS HUMPHREYS

ALFRED A. KNOPF
NEW YORK

Whitby
Ouse River
Battle of Stamford Bridge
York
Derwent River
Severn River
Stretton
Birmingham
Wenlock Edge
Malvern Hills
ENGLAND
Cambridge
Thames River
London
Battle of Hastings

BATTLE OF HASTINGS
AD 1066

ANGLO SAXONS

NORMANS

Are we walking or
are we talking?

CHAPTER ONE
LOST SOUL

He was halfway there when the crows attacked.

"Eaaaach!" The terrible screech came out of nowhere. Shocked, he twisted toward it . . . just in time to see the razor beak snap shut and strike at his belly.

Wrong! Folding his wings, Sky snatched his stomach away, using his weight to speed his dive . . . into his second mistake. For another crow waited, its talons spread, plunging in to rip a feather from its root.

"Ahh!" he screamed in agony. In the open air, his old hawk enemies would never have caught him like this. A flip and he'd have been gone . . . or turned to kill! But he'd been distracted by his desperation, and now the black devils were straddling him, blocking any escape, their yellow beaks wide and shrieking hatred.

He snatched a wing tip from grasping claws. But they were working as a team; avoiding one, he was driven into the other, its feet wide apart to snatch at him.

He got his own up only just in time. Claw met claw, like wrestlers joining fingers. Yet his opponent was bigger and its talons drove into flesh. Agonized, Sky tried to pull free . . . couldn't. Locked, they fell, twirling round and round, over and down, like some crazed gyroscope. One moment Sky was on top, the city streets rushing up; the next, below—clouds above—the yellow beak opening again in a scream of triumph.

He'd seen crows do this with each other above the fields of Shropshire. A game, he'd thought, because he'd thought as a human. But now that he was a bird himself he knew it was no game. They'd been training for this.

They were going to kill him.

Down they spiraled . . . but not so fast now, his partner in the death dance slowing them, spreading its black wings against the air, holding him like one bully would hold a boy's arms for another bully's punch. It came, in the form of a beak's jab; Sky-Hawk, twisting his head, just avoiding a pierced eye.

Despite the slowing, they were still falling fast enough onto one of Cambridge's main drags. It was the morning rush hour, the street car-choked. As they spun and tumbled, Sky thought of yet another bird: chicken! This was a game of it; the one to let go first would lose . . . everything. Yet he knew the crow was not going to smash them both into a car roof. It was getting ready for something else.

So Sky had to be ready too. He may have been exhausted—after all, he'd just spent the whole night as another Fetch, the wolf. Yet he was still a raptor. His attackers may have been bigger . . . but he was nippier. And though they wanted his death, crows usually fed on the kills of others.

But he was a hawk. . . . And a hawk did its own killing!

Down, down, rushing to the car roof that seemed to rush up . . . and it came, the moment he'd waited for, the slightest loosening in his enemy's grip. Sky darted a look at the other bird. Its talons were uncurling to receive . . .

Wait . . . , thought Sky. The grip slackened. Now!

The crow tried to release him, fling him at its partner . . . and Sky-Hawk refused to go. For it was he who shot his claws forward now, he who spread his wings to make himself lighter, so his own weight could not be used against him in the spin. It was his sharpness that sank into flesh, his assailant's turn to cry in agony. It jerked hard away, too strong and heavy to resist. But Sky had won his moment and now let himself be flung, flipping over as he went. The second crow had dropped to seize him. Sky went high and seized him instead.

His claws found throat-feather, neck beyond,

gripped, held. Wings spread, he channeled the wind, flipped again, so he was above, thrusting down toward a parked car. At ten feet, Sky loosened his hold. At five, he hurled out his legs.

The crow smashed onto the steel roof. The car's alarm blared, matching the screech of the other crow, who dived for him again. But Sky spun away, flicking the car's mirror, eluding the talons that reached. Leveling, he shot down the street, wing tip missing a pedestrian's nose by a feather's breadth.

Behind him, within the rhythmic wail of the car alarm, Sky heard a clatter and a squawk, the other crow striking something. Perhaps the body of his dead companion, splayed on the car's roof.

He'll probably start eating it, Sky thought as he rose up to the roofline. Crows are like that.

The thought of food made him instantly ravenous, and he nearly turned back. He'd killed the creature, after all! But then he remembered, with the memory of a hawk, that crows were carrion eaters and lived on rotting flesh. So they tasted . . . absolutely disgusting!

As he flew higher to scan the streets and find out where he was, Sky realized something else. It wasn't the hawk, his animal Fetch, who needed food. It was Sky himself. Sky, whose body was probably being rushed into the ER right now.

Sky paused to hover, look down. There were any number of big buildings that could have been the hospital. He didn't know Cambridge well enough. But wherever it was, as his Fetch fought the crows, his body would undoubtedly have been convulsing, panicking the paramedics. Their training wouldn't have prepared them for the marks that would have suddenly appeared—a shadow wound on the shoulder where the hawk had lost a feather, a mark on the sole of the foot where a talon had sunk in.

" 'For what the Fetch receives, so shall the body.' " Who had said that?

Sigurd, no doubt! But he didn't think it had been his dead grandfather who'd attacked him this time. On the hotel's fire escape, not three minutes before, Sky had watched Sigurd transform into his latest Fetch, a seagull. Surely not even he had grown so powerful that he could switch bird bodies in midflight, recruit a sidekick, and ambush a hawk?

As he hovered, Sky shook the hawk's head in an almost-human gesture. Sigurd had no need to try to kill him—that way! He'd already condemned Sky to a terrible fate. By organizing the discovery of Sky's human body, Sigurd had stranded his grandson in his Fetch. And within it, Sky was already weakening, like a battery running down. He had spent so much energy doing what he'd had to do to free Kristin. Soon, he might not have enough power left to rejoin himself at all. And then . . .

The words of Pascaline, his Corsican great-aunt, came back to him now. She'd been talking of a Mazzeri, a Dream Hunter who'd . . . become separated. "He never found his way back. Body without spirit wastes away. So does spirit without body. Both fade. Eventually, the body dies. But the spirit lingers on. Barely heard. Scarcely seen. Reducing slowly to the edge of vision."

Although she hadn't used the term, Sky had known what she was describing.

"A draug," he murmured. A spirit without a home, condemned to wander in life's shadows for eternity.

No, Sky thought grimly. Sigurd doesn't need to use a crow to kill me.

He was exhausted before he'd even begun his flight. And this further, terrifying thought filled his mind with mist, drove weakness into his very wing tips. He began to float down toward a telephone pole. Perhaps a little rest, he thought. Just a short sleep . . .

His talons almost touched the wood before he cried out, "No! No! No!" The words came out as the fierce shriek of the hunting bird he was. He breathed deep, and his head started to clear. He'd been going to find someone when he was attacked. Who was it?

Kristin! he thought. He was way above the rooftops now and paused to hover again. I need Kristin.

Wings spread and vibrating, he surveyed the city, spread like a map beneath him. He'd left his cousin—or rather his cousin's Fetch—there! In a boatyard hut by the river. He'd drawn the hunt away so she could have her one quiet moment and re-enter her body. Assuming she'd succeeded, it was likely she'd have returned. . . .

Hawk eyes swiveled to the two quadrangles of her college, Trinity. The one closer to the river was Nevile's Court. He saw the patch of green, the distinctive sloping roof of the college library.

Last night, he'd killed his cousin there. Then he'd resurrected her. Surely she'd be back there now?

He stooped, wings angled to send him swiftly there.

CHAPTER TWO

DUMPED

Hawk hearing heard her. Hawk sight spotted her. But perhaps only just before he'd have heard and seen her as a human. A bird of prey's keen senses weren't really required to locate someone trying so hard to kick a door in.

"I know you're there!" Kristin yelled. "Open! This! Door!"

Each word was accompanied by a hefty boot. She was wearing Doc Martens, and the blows echoed down the stone corridor and around the ornate facades of Nevile's Court. Sky swooped down, settling into a stone archway; close enough to see, not too close to be obvious to others drawn by the ruckus. There were students in the doorways of their rooms . . . and two black-uniformed college porters, approaching with the weary look of men who'd seen such things a hundred times before.

"Easy, easy!" one of them said, reaching.

"They're in there!" She jerked her arm away and banged the side of her fist on the wood.

"He's not worth it, love," the second porter said, succeeding where his colleague had failed, grabbing and holding. "And if he has got someone in there, it's against college rules, and he'll be dealt with."

"Dealt with?" Kristin echoed in a shriek of rage. She had let herself be pulled away. Now she lunged again, smashing wood with steel-cap toes. The door began to splinter.

"That's enough!" The first porter grabbed hold. Each on an arm, they began to pull Kristin away.

"No!" she screamed. Suddenly, she went limp, using her weight to drop to the ground. Then, thrusting up, she broke free and hurled herself at the door again. "Open . . . ," she began.

As if responding to her command, the door opened and she stumbled half through it, into a man in his bathrobe, one hand rubbing his eyes. "Hello, Kristin," Dirk van Straaten said. "What is all this fuss about?" His thick South African accent was muddled with sleep.

"Sorry, Mr. van Straaten, but this girl—" began one of the porters.

The other interrupted, "Have you got someone in there with you, sir?"

"In here?" Van Straaten stifled a yawn. "It's against the rules, isn't it?" He looked down and smiled at Kristin, who was glaring up at him. "Hey, babe."

She'd stepped back. The porters grabbed her again. "If you wouldn't mind . . . ," one said. Making sure that his colleague had a firm grip, he moved past the South African into the room.

"Not in there!" Kristin yelled after him. "In *there*!" She had one hand free, and she used it to slap van Straaten hard in the chest.

"Ooh, sorry, sir," said the porter, grabbing Kristin's arm again. She began aiming kicks at his shins.

"That's quite all right, Cobb. Just let her go. We had a bit of a tiff last night, that's all."

"Tiff?" The word, so inadequate to explain what had occurred, seemed to sap some of Kristin's fury. She sagged as the porter released her.

"If you're sure, sir." He stepped back fast, out of range.

The other man came back. "No one," he said. He looked up at the tall student. "But if you could try to sort out your"—he looked at Kristin—"domestic problems quietly, sir. We've had enough bother in college, what with the Cloisters awash in blood, and the wolf hunt and all."

Sky, watching from his perch in the archway, stiffened. He'd been the wolf they'd hunted. And it had been Kristin's blood on the flagstones. Her Fetch's anyway.

"Didn't catch it, did you, sir?" said the second porter.

"Nah," replied van Straaten. "It escaped." He was

staring at Kristin still, smiling slightly. Then he looked up. "And I'm sorry about all the fuss. But I won't be bothering you from now on. I'll be leaving college today." He glanced back at Kristin. "For good."

"Sorry to hear that, sir," said the first porter in a bored voice; this was something else he'd obviously seen a hundred times before.

"Need some help, will you, sir?" said the other eagerly.

"Yis." The South African nodded. "Come and grab my stuff at noon, say. There'll be some money in it."

"Oh, you've always been most generous, Mr. van Straaten," came the oily reply. "We'll miss you."

The first porter was already turning away. "As for you," he said, waving a finger at Kristin, "behave!"

They went down the stairwell. Onlookers closed their doors, some more swiftly than others. Eventually, two people and a hawk were left alone in the corridor.

"Dirk," Kristin said, stepping forward, "we need to talk."

"Sure, babe," he said. "Come on in." At her hesitation, he added, "Don't worry about the rules, I'm dropping out anyway. So we can do . . . anything we want."

He beckoned her in, smiling. And there was something so creepy about that smile, it made Sky shiver, his feathers fluffing up, sinking down.

Kristin stopped. "No," she said softly. "Let's go somewhere public."

"Why?" The smile hardened. "Don't you want to be alone with me anymore, babe?"

"That's just it," Kristin said, stepping back. "We wouldn't be alone. And Dirk"—she choked—"has never called me 'babe.' "

"I don't know what you're talking about." The smile was completely gone. The voice had a new, rough edge. "Except that it's crap."

"Dirk . . ." She began, stopped, and Sky knew why she had stopped. How do you begin to tell someone they're possessed? They'd both seen their grandfather take over the South African's body the night before, just as Sigurd had once taken over Kristin's. She'd never known there was someone inside her, controlling her, a parasite feeding off her. Hadn't, right up until the moment Sky had cut the parasite from her body. Almost literally. So Dirk wouldn't know now.

And then there was the other problem of possession. As she'd said, she and Dirk wouldn't necessarily be alone. Sigurd could be off as an animal Fetch. He could also be right there, looking out, listening in. She'd never know if she had an audience of one or two.

Sky watched her wrestle with that, as he'd done when he'd first come to her in Cambridge the previous week. "Dirk," she began, "something . . . something *happened* to you last night. Something terrible. I know, because it happened to me too. I only just got free of it. You can too. My cousin knows a way—"

"Your cousin?" he interrupted, his voice harsh. "That . . . *tree hugger*! With his beard, his earrings, his knitted hat. I knew when he arrived that he was trouble. Knew when I saw you together that you loved him."

"What? I don't," she protested. "Well, I do! But not that way. We—"

He carried on as if she hadn't spoken. "So you might as well go to him." That humorless smile came again. "We had fun though, babe, eh? For a while there? But now I'm leaving. Alone, I think. Besides . . ." His eyes went past Kristin and looked straight into Sky's. "I think your cousin might have a few problems of his own."

Kristin turned, saw the hawk. "Sky!" she cried joyfully.

She turned back, just as the door closed. Stood there, staring at it, mouthing words. Sky spread his wings. "Kristin," he called softly, briefly amazed as ever that his own voice emerged from the hawk's beak without benefit of lips and tongue. "Let's go!"

Without acknowledging him, shoulders hunched, his cousin ran along the corridor and disappeared down the stairs.

Fortunately, she didn't disappear to her own room. A hawk wasn't so mobile inside. Sky, hovering again, watched her dart into the Cloisters. He hoped she wouldn't stop there either, and she didn't. The iron-grille gate swung outward; her hunched head and shoulders followed it. Arms wrapped tight around herself, she marched down to the river.

It was still early—could be no later than eight. A freezing November morning, damp with the fog that drifted waist-deep above the grass on the far bank. He settled on a wooden post near where she sat, head on knees, and the mist's chilly gray tendrils pushed through even his feathers and down. She was wearing just a T-shirt, so he reckoned that accounted for her shaking. Till he heard the sobs.

"Kristin," he called.

"Go away!"

Her voice was tear-choked. He'd never been good with tears, his own or anyone else's. "I know," he ventured. "It's been a tough night. For both of us. I've—"

"Oh, it's been tough for you, has it, Sky? How so?"

"Ah! Well, you see . . ."

She raised her face to him, wetness shining on her cheeks. "You haven't been murdered; you're just the murderer. You haven't been . . . resurrected; you're just the . . . resurrecter-er."

Anger was easier than tears, especially Kristin's. He was used to her temper. He could provoke it. "That's not English."

She ignored him. "You're always *doing* things. I'm always having things done to me. And last night I was . . . *re*possessed?"

"I think that's cars."

"*De*possessed?"

"That's not English either."

"Sod OFF! I'm the Cambridge student. You're just a . . . tree hugger!" She faltered on the phrase, went on in a softer voice, wet with tears. "I watched my grandfather . . . my own grandfather . . . *emerge* from within me. He'd . . . occupied me for a year, and then . . ."

Her voice broke. It didn't seem like the time to say I told you so. Instead, Sky whispered, "Then?"

". . . then I watched him as he possessed my boyfriend."

Sobs came again. He thought of dropping down to the ground—but putting a wing around her probably wouldn't comfort much. So he just watched, waited.

Gradually, the tears subsided. And something else came—bitter laughter. "You know the craziest thing? You know what I'm most upset about? Dirk just dumped me!"

"Well, in a way—"

"He did. He said, 'See you, babe.' I've never been dumped before. I do the dumping, dammit!"

"You're better off anyway. I never liked him."

She sniffed. "I could see you didn't."

"And then, of course, there is that other thing."

"What other thing?"

"The fact that he's also Sigurd?"

"Oh, yeah," she said softly. "There is that."

The laughter had stopped. The tears came again. This time Sky just let them flow and didn't try to anger her out of them.

After a while, she raised her head, wiped her nose and eyes, then looked at him. "Why are you still, you know, in your Fetch? Your hawk Fetch. Last time I saw you, you were a wolf."

"Well, you see . . ." Where to begin? "Remember when I said I'd also had it tough?"

"Yeah?"

He told her, as swiftly as he could, about Sigurd, about what had happened on the fire escape, about his body being carried away to the hospital.

When he'd finished, she thought for a long moment. "So he's trying to murder you?"

"Same thing, essentially—turn me into a draug."

"That's worse than murder."

Sky sucked in air. "Tell me about it! Remember, I know all about the lost dead."

"So you don't want to go back into your human Fetch because . . ."

Sky shivered, his feathers rising over every part of his body. "You know it takes a lot out of you. By the time you've . . . wandered a night, you're ready to return, recharge. It's a bit like a battery . . . and mine's run way down. I overused it last night. Murder, resurrection. Werewolfdom." He tried to laugh but it came out more like a sob. "I'm scared, Kristin. Scared I won't have the power to transform again. And unless I hurry,

I don't think I'll have the power to get back into my body, quiet moment or not." He hopped off his perch, waddled toward her. "Please help me."

"OK," she said, wiping away the last trace of tears. "It's about time I began to *do.*" She smiled. "And I don't care if that's not English."

CHAPTER THREE
COMA WARD

Girls' purses had always been an intriguing mystery to Sky. They seemed to carry so much junk in them! Now he wished he'd left it mysterious. Kristin claimed she'd taken most of her stuff out to make room for the five runestones, one quartz chisel, one cigarette lighter, and one hawk. But some sort of brush was definitely digging into him. And the perfume that Kristin wore had doubled in intensity when he'd squirmed earlier on. He had to be lying on a dispenser, each slight shift spraying another burst of fragance onto his feathers. She'd done the zipper almost all the way up, leaving only a slight gap at the top, so there was hardly any unpolluted air. He hadn't realized hawks could sneeze. Apparently they could, and once they started they couldn't stop.

The banging motion caused by his cousin's swift surging through the streets was making him nauseous.

Could hawks be sick as well as sneeze? He thought they would be finding out quite soon. How far was this bloody hospital anyway?

Then they did stop . . . paused, anyway. The bag rose.

"We're here," came a whisper. "I'm going in."

Motion again, the hiss of a pneumatic door, street sounds fading, cut off by another hiss. In the darkness, hawk sight didn't operate, but powerful hawk hearing kept getting sharper. Heels tapping on a linoleum floor, something being rolled nearby, a squeak from one of its wheels, ten conversations at once: complaints, football results, the weather—typically English, at least five were on that subject. A child ran yelling toward them, a hushing mum in pursuit. Underneath it all, he heard the clear, high-pitched cry of a mouse. He reacted first as a human, with outrage that a mouse should be in a hospital; then as a hawk, with a sudden stab of hunger.

His surroundings halted. He heard Kristin mumbling. She'd rung the hospital to find out where he'd been taken—the coma ward, apparently. "Merrydown, Brookes, X-Ray Department, Electro . . . there it is! Hanson Ward."

She turned a hard left; Sky got another squirt of scent. A bell dinged, a door slid open. "Which floor?" came an older male voice.

"Eight, please," Kristin replied.

The elevator started, soon stopped.

The door opened, closed. Immediately he was lowered, the zipper was unzipped. Light and Kristin were above him. She was wearing a white coat, stolen from Trinity's laboratory.

"Thank God!" Sky muttered, attempting to squeeze out.

"Not yet," she said, raising a hand. "Just thought I'd give you some air."

"About time!" He sneezed. "What the hell is this scent?"

"Oh, sorry. Did I leave it in there?" She sniffed. "It's called Mystery."

"It should be called Vomit."

"Dirk gave it to me."

"Now why doesn't that surprise me!"

She reached past him, pulled out one of the objects that had been causing him pain. "What's that?" he asked.

"Voice recorder." She flicked a switch. "I examined the draug for signs of decapitation," she dictated in a formal tone, then smiled. "People don't like interrupting you when you're talking. Especially in England."

Before he could comment further, the elevator slowed, the red number settling on eight. "We're here."

Ping! She zipped the bag. Darkness, and Mystery, surrounded him again.

"Hanson Ward, left," he heard her say confidently. Then her heels were clicking again.

She's enjoying this, Sky thought, suddenly annoyed. Because he wasn't, not at all. Apart from the discomfort, every moment away from his human body was hurting him more. No, not hurting. It was almost the reverse, a sort of numbness spreading through him, as if he'd been given some drug that was slowly paralyzing him. It had been seven hours since he'd been "separated." Of course, he'd wanted to rush straight to the hospital; but when she'd called to ask after him, she'd also discovered that no visitors were allowed anywhere till after 2 p.m. And only immediate family were allowed into Hanson. Cousins didn't count. Hence the white coat, the Dictaphone . . . and her obvious enjoyment of the role!

The sound of beeps came, numbers being punched into a keypad. At the same time, Kristin started talking very loudly. "The patient appears blotchy and his temperature is—'scuse me, can you hold that door? Thanks so much!—above normal for the third day in succession. We can almost assume . . ."

Other footsteps moved away. Her voice trailed off. "Good," she whispered. "We're in! Now just find the room. . . ."

He couldn't feel his claws anymore. The tips of his wings had long gone. And when he wasn't sneezing, he was yawning, huge gulps, his beak stretched wide.

The footsteps slowed, stopped. “This looks like—” he heard her begin.

“You! Who are you? What are you doing here?” The voice was loud, female, and authoritative, and went on, “This is a restricted area.”

“Let go of my arm. . . .”

“Security!”

“Oh, no, no!” Sky couldn’t help the cry that escaped.

“What was that?” said the woman. “What have you got . . . ?”

“Kristin?” A third voice joined the conversation. But this one Sky recognized.

“Aunt Sonja!”

Mum! Sky squirmed down into the bag. How had she . . . ? Then he remembered the cell phone his mother had insisted he carry. They’d have called her as soon as they found his body in the hotel. Shropshire to Cambridge had to be six hours minimum. She must have driven like a lunatic, which was unlike her. . . .

“What’s going on?”

Dad! Of course. His dad *was* a lunatic driver!

“It’s Kristin, dear.”

“It’s an intruder, madam. Sir.”

“No, no, nurse. This is my niece.”

“She’s impersonating a doctor.”

“No, I’m not!”

“Why are you dressed like that, Kristin?”

“Uh . . .”

Sky was sure he was not the only one who craned toward the answer.

"Party. Doctors and nurses," she giggled. "Came straight here when I heard."

A snort from the real nurse. "A party? At two p.m.? Rubbish!"

"You've obviously never been a student."

"But how did you hear?" It was Henry, Sky's ever-practical father, asking.

Another "uh." Sky winced again. Kristin was digging herself deeper in the dog doo with every statement. "Text message," she said. "Sky texted me. Said he wasn't feeling well."

The woman again. "How? When he's in a coma."

"Uh . . . I only just turned my phone on?"

It came out more like a question, a plea. But before anyone could challenge her, a new voice chimed in. Male. Authoritative. With one of those pompous, upper-class English voices. "Well, you may have been the last person to hear from him, young lady. You are family, are you?"

"She's my niece, Doctor Abel. Sky's cousin."

"Then you may as well join us. Help us unravel this knot." A harrumph came. "That's all right, nurse. I'll take responsibility."

The nurse went away, muttering. Sky was carried again. The bag was set down, and Kristin managed to open the zip halfway. As she stepped away, part of the room was revealed through someone's legs. Corduroy trousers. Work shoes. His dad. Beyond him, Sky saw the edge of a bed. On it was a hand he didn't recognize immediately, which was strange because it was his own. His body's, that is.

And then another hand took it up and his mum sat down on the bed. "So where were we, doctor?"

Henry stepped away to join his wife at the bedside. A suit's trousers came into Sky's vision. "I was telling you, Mrs. March, about the tests we are running. We are trying to ascertain the type of coma your son may be in, what may have caused it. There is some response to stimuli—pinpricks on the soles of feet, that sort of thing. In the ambulance, coming in, the paramedics reported a severe thrashing around . . ."

That would be the crow attack, thought Sky.

". . . but since then, nothing. We have taken blood and should get the results back soon. That will tell us if the coma is drug-induced—"

"My Sky would never—"

"Mrs. March, if I had a pound for every time I've heard parents say that . . . I'd have about twenty pounds!" He chuckled, walked into sight, a gray-haired man in glasses, blocking Sky's view of the bed. "But the blood tests will confirm or deny. And we'll do a computerized axial tomographic scan—"

"Sorry?"

"CAT scan to you. To rule out trauma. There does not appear to be any to the head, though some strange marks have emerged on the shoulder and foot."

Bloody crows again, thought Sky as the man continued. "But if, as I suspect, there's nothing to see, and the blood tests also rule out viral encephalitis, we're left with doing a lumbar puncture for meningitis—relatively common in students, actually. . . ."

"Oh, God!"

"Yet there are few other signs of it. No rash, for example, just those strange markings." He moved again and Sky looked at his mum's anxious face. "We also have to consider psychogenic causes."

"What?"

"Once organic reasons for the coma are removed, we seek psychogenic or psychologically based reasons. Has he been very depressed, for example? Listless? Or the reverse—prone to mania? Bizarre outbursts? Uncharacteristic behavior?"

"Well," said Henry, "he has been away for a year. We have no idea where. Just came back."

"And he's always been a sleepwalker, doctor," Sonja added. "Ever since he was a child."

"Hmm!"

"And we didn't know he'd come here to Cambridge. We'd have worried because . . ." Sonja hesitated. ". . . because his cousin's here, and we had a little trouble last year when they ran away together to Norway—"

"I've told you, Aunt Sonja, it wasn't what you thought. . . ."

The doctor queried, "Which was?"

"My aunt thought we—Sky and I—were in love. Which is nonsense."

"But you did go off together, dear, and—"

The two women started to talk over each other. The doctor interrupted. "Leaving that aside, what did he come to Cambridge for? To see you, obviously, and . . ."

Maybe it was the perfume, but Sky was starting to feel drunk. Go on, tell them, he thought. I came to kill you, drive our grandfather's Fetch out of you, then bring you back to life. Stick that in your CAT scan and smoke it, doctor!

Instead, Kristin said, "It's . . . it's a bit of a long story."

"You're telling me," Sky chirruped. Except it came out in hawk speak.

"What was that?" asked the doctor.

"My cell," Kristin said quickly.

"Well, if it's a long story we might as well hear it over a cup of tea, what? My office is just down the corridor here."

He moved toward the door. Sky saw Sonja squeeze his hand. "I don't want to leave. In case he wakes up. . . ."

"Mrs. March, should he do so, our battery of machines will alert us. And we need to get all the details down. The backstory, as 'twere. Even something trivial could be vitally important. There are consent forms to sign, as well, for treatment." Sky saw his mother's hesitation. "Don't worry. We'll have you back here in moments if there's any excitement."

Sonja reluctantly rose. Henry's legs passed in front of Sky. "Coming, young lady?"

"Of course. I'll just grab . . ." The door opened behind her as Kristin reached into the bag, running the zipper all the way open. "Be quick," she hissed, then followed the others out the door.

As soon as it clicked shut, Sky thrust his beak through the opening. He blinked at the room, the medical equipment—drip, monitors, the LED showing his heart rate in green light and beeping faintly. Awkwardly he thrust his shoulders out of the bag. It tipped, sprawling him onto the floor. He hopped onto his feet, his talons clicking on the floor like Kristin's heels. Then with a beat of his wings, he rose, settling onto the metal rail at the end of the bed . . .

. . . and looking at the body on it. In Corsica, he had seen himself like this every time he'd left to "travel," and on each return. It wasn't something you ever got used to. Two versions of himself, both spirit, both flesh.

He swayed on the bed rail, nearly toppled off. "Time," he said aloud, dropping to the ground. Closing his eyes, he remembered Pascaline, in Corsica, how she'd taught him to leave his body at will, the one quiet moment needed, a breath out, a surging up. It was the same going back, a breath in, a merging. And he couldn't do that as a bird.

He breathed deeply. His exhaustion made it so hard to shake off feathers. But he did it. And then he was standing there, shivering because he no longer had down to cover him. He was as naked as he had been on the fire escape, watching his body being taken away.

This body, he thought, Sky looking down on Sky. As he stared, the one on the bed gave a little groan, his legs shifting under the sheet. The heart monitor showed an accelerating rate. If it was hard for him, the Fetch, to be separated from the body, it must have been equally tough for the body to be separated from his Fetch. "Time," he mumbled again. Taking another deep breath, he bent, eyes seeking eyes behind the lids of the sleeper, hand reaching for hand. One quiet moment, he thought. At last.

And then the hands touched . . . and those other eyes jumped open. "Hello," said Sky. . . .

. . . The one lying on the bed.

CHAPTER FOUR

DOUBLE TROUBLE

If he still had wings, he'd have shot to the ceiling. But arms and feet just froze, his eyes wide, mouth working at some word to sum up his terror.

"Ugh," was the best he could do.

"You know," said Sky from the bed, "I've encountered some serious weirdness lately. But meeting myself in a dream has to be the weirdest."

"You—you—you think this is a dream?" stuttered Sky, staring down.

Sky lifted his head from the pillow, nodded. "Of course. When the Fetch is traveling, everything happens as if in a dream. And just like when you are in a dream, you don't know it's one. You think this bizarre stuff is actually happening! Until you wake up. But when Fetch and body re-unite, dream becomes reality. The experiences become mine. The memories . . ." He bit his lip. "Except right now I'm dreaming that my

Fetch can't get back. Dreaming everything, right up to . . . well, this conversation." He smiled. "Still dreaming! But why am I telling you this? You already know."

"Except you . . . um, I . . ." He stopped. *He* stopped? Was he *he* anymore? Did Sky on the bed take over as . . . Sky? And how was he going to break this news? You never wake up someone who's sleepwalking. Just as you must never disturb the body when the Fetch is gone. What would happen to Sky, lying in the bed, when he realized that this wasn't a dream? But what choice did he—did they?—*Oh, bollocks!*—have?

"Um, listen," Sky—he'd have to keep thinking of himself as that until some better alternative came along!—said. "I think there's something you need to know."

"Ah, good!" said Sky, propping himself up on his elbows. "A message from a dream! When I wake up I'll be able to analyze it for meaning." He frowned. "It's not going to be too symbolic, is it?"

"No," Sky replied. "It's fairly simple, actually." He took a breath. "You remember that day just before you discovered the runestones, how you went to school and you—"

"Went 'Vardogr'?" Sky nodded. "My pen was warm on my desk. People had seen me. Except it was my bodily Fetch they saw. The first time it—I!—you!!—walked. I think . . . I think I saw me too." He shuddered. "Only for a moment, thank God."

"Well," said Sky, leaning down to the bed. "This is a bit like that."

"How do you mean?"

"I am not in a dream. I am your Fetch."

The patient paled. "You mean, all the stuff I think I've been dreaming has happened—is happening?"

"Yes."

He looked wildly around. "This hospital is . . . *real*?"

"Yes."

Sky looked up. "Bloody hell!"

Sky looked down. "I think that's putting it mildly."

They both laughed—an identical laugh, cut off at the exact same moment they realized it was identical. "What the hell are we going to do?" whispered Sky from the bed. "If you don't—I don't—we don't—"

"Exactly. I've got to . . ." Sky stared down. How to re-enter? Re-unite? "I've never done it when I've been awake."

"Well, obviously neither have I."

Sky could feel his heart pounding. And judging from the increased beeping of the heart monitor, Sky's was too. And that was ridiculous! He couldn't keep thinking of himself as two people. They had to be one. No, dammit, *he* had to be one.

He reached for the hand again. It gripped his, and he suddenly thought it the strangest sensation he'd ever had in a life of strange sensations.

"We can do this," gasped Sky from the bed. "The one quiet moment?"

They closed their eyes. Hands locked, they both breathed. Then both heard the footsteps in the hall.

Eyes shot open. "Hide," yelped Sky.

"Which one of us?"

"You. The Fetch! I'm"—he raised the arm that had the drip—"hooked up."

As the door opened, Sky dived under the bed.

Kristin rushed in. "I sneaked away. The old toilet excuse." She came across to the bed, took Sky's hand. "You did it! Yeah!"

"Um," said Sky, extracting his hand. "No."

"What do you mean, no?" mocked Kristin.

"He means this," said Sky, sliding out from under the bed.

It took a moment, as she stared at the two of them, before she found the breath to scream.

"Shh!" they both hissed. Too late.

Just before the door burst open, Sky flicked the sheets so they hung halfway down to the floor, a little concealment for the open side, the other blocked by the drip.

"What's going on here?" It was the voice of the nurse, the one who'd been so suspicious of Kristin. She was no less so now. "What are you doing there? Why did you scream?"

"His eyes were open when I came in. He was staring, it . . . it made me jump!"

The nurse came over to the bedside. "Sometimes coma patients have involuntary reflexes." She lifted Sky's eyelids. Somehow, he managed to keep his eyes glazed, rolled over. "Hmm! Nothing stirring." She lowered them, then leaned down and suddenly bellowed, "Sky!"

He didn't open his eyes, but he jumped. "Now, that's a positive sign. I'll go fetch the doctor."

With a glare at Kristin, she left. Sky's eyes opened. " '*Fetch* the doctor'?" he said.

"I know!" laughed Kristin. Then Sky slid out from under the bed, and she leapt back. "Oh my God, that's too weird. Don't do that!" She'd glanced down and now looked rapidly away. "And do you think you could . . . uh"—she gestured, eyes averted—"cover yourself up?"

Sky scrambled up. There was a towel hanging beneath the sink. He grabbed it, wrapped it round his waist. The panic he'd tried to force down was bubbling up again. "What are we going to do?"

On the bed, Sky's face was a mirror of fear. "They'll be back here soon, sticking pins in my feet again, shouting." He swallowed. "I won't be able to pretend I'm in a coma for long."

"But if you 'wake up,' we'll never get rid of Mum and Dad. There'll be questions. . . ."

On the bed, Sky swallowed. "I don't think we have a choice."

Sky leaned over him. "Are you thinking what I'm thinking?"

"Probably."

They said it together.

"Run!"

Sky went to the door as Sky unhooked himself from the drip. "Oh, great!" said Kristin when he stood up. She waved at him, and he tried to pull the hospital gown around to cover himself. But of course that only exposed his front.

"Oh, never mind!" she said. "I'll just have to put up with a naked cousin . . . two naked cousins!"

From the door, Sky called, "Corridor's empty. We better move."

Kristin was looking at them both again. "We'll not get far with you two . . . undressed like that." She pointed at the bed. "That's on wheels. You"—she snapped her fingers at Sky by the bed—"take the brake off and get in. You"—she gestured at the other Sky—"prop the door open, then get in too."

"But—"

"Now!" she yelled. "Unless you fancy explaining how you've . . . *cloned* yourself to your parents!"

At the bed, Sky unhooked the brake, then climbed in. At the door, Sky propped it open, then went back and climbed into the bed as well.

"One of you get under the sheets, will you?"

One of them did. Kristin got behind the bed, strained. "One of you needs to diet," she grunted, bending lower to heave.

The bed lurched forward. She banged into both door frames before she got it out. Turning left, they trundled down the corridor. Behind them they could all hear the beeping sound of a door code being punched in. They were just swinging around the corner when the door opened and they heard Sky's mother saying, "But it could be a good sign, doctor, couldn't it?"

At the end of the corridor was an elevator. The door was just sliding shut. "Hold that, please," said Kristin crisply. A West Indian man in an orderly's coat held the door, which slid back. "Thank you."

The door was just closing again when the screaming began. "Man! What is that?" the man said, reaching for the buttons.

Kristin's hand intercepted his, slapping it lightly. "Sorry," she said. "But this is an emergency."

The door shut, cutting off the tumult. The first-floor button was lit. Kristin reached forward and pressed "B."

"An emergency . . . in the basement?" the man queried.

"Didn't you hear?" said Kristin with a slight smile. "The new isolation unit's down there. Only for incredibly contagious patients."

The floor bell dinged, and the man left fast without another word. "Sorry," said Kristin, spreading herself to stop someone boarding. "Occupied."

The door closed. The elevator plunged on. "She's very forceful, isn't she?" Sky whispered from beneath the sheet.

"You should see her as a lynx," came the reply from above.

"Shh!" Kristin hissed, just as the elevator stopped. The door opened, and she nudged the trolley into the basement. "No one," she said, peering. She steered out into the corridor, managed a corner with difficulty.

"Where now?" Sky asked. But his words were lost in the sudden blaring of the alarm bell.

"I wonder what that's for?" shouted Kristin. "As if I didn't know."

They all heard footsteps running nearby. A man called, "I'll get onto the front desk."

Kristin took a turn down another corridor, this one worse lit, with older wooden shelves piled with dusty equipment, followed by several rooms whose walls were made of meshed metal. "Aha!" she said, jerking the trolley to a stop. "Sky!"

"Yes?" they both replied.

"Hop off and open that door!"

They both began to slide off. Each stopped when he saw the other move. "Which one?" they said together.

"You, Sky . . . no, you, Sky! Ach!" she grunted. "This is so confusing."

One Sky raised his hand. "Why don't I be

'Body-Sky'? Since I was the one in the hospital? So you'll be—"

"Fetch-Sky!"

"Agreed. Now, one of you . . . move!"

Fetch-Sky raised a hand, slid off the bed. But as soon as he stood, his knees gave out from under him, and he had to catch himself on the rail of the bed. "I'm not doing so good," he muttered.

"Nor me," said Body-Sky. He stood slowly, also holding tight, facing his Fetch. "Maybe if we both . . ."

Two of Sky's hands reached forward, one from each body. Together, they grasped the handle, pushed it down. The door swung in, and they stumbled into the room. Kristin pushed the trolley between them, knocking over some cans that rolled away along the floor. Then, as she flicked a light switch, they let the door slam shut.

CHAPTER FIVE
REUNION

The heavy door reduced the alarm to a distant whine. "What is this place?" Fetch-Sky mumbled, easing himself down onto an inverted box and looking about the dingy room. There was not much to see, since it was only about twelve feet long, half as much wide.

"*Janitor* was written on the door." Kristin peered around. "Looks pretty abandoned, though. Yuck!" She reached up, sweeping some cobwebs from the top of her hair.

"Looks like a storeroom for paints," Body-Sky said, bending down to pick up a tin, straightening when he was suddenly aware of his gown flapping open. "Old paints." He held the paint pot up to the light so the others could see the trail of dried red down its side.

"Not the sort of place people will come to much then," Kristin said. "So we should have time."

"For what?" Sky laid the paint pot down.

"For you two to . . . you know . . ." She made a vague gesture in the air. "Mesh!"

Fetch-Sky leaned back on the box, sighed. "It's not as simple as that. I . . . we . . ."

Body-Sky sat again on the bed. "We've never been like this before. Well, just once, very briefly. The body's always unconscious for the Fetch"—he pointed at Sky on the box—"to rejoin."

"Yes," said the other. "Because one is usually flesh, one spirit . . . even if he has flesh too!" He groaned. "We shouldn't be separate like this, talking like this, it's horrible!" His chin began to quiver. "And I'm beginning to . . . fade."

The other Sky was echo as well as mirror. "And *I'm* beginning to fade."

"Sigurd did this. He's murdered me. Us."

Both Skys began to sob. Kristin, looking in horror from one to the other, took a deep breath and leaned forward. "No, he hasn't. Because you're still here. Both of you . . . no! One of you! You are still one, but . . . apart. We just have to find the way to put you back together again."

"How?"

"How have you done it before? And I don't mean with all that 'one quiet moment' crap. We're not going to get that." Her face was swinging between the two of theirs as she spoke. "What other factors are involved each time?"

"Apart from the . . . body?" They spoke as one, right down to the pause as they realized it.

Kristin clucked in irritation. "This is a bit strange, guys. Guy! Can't one of you speak for both of you? You are the same after all."

Sky—Fetch-Sky—put up his hand. "That's what worries me. Are we still the same? Life is shaped by so many little choices—choices that then shape character. The longer we are apart . . . aren't you worried that we'll actually start to grow *different*?"

Body-Sky nodded. "Totally. And yet if we do—"

"Please! Can we save the Fetch theories for later?" Kristin looked at each of them in exasperation. "So what was there, apart from yourselves?"

"Runes," they both called out.

"Runes? We have those." Eagerly, Kristin grabbed her bag from the hook at the end of the trolley, thrust her hand inside, pulled out a plastic sandwich bag, and tipped the stones she'd picked up in the Cloisters onto the bed. Each Sky reached forward for the same stone, hesitated, then went for another that was the same.

"Let me," said Kristin, and turned all the stones face-up. "Now, these were the runestones you used"—she shuddered—"to help expel Sigurd from me, yes? So can't we use them again?"

It was Body-Sky who answered. "I don't think so. Because these were the runes I worked through in Corsica. Each was geared to freeing you. Climaxing with this one." He lifted the stone with the straight line, the diagonal slashed through it. "*Naudhiz:* rune of power, of destiny fulfilled," he intoned.

"A rune of power is what we need."

They both shook their heads. Fetch-Sky spoke. "Not this one. I chose it for a specific purpose. It combined with all the others to achieve that purpose—freeing you! It can't just be applied anywhere, instantly. We need another."

"Any of these?" She squinted down. "*Kenaz. Gebo. Berkana—*"

"No." They interrupted, then began to speak one thought, in two voices.

"These are too linked . . ."

". . . their power geared to one goal . . ."

". . . I released the energy within them to achieve it . . ."

". . . I need another now . . ."

". . . Am I thinking . . . ?"

". . . what I'm thinking . . . ?"

". . . Of course. It's obvious . . ."

". . . Totally!"

The flow stopped. The two Skys stared at each other, the same grin on both faces. "Um, hello-oh?" said Kristin at last, waving a hand.

Both turned. Body-Sky spoke first. "It's in the poems."

"The poems?"

"The Rune Poems. Where the ancient masters left clues to each rune's power, hidden in the lines—"

"I know what the poems are!" Kristin exploded. "I've studied them more than you two . . . put together, I'm sure!" She settled. "Which ones are you thinking of?"

"Just one," Fetch-Sky went on. "Here's the first line: 'Man is the increase of dust.' "

"That's *Mannaz,*" Kristin said. "Meaning: 'Man.' "

Body-Sky leaned forward. "But the second line makes it the one for us: 'Mighty is the talon-span of . . .' "

" 'The hawk'!" They all three said it.

"I see! It's you," Kristin went on, leaning forward to tap Fetch-Sky on the knee. "The bird of prey. But *Mannaz* is much more than that, isn't it?"

"Exactly!" Each Sky chimed in, overlapping the other.

"It's the rune of the perfected being . . ."

". . . the journey . . ."

". . . along the road to Valhalla . . ."

". . . the ultimate destination . . ."

". . . where all things will be unified . . ."

". . . body and soul . . . united!"

Each gasped. Each repeated in awe, "Body and soul united!"

They'd reached out one hand to the other, grasped. Kristin leaned forward, laid hers on top. "It *is* the one, isn't it?"

"I think so."

"So what do we do now?"

"We need to make the rune."

"Can't we just use the one from your set?" Kristin rose. "They must have your possessions at the hotel. I could—"

"No time." It was Fetch-Sky who spoke. "I'm getting weaker by the minute. We have to do it now. Here. With what we have."

Kristin reached into her bag. "Uh, I have this."

She held out the quartz chisel. Neither reached to take it. "No," said Body-Sky. "I know it's a rune carver. But it's also a weapon of murder. Yours. Emilio Farcese's. And murder is what we are trying to reverse here." Both Skys looked around. "What else have we got?"

"Paint," said Kristin, eyeing the tins. "You'd need red, wouldn't you?"

"It's the color of power, sure. Of blood. My runestones are dyed red." Body-Sky gestured down. "It was definitely the color for journeying to ancestors. But for this, it has to be less connected with blood, more with pure spirit. With healing." He turned to his twin, still sitting on the box. "Do you agree?"

"You know I do. Green is the color we want."

Kristin began looking, found a can straightaway. It was hard to pry the lid off, but with the help of the chisel she managed. "There! Some left. Will it do?"

Both Skys nodded. "Paper?"

Kristin reached. "What about wallpaper?" She lifted a roll. On their nods, she pushed the bed deeper into the room, clearing a space before them. Then she unrolled a section about the size of a poster, ripped it off. It curled on the floor and she weighted it down with paint cans.

"Now what?"

The Fetch had found a paintbrush soaking in cleaning spirits. Shaking drops off to dry it, he leaned forward. "Now, we paint."

"Wait!" said the other. "We can't rush this. I think we'll only get one chance at it."

"You see," replied the Fetch. "That's what I was talking about. We're already becoming different. I would have rushed ahead. We need an invocation, don't we?"

"Uh-huh." All three bent their heads. "Ancestors," both Skys called. "You whose blood sings within us. Be with us now."

A silence came over them. Into it, Fetch-Sky sang out, "Odin. All-Father. Giver of the runes. Guide us in our quest. Help the separated to reunite."

"All-Father," the others cried.

Each of them closed their eyes, breathed deeply. Each visualized the rune floating in green in the air before them. All saw it form—two straight lines down, joined by two that went diagonally from the top to halfway down, forming two conjoined triangles.

"*Mannaz:* Man," they all breathed.

"It's a mirror," Kristin whispered, "just like you two."

Fetch-Sky dipped the paintbrush in the pot, then

leaned forward. With a last deep breath, he ran the brush in a straight line down the left side of the paper, chanting as he did.

"*Mannaz,* Man and Hawk . . ."

Body-Sky took the brush from him, dipped, bent, chanted as he daubed.

"Sundered by evil . . ."

Hand joined hand. As one they dipped, traced the diagonal across from the top left.

"Reunite to live. . . ."

The brush flowed, slowly bringing the opposite diagonal down.

"Separate, together, one is one."

The chant finished as the brushstroke ended, joining side to side, completing the symbol. The images faced each other, separate, linked.

"It is complete," the two Skys said. "A mirror made. Each of us reflects the other."

"And you know what else you've mirrored?" Kristin whispered, awe in her voice. "The words! If you held 'evil' up to a mirror, what would you see?"

Sky breathed deep, seeing it. " 'Live' equals 'evil,' reversed. Life, the reverse of the death Sigurd condemned me to."

"Live," said his Fetch, putting the paintbrush aside, reaching to take up one side of the paper.

"Live," repeated Sky, doing the same. They each held their side, mirror images on the paper, holding the paper.

Kristin stared at them, unwilling to break the silence. It lengthened, on and on, until the paper began to shake. At last, she could bear it no longer. "What can I do?" she whispered.

They spoke as one. "Burn it."

"Why?"

"Burn it. . . . Now!"

Sky's lighter from Corsica was in her bag. With shaking hands she reached into it, her fingers straightaway encountering brass. She pulled it out, pushed up the metal arm, flicked at the wheel. Once, twice, it sparked, didn't catch.

"Hurry," came the plea from two mouths. She looked at them. On each face an identical line of sweat ran down the forehead.

She flicked again. Spark turned to flame, yellow and blue. "Here?" she said, reaching it toward the middle of the paper.

"Yes," came on a strained exhalation, as if it was their last. She touched the flame to the very bottom of the paper, directly under the middle of the symbol. It caught immediately, brown chasing yellow across the paper, smoke pouring from it. Smoke that, as soon as the flame encountered paint, thickened and turned acrid.

The flames shot along the green lines as if following trails, speeding ever closer to the hands that held it. "Let it go," Kristin called.

But they didn't. Just stared into each other's eyes, sweat-gleaming faces pushing closer and closer through the thickening cloud. Paint and paper dissolved in flame, which flowed like liquid fire onto flesh. Still they held, and then Kristin could see nothing more, so thick was the air with smoke, so dizzy her head from the breathing of it. "Sky," she croaked, falling backward. "Sky! Let go!"

Smoke muffled all sound but the crackling of the paper each Sky held, obscuring all sight but the one directly before them, the eyes of the other, eyes in a mirror—Sky's eyes, staring from two faces. Flame licked flesh, but not even pain could break what bound them. And then the twin triangles of *Mannaz* succumbed to fire, flowed into one, vanished entirely. Fingers merged, but without entwining. *Sinking,* skin into skin, bone into bone, blood mixing with blood, its every cell melding with its exact double.

At last, four eyeballs pushed together. Each felt it, like a thumb pad pressed onto the lens. Until something gave.

It was the water that brought her back. It sprayed out at all angles from the sprinkler above. Another alarm was blaring, different from the one they'd heard before. Much louder, because it was the smoke alarm in the ceiling.

She sat up, staring through the deluge, the banks of smoke that still drifted. She could only have been out a moment.

On the floor lay a body. Absolutely still. Coughing,

she staggered across to it. "Sky," she gasped, desperately tugging at his shoulder.

She rolled him over. For the longest moment he did not move. Then his eyes fluttered, opened. "Kristin," he murmured.

She glanced up, frantically looking around the small room. Seeing nothing, she looked down again. Drops ran off her hair onto his face. "Where's your friend?" she muttered.

"Here," he said.

"You . . . got back in?"

"Yes." He coughed, struggled up to one elbow, winced.

"Oh, Sky. Your fingers are burnt."

"This?" He peered at his hand. "This is nothing," he said, remembering the cave in Corsica, his arm ablaze. He looked up at her. "Why's it raining in here?"

She helped him up, and they staggered out of the room. The alarm was sounding in the corridor too. They heard some muffled shouting, footsteps in the stairwell.

"Elevator will have cut out with the fire alarm," Sky said. "They'll be coming down to check it out." He turned to her. "You should go. If they find you, they'll blame you for stealing the bed—and me in it."

"I'll split. But what will *you* say?"

Sky smiled. His body was whole again, and so was his confidence. "Big advantage of being King of the Sleepwalkers," he said. "You can get away with anything. Arson's nothing. I heard of someone in the States who got away with murder!" He laughed at her flinch.

The feet pounded down the last stair. "Go," he said. "I'll be here. I have a feeling they're not going to let me out for a while."

Saluting, she grabbed her purse and ran. Sky stayed put, facing the door. As the first hospital orderly came through it, waving a fire extinguisher, Sky stepped toward him. "Excuse me," he said, holding a hand to his head, "but where am I?"

CHAPTER SIX

HOME

Sky stared up. The ceiling of his bedroom hadn't changed at all. How often had he lain there, watching the fantasy film version of his life on it? He'd scored the perfect goal—in that crack by the light fixture. He'd asked Alison Freeman on a date—right beside the water stain from the burst pipe.

He was the one who'd changed. Because ever since his return to his parents' house two weeks before, he'd been unable to see anything so innocent up there. Nightmares had replaced dreams. Fantasy couldn't keep up with reality. He'd look up . . . and all he'd see would be his own face, staring back.

He closed his eyes, brought his knees up, groaned slightly. They ached, his run that day longer than any he'd ever taken before. They hadn't let him exercise in the hospital, so he'd overcompensated when he'd gotten back, pushing himself farther and farther each time. He'd be fit for the Shropshire Marathon soon. Perhaps he'd win it!

He shrugged. He knew why he was driving himself so hard. Trying to get all the junk that they'd shoved into him at the hospital out. The drugs had made him feel sluggish, barely able to do much more than watch TV. And answer their questions, of course. Smart people—usually bearded men wearing glasses—gently probing him as to why he'd shut his body down, all other causes having been ruled out. And why he'd tried to set fire to the hospital, of course. He'd nearly told them the truth, blurted it out just to get them off his back.

"Thing is, doctor, I'm a time-traveling berserker; I've murdered people in different centuries. I'm also a hawk and a werewolf! Oh, and every person or beast I've ever been still lives in me, just waiting for the right trigger to . . . oops! Sorry, doctor! You didn't need your throat, did you?"

Sky laughed and winced at the same time. If they'd pushed him much more, it wouldn't be his old bedroom he'd be lying in now but a padded cell!

Swinging his legs off the bed, he went to the window and sighed. It really was depressing here this time of year. He'd spent last winter in a freezing cave in Corsica . . . and missed it! England didn't have extremes of season anymore. Rare snow, quickly gone. Only this bleakness, a world reduced to gray and black; leafless trees, branches like bones. Below him, the apple trees looked like a dozen scarecrows, their branches like skeletal arms, their fruit rotting on the ground. It had been a late fall, so his parents had delayed the harvest. Then Sky had shown up again.

He shivered. It had been down there in the orchard that he'd seen his first draug, the headless corpse that had stalked him. He'd thought then that the bony hand reaching for him was just another of his nightmares. It wasn't. It was the start of something else entirely.

"Entirely"? The word sounded familiar in his head. Where was it from? Then he remembered. *"Non Omnis Moriar"*—"I will not die . . . entirely." The epitaph carved on the headstone of Sigurd's grave in Norway. Well, his grandfather had proved the truth of that. He was out there somewhere now. Not entirely dead. Not dead at all. It was why Sky ran at noon. It was the lightest part of a winter's day.

Headlights came round the corner, swept up the driveway. It was only two in the afternoon, but it was the shortest day of the year. And Mum was always cautious.

Two women got out. One of them was Kristin.

For the first time that day, Sky smiled.

"Mum," Sky called. "We're just off for a walk."

His mother appeared in the kitchen doorway, instant worry on her face. It had taken all Sky's gifts of persuasion to get his cousin invited for Christmas as usual. Sonja still suspected that they'd run away to Norway eighteen months before because they were in love, despite all evidence to the contrary.

"Really? I was just about to put the kettle on."

"Mum," he laughed, "you're trying to drown us. We've had two pots already."

"Well . . ." She turned back into the kitchen. "Henry, why don't you join the kids? You could do with the exercise."

"Hmm! What?" Sky's father shuffled into view. He had his slippers on and was clutching a beer-brewing magazine. Taking off his reading glasses, he saw Sonja's look. "Oh, well, yes, love to. . . ."

"Oh good, Uncle Henry. I was just going to tell Sky all about my new boyfriend. He's had this hot tub installed in his bedroom, with candle holders and—"

"I'm sure they'll be fine on their own, dear," said Henry hastily. "Don't fuss so."

Sonja gave up the battle. "Just make sure you take your scarf, Sky. It's bitter out."

When the door closed behind them, Sky said, "Hot tub?"

Kristin smiled. "Be nice if it were true." She shivered. "It's cold, isn't it?"

"No new boyfriend then?"

"Nah. When you've seen your last one possessed by your grandfather, it kinda puts you off men. Except you, of course." She took his arm. "So? Tell me everything!"

Sky laughed. "Not one for small talk, are you? I haven't seen you for seven weeks."

"They wouldn't let me visit. Your mum still thinks I'm at the root of your . . . illness. Plus I had exams to write." She squeezed him hard. "Come on. What's going on? Your e-mails were so bloody cryptic."

He looked around. "E-mails can be read by others."

"Bit paranoid, Sky?"

"Well, you know what they say: just because you're paranoid doesn't mean they're *not* out to get you."

"What, Sigurd read e-mails? A ninetysomething Norwegian?"

"He's trying to take over the world," Sky replied. "I think he can probably handle cyberspace."

She frowned and held his arm a little tighter. "Dirk was pretty good with computers. And that's who Sigurd was . . . in, last we saw." She shivered. "Have you, uh, heard from him, at all?"

"Oh, yeah."

"What? When? How?" She stopped. They'd crossed a stile, were climbing a field up toward the forest.

"Keep going," he said, pulling her along. "And when we reach the fence, look back quickly, then turn and tell me what you've seen."

"It's like a kids' memory game."

"So play."

The rich, turned soil was wet, clinging to their boots, slowing them. Wheat husks were scattered in the plowed furrows. He remembered walking this same route with her, with the crop just knee-high, on the way to his second rendezvous with both Sigurd and Bjørn.

They reached the fence. "Now?" she asked.

"Now."

She turned, stared, turned back. "Right," she said, "there's the hedge along the road, a delivery truck driving along that, your house. This field, a scarecrow in it, field across the road has cows—"

"That's enough. Now do the same thing again."

She did. "Your mum's in the window now." She waved. "Truck's turned the corner, one cow's mounted another, which seems weird, and . . ." She stopped. "Wait a minute," she said. "Where's the scarecrow gone?"

She began to turn again. He stopped her. "There isn't one," he said.

"You mean . . ."

"Draug."

She gasped, let him tug her toward the fence. "How long have you seen it . . . him?"

"From my first day back here."

"But Sigurd must know you'll spot him?"

"Them, actually. I'm sure there's more than one—though it's a little hard to tell, what with the black cloaks and the headlessness and all."

He was trying to make light of it, and Kristin picked up on it. "Couldn't Bjørn have sent them? Like: 'Contact Sky for a good time! He helped me move on, he'll do it for you.' " She laughed. "You could charge a fortune!"

It wasn't something Sky could find funny for long. "I think Sigurd just wants to show me how powerful he's become. How he's ripped more souls from their rest."

Kristin climbed over the barbed wire, held it down so Sky could do the same. "So he's challenging you. It must mean he's—I don't know—scared of you somehow?"

"Doubt it." Sky led them up a leaf-slick path into the woods. "Except he's always said how I could be more powerful than him. But that could be just another trick. Trying to flatter me into helping him?" He shrugged. "There's still a lot I don't understand."

"Well, maybe you can understand this." She reached into her bag, pulled out a sheaf of papers.

"Not here," said Sky. The rain had started again. "There are some pines up ahead. A bit of shelter."

Near the hill's crest, Sky found the tree he was looking for. On his knees, he led her under the low branches into a sort of cave of needle and cone.

"Cozy," she observed. "And I have this." From her bottomless bag, she produced a flashlight with a lamp bulb on top of it. Its light filled the hollow. Lifting one of the papers—he saw that it was a flyer—she said, "What do you make of this?"

She tipped it toward the light. It was glossy, the paper thick and creamy. Embossed on the top was a symbol. A rune. A jagged "S."

"It's our old friend *Sowilo,*" Sky muttered. Taking it, he began to read aloud.

SOWILO: the Sun. Ancient runic symbol of the journey within, guide to the mysteries of one's true self.

Have you ever felt that there is another "you" within?

Have you ever woken from a dream where your body, liberated from the shackles of illness or injury or daily labor, has soared above the world? A dream where your mind, cleared of everything that others have told you to believe, was freed to believe only in itself?

And, on waking, did you not wish that the dream was reality, reality merely a passing dream?

It is. Freedom is here. Revealed in ancient tradition, guarded and passed down by a select few through the centuries.

And only a few can learn its secrets now.

Are you one of us?

Are you ready to soar beyond the limits of your body? To cast off the chains that hold back your mind?

Freedom is yours!

Sky looked up. "Sigurd," he said.

"No doubt. And did you notice that?"

She tapped the very bottom of the page. There, in tiny print, was a title.

"The Church of the Freed Spirit," he read, looked up. "Where did you get this?"

"It was an insert in a magazine I subscribe to—*Mythology Today.* Then I went down to the shops and looked through some other mags." She handed him a photocopy. "This was an ad in *Biker Monthly.*"

He scanned it. One half of the page was occupied by a woman in a bikini straddling a large motorcycle. The other half had words. "It's a bit different," he said, handing it back. "More 'Meet the Sacred Warrior Within.' More runes too."

"And this one was in *Gaia Weekly.*"

Sky read. "Different emphasis again. More . . . New Agey."

"Oh yeah. Total granola! But you know what's common to all? They're all magazines published by Springbok Media, Inc." Sky looked his question. "Oz van Straaten's company. Dirk's dad. The media mogul?"

Sky nodded, then squinted at the bottom of the page. "He's having a meeting in . . . Birmingham. Why Birmingham?"

"It's not just there. It's all over." Kristin was flicking through the pages in her hand.

"All over England?"

She handed him the sheets. "For now. But by next year . . . all over the world."

Sky looked down. These were printouts from a Web site. He looked at the URL. "Fetch.org.uk? You're kidding me!"

"Why not? Who actually knows what a Fetch is?" She leaned forward. "You know what this means?"

Sky nodded. "Sigurd's recruiting. That's what he told me he'd be doing in Cambridge. Seeking out those"—Sky thought back to the conversation with his grandfather on the fire escape—"who were 'gifted.' He's after disciples, isn't he?"

"Yes, but disciples are always a limited number, right? Like twelve?" She tapped the sheets. "This looks more like he's trying to start a mass movement."

Sky stared at pine needles for a long moment. "You know what he's doing?" he said. "He's forming a cult." He began flicking through the pages. "He's been busy. And it looks like he *has* mastered cyberspace."

"I told you my former boyfriend was always pretty good at that stuff. And remember Dirk's connections. His dad doesn't just publish magazines and newspapers. He owns TV companies, film studios. . . ."

"Maybe he got some help with the phrasing too." Sky was reading the flyers again. "It's pretty smart, isn't it? Appeals to anyone who feels 'different.' Who has a dream. Well, who doesn't? And that 'ancient tradition' and 'select few' stuff. Everyone wants to feel part of something secret. But all these meetings? Perhaps he's already got some disciples. He can't attend them all, surely."

Kristin riffled the pages. "Every one is on a different day. I checked."

"Still, that's an insane amount of traveling. Unless . . ." Sky whistled. "You know, he told me the very first time we met that eventually my Fetch would be able to . . . 'cross the world in a heartbeat.' " He lowered the pages so she wouldn't see his hand shaking. "How powerful has he become?"

"Plenty. And did you notice something else about the first flyer?"

"What?"

"The meeting in Birmingham? It's on December twenty-third. Two days' time."

Sky suddenly felt really cold. "So?"

Kristin echoed him, incredulous. "So? So we have to go. Birmingham's, what, an hour away?"

"By car, yeah."

"There you go. I passed my driving test last summer. We'll just borrow your folks' car and . . ." She paused, seeing his face. "You all right? You've gone very pale."

He swallowed. "I'm OK. It's just that I'm . . . I'm not sure I'm ready for Sigurd yet."

"Ready? You mean, like, to fight him?" She put a hand on his shoulder. "Course not. But we have to know what he's up to so we can fight him eventually."

Sky blinked. Behind his cousin, in the shadows thrown by lamp onto pine needles, he thought he'd glimpsed another pair of eyes. "So you're suggesting . . . ?"

"We go to the meeting, in disguise perhaps, sneak in, listen, sneak out." She smiled. "It'd be like wall-walking again when we were kids." She squeezed his shoulder, put on the cowboy-movie voice she'd always used when they'd set out to walk the walls at night behind his old house in London. " 'So, are we walking or are we talking?' "

He shrugged her hand off. "Kristin, he'd know we were there."

"Well . . ." She blew out her lips, then looked at him with a new glint in her eye. "Then let's sneak in as our Fetches." Before he could protest, she hurried on. "Come on, cousin. You promised me in Cambridge you'd show me how to, you know, walk. Without all that 'blood and sacrifice' crap. As easy as breathing out, you said."

"It's not that—"

"Then we'll adopt some guises. Not a lynx and a wolf perhaps. Too bulky. We could, I don't know, become mice." She suddenly thrust her front teeth out, wrinkled her nose, and he couldn't help but laugh. "He'd never spot us!"

"He might. And anyway . . ."

"What?"

"Who would guard our bodies?"

Kristin wasn't going to be put off. "We'll park in some obscure place, leave them safe—"

"No!" Sky shouted, and Kristin jumped. "No," he continued, more quietly. "You don't know what it was like, coming back, watching . . . myself being taken away. And then, to . . . *meet* myself? You can't imagine, it"—he put a hand over his eyes, closed them—"was horrible. Terrifying. Bollocks! Such useless words." He opened them again, looked at her. "I was . . . *sundered* from my body, Kristin. Condemned to fade away, turn into a draug. You've seen 'em!" He shook his head. "Walking the world forever. Barely heard. Scarcely seen. Dead but not dead . . . *entirely.*" He shuddered at the word. "I don't think I'll ever want to walk again."

Kristin went to speak, to react, then silenced herself. Sky watched her, realizing that all he'd been through, the fighting, the murders, the transformations into human and beast, had ultimately been for her. For love of her, of course. But also because he wanted his older cousin to admire him. What would she say now to his cowardice?

She reached forward, took his left hand in both of hers. "Sky, I totally understand. Well, of course I don't, I can't imagine the terror you went through. But"—she leaned closer—"don't they say, 'For evil to flourish, it takes only a few good people to look the other way'?" She shook his hand gently. "Can you look away from this evil? When you have a chance to stop it? When maybe you are the only one who *can* stop it? Well, you and me, but I don't have nearly your power . . . yet! But *together* I think we are a match for Grandfather, don't you?"

Her hands had moved down onto his wrist. Suddenly, she twisted the skin opposite ways in a Chinese burn.

"Ow!" he yelped, jerking his hand free. He rubbed his wrist, studied her, her certainty. Nothing she'd said was new to him; he'd thought it all himself, terror and courage chasing each other through his brain ever since he'd gotten out of hospital. He knew what he *should* do. What he should oppose. For Sigurd was going to force everyone on the planet to walk side by side with their Fetches, to visit ancestors and learn their secrets. And from the look of the flyers and his Web site, his plans were quite advanced. He saw it as liberation, when Sky knew it would be pure chaos—anarchy, not freedom. Each time he'd traveled, there had been a price to be paid. Some crime had been committed, some experience forever lodged within him, part of his nature now—something, given the right stimulus, he might have no option but to repeat. He had a werewolf within, a killer—two killers!—within. And if everyone on the planet was to do the same . . .

He sighed. He was just so tired of "shoulds." All he wanted was to be a normal young man again, score the perfect goal, ask Alison on a date. And yet, with Sigurd loose in the world, and recruiting disciples now, could he turn away?

"I'll go," he sighed, "on one condition."

"Excellent. Name it."

"I won't leave my body unguarded."

"But who could we get to look after us? We can't very well—" She stopped, seeing his face. "Oh, no. No. No!"

"Yes."

She raised her head to the pine-needle canopy. "Oh, great!" she shouted. "I get to be the bloody Gatekeeper . . . again!"

CHAPTER SEVEN
CULT

Every creature Sky had inhabited had also partly inhabited him. The hawk, the wolf, each had their distinct ways of being, urges that drove them. Both of them longed to hunt, to kill. In the past Sky had let them have their way, get the taste of still-pulsing flesh into jaws or beak. Sated, the beast was more easily mastered, bent to his will. And surrendering to an animal's instincts—what a rush!

But a weasel's very different, Sky thought. Curiosity had to be a major characteristic of the species—the bloody thing just wouldn't keep still! There was always something it wanted to see—over here! over there!—and once seen, give it a damn good sniffing! Sky had thought he'd just be able to curl up in a corner of St. Mark's Church Hall, watch and learn. But there was no resting in a weasel. And trying to stop it was harder than letting it go.

Fortunately, he'd found the beams. A framework of them held up the ceiling, a roadway of dust and cobwebs twenty feet above the floor. Sky could let the weasel body go and, with a small exertion of will, direct its energies the length of the long room. He could hover above the stage, where a screen had been set up, a single microphone on a stand before a lectern. He could run back, stop directly above the pile of blue mats from some yoga or martial arts class, and watch the doorway for the first arrivals.

He and Kristin had gotten there early, three hours before the meeting was due to start. Partly to find a safe place to park—they'd found an alley of abandoned garages with a view of the church hall—partly to give Sky time to . . . transform. Which was harder to do than usual, given the intense scrutiny.

"Go on, then," Kristin had said, turning off the engine, folding her arms, staring at him.

"It's like undressing in front of someone!" Sky had protested. "Can't you at least look the other way?"

"No. Since you can't be bothered to sit down and teach me—"

"There hasn't been a lot of time. Besides, it can't really be taught. It's more—"

"Exactly! I will observe you, O great master! Perhaps then I'll be able to learn to do it myself."

Grumbling, Sky had tuned her out, focused inward, as Pascaline had taught him to do in Corsica. But this was not merely stepping out of his body on a breath. This was . . . borrowing the form of a creature. One that suited his requirements. Kristin still thought the mouse the best choice—small, easy to hide. But Sky had wanted something with a little more power. And teeth.

Now, as the weasel's body drove him for the fortieth time back along the beams, he was not so sure. Then the first people arrived, and he managed to stop and stare.

He'd wondered if any particular type of person would be drawn by Sigurd's words. But the first two could not have been more different—a huge Hell's Angel in full leathers and chains, pushing a wheelchair containing what was probably his mum, a tiny lady in a blue wool dress. Behind them came two middle-aged couples, all wearing glasses, all in tweed and corduroy. One of the men was talking very loudly.

"Of course, Gudjonsen made a fundamental error in his translation from the Icelandic Eddas. . . ." The other man began talking at the same time, and Sky lost all sense of it in the six-syllable words. They were followed by a group of seven students chattering excitedly, each clutching the flyer.

More and more arrived. The hall was nearly full when the doors were finally shut. Running the length of the beams, Sky noticed that though people were jumbled together, there were distinct subgroups within the mass. Right before the stage, ten wheelchairs were placed, with several sets of crutches beside men and women on the front row. The next three rows were occupied by well-dressed people, mainly middle-aged. Behind them were the students. At the back, arms folded over beer bellies, disdaining chairs, stood a dozen bikers.

There did not seem to be any organizers amongst them. If they were there, they blended into the crowd. Scanning it, Sky had just passed the midpoint of the hall when the lights dimmed, then went out. For a moment, the only light came from the fire exit signs. Then the screen began to glow.

Even the weasel's desire for movement was halted by the jagged "S," the rune *Sowilo,* that burst through swirling clouds to fill the white canvas. There was music, some type of flute, a solo note, pure, joyful. In a moment, it was joined by panpipes, the two voices harmonizing, while the rune gradually dissolved into the soft beams of a rising sun. One by one, three figures appeared, shielding their eyes. The first was an old woman, upright and strong, in comfortable purple. As she lowered her hand, Sky could see she held secateurs in it, that she was standing in a beautiful garden, banks of flowers surrounding her, daisies, lavender, violets. She turned to a rose, reached, faded . . . and was replaced by a man, leaning forward across a table. Slowly, the camera pulled away; Sky could see that the man was in a wheelchair and that he was helping a student, also wheelchair-bound, with a science experiment. As they, too, faded, a drum, an Irish bodhran, began its knucklebone dance across a stretched skin; the flute and pipe picked up pace to a military beat. The third figure came clear—a soldier, dressed in modern fatigues and camouflage paint, with gun smoke staining his face.

Next, all three of them appeared side by side. They closed their eyes, their figures merging with mist. Out of it came a white stallion, mane and tail flowing, racing over a great green hill.

Sky's weasel eyes, which had stayed wide to take in all these images, suddenly snapped shut. A moment, a wink, nothing; but it was odd because in his time as the creature he had never blinked.

The horse plunged across a wide blue river; swimming strongly, it emerged onto the other bank, shook itself dry, galloped on. It took a path between fields: in one, the wheat sheaves stood tall, crowned in white; in the other, they were already half fallen. There was the teacher again, but dressed in the clothes of an ancient time, a simple woven smock and breeches tucked into boots. He leaned on a stick; one leg was withered. But in his other hand was a flail, and he was beating at the wheat sheaves laid on the ground. More were thrown down beside him by the soldier, now stripped to the waist, his muscled body glistening with the sweat of labor. As the horse plunged past them, each raised his hand to salute it.

Sky blinked again. It was the oddest thing, like he'd developed a twitch. But his eyes were clear as the horse swept through the village, past the grass-roofed house in which the old woman stood, crumbling bunches of sweet herbs into a cauldron upon the hearth, preparing her healing salves. She straightened, rubbed her back, waved at the horse as it passed her . . .

. . . to a blink! Sky's eyes opened again, to the horse approaching darkness, a roiling gray cloud. The music changed, too, no longer pleasing, turning harsh, jagged, fearful. A trumpet blared, the horse reared onto its hind legs . . . and a man stepped from the cloud. A warrior, huge in jet-black armor, cruel desire clear in his too-close-together eyes. He turned, shouted back to shadow figures forming in the mist.

The trumpet sounded. In the field, the warrior drew a sword. The farmer dropped his flail and picked up a hand scythe. In her hut, the wise woman lifted her bow down from the wall.

The battle began with a cascade of drums. Indistinct shapes moved through smoke, there was the flash and clash of blades, cries of pain, triumph, terror. Lightning struck, a war in heaven as well as on earth. Sky, within the body of the weasel, felt something move even deeper within. Memory. Desire. He recognized the warrior he'd once been, his ancestor, Bjørn, stirring for a fight.

Then the music dropped to the merest caress of bone upon stretched skin. The pipe came, a lament now. And there was the woman, lying in her doorway. There, the farmer, beside him, the warrior. All dead.

But they lay amidst the heap of their enemies, and in the distance, the black army fled.

The horse returned; Sky blinked. It nuzzled the bodies in turn, and as it did, a living spirit arose from each of the dead, stood above its flesh, upright, strong. Whole and healed of wound, of disability. The horse reared up . . .

While back in the garden, a flower fell from lifeless fingers. Fell slowly, because before it even reached the ground, the woman rose, to stand behind her body and smile straight out. . . .

And on a basketball court, that same student from before threw a ball from a wheelchair, scored the winning points. As he was mobbed by his teammates, the camera moved courtside, to a man seemingly asleep in another wheelchair—the same man standing behind him, applauding the shot . . .

While on a street in a desert town, the soldier pulled an unconscious man from a burning jeep, carried him to safety through a firefight. Laying his burden down, he reached inside his flak jacket . . . to the blood there. Yet even as his body crumpled, another identical one stood tall behind him.

One by one the three of them turned—warrior, teacher, healer. One by one they raised a hand to the sunrise. And in that instant, Sky knew what was going to ride into it. So he blinked, deliberately, in the microsecond before the horse appeared and so saw what he'd missed before. It was the briefest glimpse of something, barely there, instantly gone. But it *was* there.

"Ehwaz," Sky murmured.

A rune. Not just any. It was the symbol that meant "horse." It was unity of the tribe against all others. It was obedience, loyalty beyond death, the sacrifice of oneself for the good of one's people.

Ehwaz was all this and something else.

Ehwaz was the rune of the Fetch.

Whoever had made the film had slipped the rune into it, so that it could only be seen by the unconscious mind.

It was Sky who moved now as much as the weasel, for he could not keep still. The film was clever, because even Sky, who could see its purpose, had been stirred by it. It was beautifully made, expensive. Sigurd, possessing the media mogul's son, had been busy. It made you want to belong to the tribe of your ancestors. It made you dream of sacrifice for a cause. A sacrifice that was an end, and a beginning too. Summed up in the words that now appeared on the screen in glowing red, in lettering that was almost runic.

NON OMNIS MORIAR.

Sky had moved back till he was above the door end of the hall. He settled again, in time to see two things happening: a cat leaping from the top of a cupboard onto the beams at the far end; and, on the stage, as the words faded and the screen light dimmed, another light softly growing. It fell on a figure standing at the lectern. He had not been standing there before, and a gasp came from the people as they noticed him.

It was not someone Sky had ever seen. Bearded, middle-aged, dressed in a dark blue suit. Warmth radiated from him as he smiled down. His voice, when it came, was as welcoming as the smile.

"It means," he said softly, gesturing to the screen, to the Latin words merging into sunlight there, " 'I will not die entirely.' " He leaned on the lectern, bent toward his audience. "I do not ask that you believe this now. I only ask that you consider it. Many of us do believe that we have something—some*one*—within us, ourselves and yet not quite ourselves. Something pure, unsullied by experience, by illness or disease." He gave the faintest of nods to the wheelchairs lined up below him. "By death. And if we do believe that some part of us goes on, can we not believe that that same part is here with us now? Not side by side. Closer than that."

Sky shifted, his eyes drawn by movement. The cat had immediately paused to clean its paws. Now it set off, meandering toward him. Sky leapt from his beam to another that intersected it. There was a network of them up there, crisscrossing. He didn't know if the cat had seen him. But the animal distracted him, annoying because he wanted to concentrate fully on the man below.

He'd stepped away from the lectern and come forward to the edge of the stage. The phrase had disappeared on the screen, to be replaced by the rune

Sowilo. "Our ancestors certainly thought something else lived both here and . . . beyond. Energies that were usually—*usually!*—invisible to the eye. They felt them, used them, explored them. Today we'd call it magic. To our ancestors, well . . . magic was just part of life."

Another rune appeared on the screen, two arrowheads pointing away from each other. *Jera,* Sky thought. Harvest. Working together to bring it in.

The man gestured to it. "And our ancestors turned these energies into symbols. Carved them onto stone, onto weapons and tools. Onto parchment. Energies that could be released later to help them in their lives. Any aspect of their lives. Healing. Crops. War. Love." He smiled warmly. "Our ancestors called these symbols of magic 'runes.' I am sure some of you will have heard of them, even studied them. Others, maybe not. But would you all try an experiment for me?"

The cat had definitely seen him! Worse, it was coming to check him out. It had leapt, with that easy feline grace, onto his side of the network of beams. After letting it get a little closer, Sky suddenly moved fast down an outer straight. The cat stopped and watched him.

"Under your seats—for you at the front there are pouches on the edge of the stage—you will find a pad of paper and a marker. Take them up."

There was a rustling as each there sought, found. "Good," said the man when everyone had settled.

"Now, I want you all to close your eyes, breathe deeply in, that's good, now out, shallowly in, deeply out, shallow in, deep out." Exhalations filled the hall. "Excellent! Keep breathing! That's it. And when you are ready, draw a symbol. Use straight lines, no curves. Big, bold strokes. Not one of the ones you've seen on this screen. Anything else you like. One from your imagination. One from your . . . spirit."

Breaths taken, sharp, fast. Someone groaned. Then there was a frantic scribbling, followed by silence. The screen came on, with a hidden camera trained on the audience, showing them to themselves.

The cat leapt again. It crossed to the beam beside Sky. Closer now, he could see that it was a brindled tom, a big one at that, its ears torn from many a fight. They eyed each other across the divide.

"Good, good! Now, when I say, could you all lift your papers. Not yet! On my word. Take a breath!" He paused. "Now!"

The papers were raised . . . to a huge gasp. Sky, looking away from the cat, looked at the screen . . . and gasped too.

They were not all identical. But of the hundred or so people in the room, ninety were holding up the same symbol. The same rune.

Ehwaz.

He shook his head angrily. Of course, that's the rune they'd choose. It was hidden in the film, planted in their minds. But they didn't know that, and so the astonishment and pleasure was clear on their faces, in their exclamations of joy. The man had bonded them together already. Except for the few, whom he wouldn't care about.

Sky's anger distracted him. Looking down, he'd taken his eyes from the other beam. Looking up now, he saw that it was empty.

The cat had moved along, jumped behind Sky, unheard. It startled him; but since he knew that a weasel could outrun a cat, it didn't worry him too much.

Until the cat said, "You must be Sky," and, with barely a twitch of its back legs, leapt.

A weasel could outrun a cat . . . but not when it was so surprised it forgot to run. Claws sank into Sky's rear legs, raking him as he tried to twist away, the twisting causing his grip on the metal beam to slip. For just a moment, the only thing holding him aloft was the cat's grip on his legs. Then he scrabbled with his front paws, caught hold, kicked out with powerful back limbs, finally knocked the cat away. It bared its teeth, its huge incisors lined in yellow film. Then, with a shriek, it leapt again.

Sky screeched too. A weasel could run or it could fight. Sky launched himself under the cat's widespread paws, aiming his own fangs at the throat; but the cat bunched in on itself at the threat and Sky took a mouthful of chest fur. Chomping down hard, he reached flesh. He had the strangest sensation that he was biting his grandfather. But then he remembered the cat's voice—working-class English—and suddenly he knew. . . .

Sigurd had his first disciple.

Shouts and the squeal of pushed-back chairs told Sky they had been spotted; but still the animals rolled and twisted, each fighting for dominance while keeping balanced on the beam. Then Sky began to kick his back legs, raking the claws hard against the cat's stomach. It couldn't free itself, so instead it used its bulk to flip them both over. Each lost contact with metal. It was replaced by air.

Falling, for a moment Sky thought he was a hawk. But he had no wings to slow him, the cat's weight pushing him even faster down. He braced himself for a crash that would certainly break something—some injury that his body back in the car would also receive. . . .

It didn't come. Instead there was softness, a slight give to the impact. It still hurt, knocked the air from him. But it wasn't the wood of the floor or the back of a chair.

Cat and weasel rolled from the pile of exercise mats. For a moment, each was too stunned to renew the fight.

"It's a rat," someone yelled, causing immediate shrieking, chairs being thrown aside, people hastily backing out of the way.

"I'll get it."

Winded, Sky looked up. It was one of the bikers,

huge and tattooed. He was unwinding a length of chain from his leather jacket. Then he ran forward, swinging it.

The chain arced down and Sky only just rolled away in time. Links crunched into the floor where his head had been. He rolled onto four paws and one buckled. But then he began limping fast toward the benches stacked at the side of the room, toward some kind of shelter.

Other bikers had the same idea. More chains were unwound, and metal again smashed down beside him. Sky leapt onto a pile of benches—and greasy links flew at him. Scrunching down saved him, the chain raising fur as it passed over his body. It smashed, not into the wall, but into the fire alarm. Instantly, the bell's blare filled the hall.

As he squeezed down behind the benches and ran along the floor against the wall, having no clue where he was going, someone began to shout, "Clear the hall, please! Assemble outside the building."

There were a lot of shifting chairs; wheelchairs pushed rapidly out, the doors finally swinging shut. Beyond them, the noise of the crowd faded. Though the alarm still clanged, the loudest sound was undoubtedly Sky's weasel heart beating wildly.

With his keen animal hearing, under the clanging, Sky heard footsteps. Approaching slowly. Run or stay still? Did they know where he was, scrunched down there? Then the feet halted. Sky raised his head just a little, saw a dark blue trouser leg. Almost immediately, a furry head pushed against it.

A hand came down, stroked. "Yes, Peter. I know he's there."

A second cat appeared. This one spoke, a female voice. "Shall we drive him out for you?"

"Why not, Lucinda?"

She came at him from behind. Wedged between bench and wall, he had no room to maneuver, to use his weasel agility. Cat claws drove him forward, into waiting cat claws. The male cat he'd fought before seized him now. One he could escape. But just as he was about to twist free, the other grabbed his haunches. He felt its claws sink into fur and he stopped twisting. The cost of breaking free, even if he succeeded, was torn flesh. And, safe in the car, his body already carried enough scars. While this close to the cat's oval eyes, Sky felt his courage begin to slip away.

The footsteps came again, halted. The man bent down. "Hallo, Sky," he said, and even though he spoke in the gentle tones he'd used to lecture before, even though there was not a trace of a Norwegian accent in the voice, the man who spoke was, undoubtedly, Sigurd.

"So here you are once more, Grandson. Getting in the way again," he sighed. "And I'd thought that being separated from your body might make you more cautious. But I always forget: you have my blood in your veins. The blood of Bjørn the Berserker, of all our ancestors. And that blood is hard to restrain, isn't it?" He bent lower. "I always knew we were alike, Sky. Truly, there's little that keeps us apart. It would be interesting to find out how little." He turned to the two cats. "Hold him tight."

"No!" Sky screamed. His terror was so great, he might have broken free of the cats' grip and paid the price later. But then a man's hand pressed down on him, crushing the breath from him, and he could not move.

"I'm sure you know this one, Sky. *Ehwaz,*" Sigurd said in his new, cultured English tones. In his other hand he held a runestone, the "M" carved upon it. "It is the key, of course. So useful in our little film here." He gestured into the hall. "These people here. They were on their way to joining us. At least, a select few were. But your interference has quite broken the spell." He laughed, a sound without humor. "It seems that Birmingham will have to do without Fetches. But maybe my time here hasn't been a total waste."

He lifted the runestone high, intoning as he did so, "I call on Loki, Trickster God, Lord of Misrule, of shape-shifting. Of possession."

He looked down, his voice once more normal. "*Ehwaz,*" he said. "Rune of the Fetch. Of sacrifice for the tribe. Of belonging." A light came into his eyes. "I wonder what it will be like when you belong to me."

Smiling, he thrust the runestone down.

It was as if someone had opened up his skull and

driven a red-hot blade into his brain! Sky tried to scream, his cry muffled by lack of breath, by the pressing hand. And the thought came within the pain . . . So this is what it is like to be taken over. This agony. This desolation.

But then . . . then the pain faded, faded fast, vanished, taking the terror with it. He started to feel . . . amazing! Was *this* possession then? Being possessed. What should have felt like a violation, everything he'd fought against, felt . . . wonderful! Like the time when his Fetch had gone into his ancestor's Fetch, Tza's Fetch, when she was a Dream Hunter, when she'd killed and healed as a Mazzeri Salvatore. He'd given up the loneliness of himself to become one with another. Wouldn't he do that now? Dissolve into another as he had dissolved into Tza? Merge and mingle so completely with someone, blood of his blood?

"Ah," said the wise old voice. "Yes! Now I begin to see. You've always been so alone, Grandson, haven't you? How sad that has been for you!"

He didn't need to be held. He wouldn't give this up if he could choose to. This . . . togetherness. Maybe they all felt it, for the cats' claws eased their grip, the man's hand barely touched him. He thought his question. Where did you learn this, Grandfather?

He felt it as if he was living it—the spasm of pain, the shadowed memory. "Another ancestor. A witch. And in those days in England, how a witch suffered." He shuddered. "How I suffered—so you won't have to.

There's always a sacrifice to be made for knowledge, isn't there, Sky? A price to be paid. This one, the greatest ever. But it was worth it. For moments like this. This and a little deeper."

There was a last surrender to be made, to end the loneliness. So easy to do, to sink into those clear blue eyes. . . .

The spray took Sigurd in the face. Though it was as if it had taken Sky, too, so close had they become.

"Let him go!"

Chemical foam dripped down on him as Sigurd shrieked and fell back, his shriek echoed as the cats leapt forward and were hit in their turn.

The only one unblinded, Sky looked up . . . and saw Kristin standing three feet away, a fire extinguisher in her hands. As Sigurd tried to step toward her, she hit him with another burst full in the face. He reeled back.

"Come on, Sky. Come!"

He'd found his legs again. Leaping, he landed on her shoulder. Flinging the extinguisher at the three yowling figures on the floor, Kristin turned and ran.

They burst through the crowd outside the doors, just as the fire engines pulled in. Everyone was focused on the rumpus, so they were able to pass through unnoticed.

They were halfway up to the car when Sky remembered, "You left me!"

"I know I promised not to," replied Kristin, "but you were thrashing around so much, I knew something bad was up. Then I saw all those people pouring out. Sorry, but—"

"Thank God you did. Because if you hadn't . . ."

They reached the car. "Was he trying to kill you?"

"Worse," shuddered Sky.

"Tell me."

"Let's get away first. Far away." He jumped off Kristin's shoulder. "Get in," he said.

"After you," she replied, and pointed at his body curled up in the car.

CHAPTER EIGHT
THE PLAN

Kristin had frightened Sky enough on the drive to Birmingham. She seemed to consider red lights optional and speed limits a challenge. But the return journey was worse. Mainly because she kept looking over at him in amazement as he described what had happened in the hall.

"Look, will you keep your eyes on the bloody road!" yelled Sky as yet another oncoming car blared its horn.

Casually, his cousin pulled the steering wheel back. "Stop being such a wuss, Sky, and tell me more!"

"I won't be able to tell you anything if you kill us."

"You will." She shot him a grin. " 'We will not die entirely,' remember?"

"I don't want to die at all, thank you very much. Slow down, or I'm shutting up!"

Reluctantly, she eased up on the gas. The car dropped to a more reasonable fifty, though the signs still said she should be ten miles an hour slower. "So this film? It wasn't like a home movie?"

"Hardly. It wasn't very long. But it was very slick. Big budget."

Kristin bit her lower lip. "I don't get it. How could Sigurd, inside Dirk, even with the van Straaten media empire behind him, organize that in, what, seven weeks? Not to mention all this cult stuff. I mean, doesn't the guy sleep?"

"Maybe not." A chill had run up the back of his neck at his cousin's words. Sky turned to her. "Oh, my God! Aren't we missing the obvious? That bearded guy back there—it was definitely Sigurd. But Dirk's too valuable to abandon, so . . ."

The speedometer rose again. "So . . . Sigurd, what, body hops?"

"Well, apparently he can. And if he can move between two people, why not four?" Sky whistled. "Why not possess anyone you need? Screenwriter. Producer. Cameraman . . ."

She pointed to one of the cult flyers on the car floor at Sky's feet. ". . . Secretary. Printer . . ."

"Plus, who says he just began after he possessed you? He's been planning something for years, right? When the opportunity came . . . a lot of it was probably already in place."

"But surely possession's not that easy, even for him. I mean, when he went into Dirk that first time"—Kristin shivered—"it looked so . . . so painful!"

"Maybe it was. He'd been thwarted that night, remember. Beaten for the first time. Perhaps even the almighty Sigurd was a little upset." Sky caught the shiver. "You'll recall how tough it was for me to get back into my body when I was exhausted."

"But even so . . . ," she sighed, words obviously failing even her. "Jeez! He's gotten pretty powerful, hasn't he?"

"Oh yeah. I think we've got a bit of catching up to do."

That silenced them for a little while. Then Kristin said, "You say this film was also, like, hypnosis?"

"Definitely." He rubbed at the back of his leg. He could still feel where the cat's claws had dug in there. "It was all very stirring, but then it had this . . . this extra frame, or something. You couldn't really see it with the conscious mind. I only caught it because . . . well, it was a rune."

Kristin accelerated to overtake a truck. "Like a subliminal thing? Didn't they ban that in advertising? Like flashing a shot of an ice-cold drink, to make people thirsty, so they'd buy more soda." She glanced over. "Which rune?"

"Ehwaz." He looked over to see if she got it.

She had. "Ha. Rune of the Fetch. Planted it in their minds . . ."

"Then he got them to draw a symbol. And, surprise, surprise . . ."

". . . they all drew *Ehwaz.*"

"Most of them, yup."

"And all were amazed, yet felt part of something too. Something big!" She grunted. "Not too dumb, our grandfather, is he?"

"Runs in the family, eh?" Sky tried to stretch his leg out. "And I'm sure there was more trickery to come. His audience was lapping it up."

"Course. Give each individual a sense of sharing some mystery, some ancient truth. They're no longer alone, but with people who are, like, their spiritual brethren, blah blah blah. . . ."

"Like a religion. . . . Kristin!" he yelped.

She ignored him . . . and accelerated through the yellow light. "Or a cult. Get people to believe enough, then they will do the cult's work. Obey the orders of a leader-slash-priest unquestioningly. In Norse history, there's a lot about the Cult of Odin." She whistled. "Sounds like you saw the beginnings of the Cult of Sigurd!"

Sky thought about the flyers she'd shown him, the Web pages. "And he's recruiting all over the world," he murmured.

She chuckled. "Well, we stopped his recruiting drive tonight."

"We didn't stop it. He stopped it . . . by sending his cat-disciple to hunt me down." He looked across. "He knew I was there from the beginning. He expected me to come. Like I walked into his trap. And then . . ." He shuddered. "Well, you saw."

"I saw two ugly felines with their claws in you. And I saw a man holding you down. I didn't realize it was Sigurd." Reluctantly, she stopped at a traffic light, since it was definitely red. She studied Sky. "What was he trying to do to you?"

Sky reached to turn the heat up. "When you came along? Nothing much. Just trying to possess me." He'd tried to keep his tone cool but it came out in a quaver.

"Oh, Sky! That's . . . that's horrible."

"Yeah. Yeah, it was." Sky looked out the passenger's window. An old man in gaping shoes and a threadbare coat was rooting in a garbage can. He glanced up at Sky, then returned to his search.

"When he did it to me"—she shuddered—"I can't remember feeling anything."

Sky looked back. "No? You screamed like a banshee."

"Did I? I don't remember that. And I didn't believe it, of course. Well, as you know. But did you . . . did you actually feel it? Him trying to get *into* you?"

"Yes. But he didn't just dive in. He took his time."

Someone tooted behind them. The light had turned green. As Kristin pulled the car away, Sky looked again at the homeless man, who pulled a newspaper from the bin and shook it as if waving them goodbye.

"Like torture! Yuck!" Kristin was moving up rapidly through the gears. "Was it terrible?"

"Terrible. And also . . ."

He'd paused, and she glanced at him. "Also?"

No. He couldn't tell her. Not now. Not when he didn't understand it himself. Understand the worst feeling of all. How he'd almost . . . wanted it.

"Nothing. I don't think I can talk about it right now."

"OK," she said carefully. "Later, maybe?"

Silence again, though Sky could sense the questions roiling inside her. Somehow she managed to restrain herself until they were turning in to the driveway of his parents' house. Switching the engine off, she turned to him.

"So what now?"

"Now? Bed?"

"I don't mean *now* now. I mean, what do we do now about Sigurd?"

"Do?" he asked, as if there was a choice. A huge part of him wanted to believe there was. That he could choose not to look at something—and then it wouldn't be there. Like the draug that waited in the apple orchard even now, the winter wind filling its black cloak. If he didn't look at it, maybe it wasn't there?

But he did look . . . and there it was. Yet, even as the sight of that headless cowl chilled him, another feeling came—the sense of a lost soul yearning for life. Or rather, like the draug Bjørn had become, yearning for the finality of death. When Sky had realized in that churchyard that Sigurd had ripped a soul from its rest, it had made him angry.

It made him angry now.

"Do?" he repeated, but in a different tone. "I'll tell you what we have to do. We have to find a way to stop him possessing us. Possessing anyone." He leaned in to her, and starlight was reflected in his eyes. "And then we have to find a way to beat the bastard."

It was Christmas Eve. In a Norwegian house, that meant a party. Henry, the Englishman, had long surrendered to the Norse way of doing things. It meant there was no turkey, but roasted pork belly, thick with glistening crackling. It meant cabbage, not Brussels sprouts; Yule sausages, not stuffing. It meant presents around the tree after supper. But it also meant Henry could lie in bed on Christmas Day, while his English friends got up early and fussed.

Between Sky's dad's extra-strong Yule ale and the five helpings that Sonja insisted everyone have of everything, it was two somewhat bleary teenagers who hauled themselves up the attic stairs after the parents had gone to bed. But once Sky had pulled up the ladder behind them, once the trapdoor had closed them off with its solid *clunk,* the room itself removed all their tiredness. It was chilly, but that wasn't what made them shiver.

This was where it had all begun.

"It seems so long ago, doesn't it?" Sky whispered.

"Yes. And like yesterday," she replied on a breath that plumed in the air.

Both looked up to the skylight. Henry must have fixed it after the bat smashed it in. The creature had fallen onto them, bitten and scratched. Sky had stabbed it with his knife, pinned it to the ground . . . sacrificed it. Its death had enabled him to travel, the first of the journeys back. Each one demanding further sacrifice.

As if thinking the same thought, they both shuddered, both looked away, down . . . to Sigurd's sea chest; still there, though empty now. Sonja must have cleared it of furs and photo albums. The secret compartment in its lid was sealed with tape—if she'd discovered it, Sky's mother had seen its emptiness and not looked further.

Kristin reached in, tapped. The compartment gave off its hollow sounds. "Where are the runestones, Sky?"

"You asked me that once before up here. Except it wasn't you doing the asking. It was Sigurd."

"It's me now."

"And I'll tell you the same thing now. They're safe."

She frowned. "Still don't trust me?"

He took her hand. "Course I do. But until we know how to . . . protect ourselves from Sigurd, why share that knowledge? He probably doesn't need them. He'll have a new set now."

The memory came, of *Ehwaz* being pressed into his skull. It brought both a shiver . . . and something else. He shook his head to clear the feeling. "But his old set would still be a weapon, and I reckon he's got enough of those."

She tried a French accent. "You mean, he might torture zee truth out of me?"

"No. I mean he might not need to torture it *out*. Because he'd be . . . *in*."

She jerked her hand away, rubbed it across her eyes. "So, why are we up here?" she said brusquely. "What secrets *can* we share?"

"Well, I haven't had a chance to tell you everything that happened—"

"I know! It's so annoying. . . ."

"—but I've been thinking a lot about what went on in Cambridge. Do you remember when we went into the hut to get your body back, and there was Sigurd, as a gull, sitting on Dirk's chest . . . ?"

"Oh, yeah, *that's* something I'm likely to forget. . . ."

"And he talked about how possessing you that first time had been the hardest thing he'd ever done? How it had nearly killed both of you?"

"Yes." Kristin leaned closer. "But then he said he'd had to find another way. Learn from another ancestor, right?"

"Right. He talked about it when he was trying

to . . . you know . . ." He tapped his head. "Said something about a witch. An English witch."

"Really? A witch?" she gasped. "Actually, that's kind of cool . . . in a creepy sort of way." She rubbed her hands. "And I can see where you're headed . . . back, right?" Her eyes were bright even in the dimness of the attic. "So all you have to do is pick the runes, put them in a cast, and go!"

He laughed, a bitter sound. "So simple, eh?"

"Isn't it?"

"Course not!" Sky sat back into the shadows. "I'm never *exactly* sure how I do it. There are the runes. There's the question. And there's my need—what I am trying to learn has always drawn me to the ancestor who can teach it to me. But what if it doesn't? What if I ask the wrong question and go somewhere . . . some*when* . . . into someone else?"

Kristin's forehead creased in concentration. "Well, you've never traveled into an ancestor who you didn't need something from. Why would you start now?"

"I suppose. . . ."

"Although . . ." She cleared her throat. "It's not only about what *you* need to learn, is it? When you traveled that first time into Bjørn, it was with Sigurd's runes. *His* need."

"But that," said Sky, seeing it, "that would mean that Sigurd can—can—"

She finished for him. "Can somehow control who he goes back into."

Sky closed his eyes, thought about it for a moment before he spoke. "And you know what that also means? All his talk about being drawn to the ancestor you are like. Bunch of crap. We're like them all, blood of our blood"—Sky faltered on Sigurd's familiar phrase—"and it's only our need that draws us to this one, not that one. Our need for what they can teach us. Good or bad."

Kristin nodded. "Yup. Sigurd lied again. Big surprise."

It wasn't, of course. But it still hurt, the knowledge that he'd been used. Dangled like a puppet by his grandfather, yet again. He felt like one, his arms suddenly weak, not his own. He dropped them onto his thighs. "So if—*if!*—I went back again . . . how would I know he isn't controlling me? Sending me back to learn something else . . . for him?"

She leaned down till she was sure he was looking into her eyes. "You'd know because it will be your runes, your question . . . and your choice what you do with what you learn."

For a moment, her certainty almost drove his weakness away. But then he remembered something else. He looked down. "I'll tell you what I'm sure he didn't lie about," he said softly.

"What?"

"The price to be paid for the knowledge." He covered his eyes with his hand, the last of the courage he'd felt earlier leaking away. " 'The greatest ever,' he said. I'm not ready for that. Not even close. Not ready to take . . . something else into me. I'm feeling weak. The hospital. Sigurd's . . . probing." He lowered his hand, looked at her. "I'm not sure I will ever be ready, Kristin."

She reached forward, took the hand, squeezing it gently. After a long silence, she spoke. "I totally understand, Sky. I can't imagine what you've been through . . . well, actually, since you 'murdered' me, I can, a little." The faint smile vanished. "So it's clear to me that there are three things we have to sort out before we even think of going."

"We?"

"Of course, 'we.' That's the first thing. There's no way I'll let you go alone."

He shrugged. "I'm not even sure how I get back, let alone taking someone else, and—"

"*And* you leave that to me. You may have spent a year brooding in a cave in Corsica. But I didn't just sit around doing my nails."

"But—"

"TWO!" she overrode him loudly. "We have to find out what our need truly is. As you say, get drawn to the right ancestor. And have you considered this: would learning how to possess also teach you how to resist possession?"

"Huh. Like . . ." He stared up at the sloping roof. "Like if you knew how to pick a lock, you'd be able to build a lock that's hard to pick?"

She smiled. "Nice! So—three! In order to get the question right, absolutely right, we have to know a lot more than we do right now. Knowledge is a weapon, yes?" She shook his hand excitedly.

Some of her courage reinfected him. "Well, knowledge is one of the reasons we're here." He gestured to the attic, then slid over to the bookcase. "I thought this might help." He pulled the *Compendium of Horror* off the shelf. On its cover, in glowing colors, a zombie wrestled with a vampire.

She cocked her head. "Horror stories might help? Isn't living them enough without reading them?"

He handed it across. "Open it."

She did. Inside the pages were all stuck together, their center cut out to form a compartment. Two objects lay within. "What's this?" Kristin said, lifting up a small leather pouch.

"My caul. The skin that covered my face at birth, remember?" He took it from her, felt the hardness within the soft leather of the sack. "It helped me travel that first time, helped me get back."

"You used to wear it all the time."

"I know, I stopped." He turned it over in his hands. "It was a link to the Norse bloodline, which was also Sigurd's. In Corsica, I was trying to hear other secrets, in different blood. But it's Norse blood we're going to have to explore again now, so . . ." Uncoiling the leather cord around the sack's neck, he slipped it over his head.

Kristin nodded, then looked down into the hollow again and whistled. "Sigurd's rune journal."

"Yeah. I took it to London, and before I went to Corsica, I left it in a safety deposit box I have there. Remember the diamonds Sigurd gave me?" She nodded. "They're in there too."

"And his runestones?"

He smiled. "Maybe." He pointed at the journal. "I thought it might be useful, so I brought it back."

Kristin picked the book up. Immediately, it fell open to the page with the runecast they'd first followed. But she didn't linger long on that. Flicking other pages revealed more writing, more casts.

"Now I know he wrote all this before he learned to possess," Sky continued, "but since he was trying to gain that power, maybe there's a clue, some speculation that could point us in the right direction." He sighed. "Though I haven't figured out how to get it translated. I mean, who could we trust?"

She kept flicking the pages. "Me," she said, without looking up.

"What? You speak Norwegian suddenly?"

"Hardly suddenly. I spoke some before. And I told you that I had to choose a language component for my degree, that I spent most of last summer in Norway, studying, remember? Not far from Lom, actually." She glanced up briefly, kept flicking, reading.

"But this"—he pointed—"is probably quite technical, isn't it? I mean, do you know enough?"

"Yeah, I think so. Certainly enough to know that this"—she tossed the book to him—"is a fake."

"Wh-what?" he gasped, catching it. "You mean, it's not Sigurd's?"

"No, I'm sure he wrote it. Even used different pens to make it look like it came from various times. But it's so . . . entry-level." She wrinkled her nose. "Rune 101. As if copied straight from a 'teach-yourself' book. Which it probably was." She leaned forward, flicked the book open, pointed. "I mean, look at that: *'Laguz:* flowing water. Thus the female in . . . in everything, linked to the phases of the moon.' Please!"

"But why?" Sky sat back stunned, staring at the journal in his hands. "I mean, Sigurd knows runes. Why wouldn't he write something good?"

"First thought?" She stretched her arms out. "He needed something fast. Something to fool a novice. You, bright boy!"

"Why fast?"

"Perhaps our grandmother's death gave him the way to reach you. Remember, all her stuff was going to be sent here. Plus he was getting older, sicker. He had to take his shot. So he cobbled this together, sealed it up in the chest . . ." She leaned forward to tap the book. "And it worked, didn't it? You were hooked. He didn't think you'd look any deeper into it before you were his."

"Well, you were hooked too!" Sky grumbled. Now she'd said it, it seemed so obvious. Sigurd had played him like a trout on a line from the start. But what pissed him off most was that his plan—to seek the ancestor he required through Sigurd's writings—was blown.

"Bollocks," he said, heaving the journal into the open chest. "Bloody bollocks!"

"You know what, though? I think you're on the right track."

"How?"

"If this is fake, all the rest won't be."

"What 'rest'?" he said. Then remembered. They'd spent an afternoon in Norway lugging all Sigurd's papers, all his years of rune research and Fetch speculation, into the stone shed behind his mountain hut, preparing the room for the ambush of Olav. The hut had been destroyed by fire, of course. But . . .

He noticed the smile on Kristin's face. "Are you thinking what I'm thinking?"

"Depends," she replied. "Because what I'm thinking is: Can you ski?"

CHAPTER NINE

"IT TAKES A RUNE . . ."

He could. But this wasn't skiing as he knew it: whooshed to the top of a mountain in a gondola, shooting down, carried up again on a lift. This was hard work on long, narrow cross-country skis that, after the initial run in from the town of Lom, spent much of the time slung across his shoulders as they climbed up the snow-clogged forest path. Since they were also packing winter-camping gear and enough food for their stay, what would have taken them two hours in summer took closer to five.

They struggled up a last rise, breaking clear of the tree line into a valley. "There," Sky panted, pointing up. "Top of the hill."

They struggled up. When they'd come before, they'd pushed along paths through a fern sea, to a huge, flat rock on the summit. Now, in a world of concealing white, they just aimed for the highest point, reached it, dropped their packs and skis, looked around. It was the same land, transformed, the ice wall of the glacier beyond shutting off the valley's end, the slopes dropping away from where they stood to their right, leading to other snow-capped hills in the distance, a forest in between. Four paths led into it.

"That one?" queried Kristin, pointing.

"Think so." Sky looked down. When they'd first come here, they'd been guided by a rune carved into the rock—*Othala,* rune of ancestors, had pointed the way down one of the paths. But since that signpost was probably six feet below them now . . .

"Yeah, think so," Sky repeated. "Shall we . . ." He pointed at the packs.

Kristin shook her head. "Nah, let's come back for them. Check it out first. Let's ski, man!"

It was great after the grind to just let go; to race each other, build up speed on the slope, barely slowing for the narrow path entrance between two silver birches. They were even laughing as they threaded between trees barren of leaf, branches lined in white. And then, all too suddenly, they were there, and the laughter died. Heat rose from their bodies, combining with their heaved breaths into columns of steam above them. They could feel, in their nostrils, on the tips of their ears, how cold it was. Still, for the longest time, neither of them moved, just stared at the hummock of snow that covered the burnt remains of Sigurd's hut.

If the attic had been the beginning of the journey,

this was where the path had led. To a dead grandfather who wasn't; to the murder of a man and the stealing of a soul—the soul of the girl breathing hard next to Sky now. But in the end, this clearing in a wood in Norway hadn't been a final destination either, just another way station on the road to more extraordinary things. And now they hoped a clue would be found here to point them toward the ancestor who would teach them what Sigurd already had learned: to possess and so to resist possession. Yet, as he looked around, Sky knew there was something else he sought here too: the courage to go back again.

Both shivered. Both knew it had little to do with the cold. "Come on," said Sky at last. "Let's get the gear, get a stove going, have some tea."

"Tea," laughed Kristin. "The answer to everything."

"If only," muttered Sky, turning his ski tips back.

In activity there was distraction from their thoughts. It was a race, too, because they knew that in the mountains of Norway the sun set early. Fueled by sugar-rich tea, they hustled. They stretched a tarp between branches, slanted it at forty-five degrees so it would catch and hold some heat from the fire pit they dug under it. The wood store—it was to the side of the hut and so had survived the blaze—was clear of snow, the logs dry beneath a covering of yew boughs. Kristin laid the fire while Sky set up the tent. With the beginnings of dusk graying the world around them, they heated canned stew and wolfed it down. Afterward they sat, side by side, staring at the flames, not speaking. Sky found himself slipping into "cave mode." He'd spent a year in that *oriu* in the mountains near Cauria. Much of the time—all of the winter—he'd sat like this, making worlds out of flame and crumbling ash. He'd have been content to do that all night now.

But Kristin wasn't. "C'mon," she said. "*Op igen,* as they say in these here parts."

"Which means?" he asked, though he thought he knew. His mum had said it to him as a kid anytime he fell over.

"Up again!" she said, rising.

He joined her, reluctantly. "It's nearly dark," he complained.

"So? We can't just work in daylight—there's only about six hours a day this time of year here. And what have we got? Five days before our flight back?"

"Yeah."

"I think, given your recent 'history,' your parents were quite cool to let you go skiing at all. Even if you are with your 'old friends' in . . . " She looked around. " 'Switzerland.' So you better not miss your flight because we haven't looked hard enough."

"You're right. Let's go!"

They hadn't yet checked out the little stone shed behind the cabin. A delaying tactic perhaps; because if it wasn't there, or was damaged, the whole journey was a waste of time. But it was still there, also buried in white. Digging revealed the double doors, the padlock locking them together. Which presented the next problem.

"Where's the key?" she asked.

"Haven't a clue."

"Smash it with that?" She pointed to the spade in his hand.

"Too flimsy. But I've got something else." He didn't have Death Claw, Bjørn's ax, used to kill again here that terrible night. But he did have a small wood-chopping hatchet.

It was no Death Claw, but Sky still had an axman's skill; the padlock was soon hacked from the wooden frame. Sweeping the area clear of snow, they grabbed a door each and, on "three!", jerked them open.

The shed was small enough, less than Sky's height tall, about his height across. But they'd forgotten how much they'd packed into it—Sigurd's long lifetime of studying runes and Fetches. They stared at books and folders, manuscripts and sheaves, plus thousands upon thousands of loose pieces of paper.

"Oh, crap!" Kristin muttered. "Do the words 'needle' and 'haystack' come to mind?"

"No. Because at least you know you're looking for a needle. Here . . . we don't even know what we're after. A single sheet? A journal? And maybe we're wrong. Maybe there are no clues here at all." Sky sighed. "We're bloody bollocksed!"

"We've got to try anyway. We've come all this way." She leaned in, grabbed a wedge. "Come on."

They returned with an armful each to the tarp under the trees. The light had gotten poorer, so Sky had to hang a lamp from a branch. It illuminated nothing.

"This is ridiculous." Sky added yet another page of scrawled runes to the huge pile in front of Kristin. "Five days! We won't get through this in five years!"

"I know!" Kristin sat back with a groan. "This trip's a bust."

Sky looked up into the silver birches. And maybe it was a trick of the fading light. Maybe just that Sky had been seeking some sign. But he saw it, in the curiously regular pattern of mold across the white bark. "Yew," he muttered.

His cousin looked where he was looking. "Birch, you twit."

"No," he replied, pointing. "That mold on the tree. It's a rune."

She looked closer. "Oh, yeah. I see it. *Eihwaz*. The yew. Big deal."

He sat up, went to the tree, ran his fingers down the line of mold. "I think it is, actually." He turned back. "Isn't there an expression: 'It takes a thief to catch a thief'?"

"Yeah, so?"

"So maybe we need a rune to catch a rune."

"Meaning?"

He gestured at the pile of papers before her. "We'll never get through a tenth of what's in the shed. Not with our conscious minds. But when have our conscious minds helped in all this? We need the runes." He tapped the mold. "And, if you remember, this one, *Eihwaz,* is all about solutions."

Kristin came to stand beside him. "Yes," she said, "but I also remember it's usually a solution *delayed.*"

Sky was undoing the flap of his backpack. "But runes rarely exist in isolation, do they? What if this one's linked with runes that, you know . . . speed it along?" He pulled out the red woolen bag. The sound of stone on stone made him shiver. He shook it, to hear more clinks. "Shall we?"

She was as excited as he was now. "Do you want a cloth to lay them on?"

He fiddled with the leather neck cord. "Why? If the myths are anywhere close to true, then Odin took up the runes in a land of snow." He smiled. "This is home turf!" And saying it, he opened the neck of the bag and spilled the stones out.

Gray on white. But that wasn't why they stood out here in a way they hadn't on the earth floor of his cave in Corsica. He'd fashioned each one there, granite from the Granite Island, each runestone invested with his beliefs, his prayers, his musings by day and night. Yet they hadn't belonged there. The stone, yes, but not the symbols carved upon them. For they were from this land, a Northern world of ice and snow far removed from the maquis-scented warmth of the Mediterranean. And, just as Sky had felt when he'd first come here, under his spread palm he could sense the stones surge as he had surged, with the blood of ancestors, the secrets whispering in it.

These runestones, like him, had come home.

"Sky?" He heard a snapping nearby, looked up to see Kristin clicking her fingers. "Thought I'd lost you there! You OK?"

"Fine," he replied. "Shall we begin?"

"Sure. Uh, how?"

"You've done runecasts before, Kristin."

"Of course. But mine have usually been aimed at freeing my Fetch. Apart from the odd attempt, I was saving divination for later."

"It's the same deal. We seek something. We need help." He stood. "So first we have to ask for it."

He tipped his palms up; Kristin did the same. They closed their eyes. As one, they intoned the invocation: "Odin. All-Father, guide us now."

He bent again, reached for the runestones. She still stood. "C'mon," he said.

"I thought you'd want . . . you know . . . your stones and all."

Sky smiled. His cousin was not often hesitant about anything. "After all we've been through, I think we're in this together. All the way."

"Right-ee-oh!" Excited now, she crouched. "Turn them all over?"

"All except this one." Sky reached, set aside one stone. *Eihwaz*. He jerked his thumb to the tree behind them. "It's already chosen itself. Now we need two more."

Swiftly, they turned over all the stones that showed their faces, until all twenty-three were symbolless granite. Then Sky laid his hand upon hers, and they pressed down, cracking the crust of ice that lay on top of the snow. Each taking a deep breath, they began to swirl the stones clockwise, knowing that the other way, widdershins, was a swirl to send away something, not draw it toward them. They stopped as one, looked down. The stones had churned up snow, the heat from their hands causing some of it to melt.

They stared in silence at the unrevealing backs. "What's our question?" Sky murmured.

Kristin frowned. "Help us to cut through these mountains of paper, so we can learn the secret of Sigurd's journeys to the ancestor who taught him possession and—"

"Simpler!" Sky interrupted. "Everyone thinks the runes are so complex. But they were simple tools for a simple people who needed help with things like crops, or swords, or love. Magic was practical."

She nodded. "So . . . 'Something's hidden and we need to discover it'? Or 'Help us find what is hidden'?"

"Perfect." They each closed their eyes. "Help us find what is hidden."

With eyes shut, they reached down, hovered for a moment, then picked.

They opened their eyes, looked at each other. "You first," he said.

She placed her stone next to *Eihwaz*. "A diamond," she said. "Sigurd gave you diamonds, right? But of course it's actually . . ."

"Ingwaz!" they said together.

Sky leaned closer, peering. "And as you know, it means 'seed sack.' Holding what will be sown for the future harvest and—"

"Or 'scrotum,' " she interrupted, smiling when he winced.

"Anyway," he continued, "um, a place for storing power to be used."

"And didn't we say before: 'Knowledge is power'?" She gestured in the direction of the shed. "That's a storehouse of Sigurd's knowledge, his power." She nodded. "Good. We're on the right track. Your turn."

Sky opened his fist, laid the stone down. "Hmm! One I've never really used before. *Jera,* a harvest. So totally linked to the seeds in *Ingwaz.*" He shivered. He was cold but that wasn't why. "It was also at the cult gathering."

"Forget that. This is our cast, your stones. And a harvest is what you strive for all year, right? It's, like, rewarded effort." She looked at the papers piled up by the fire. "So where's our reward?"

"In the hut?"

Snatching up the three stones, they walked over, stared at the piles of paper. Nothing had changed. A chill wind riffled them, nothing else.

Sky didn't know what he was expecting . . . but nothing wasn't it. It was Kristin who spoke. "Maybe . . . maybe we have to do something else."

"Like what?"

"Well . . ." She bit her lip. "When we were in the hospital, and you . . . were two—uh, still deeply weird, by the way—you got back together by painting a rune, didn't you?"

"And burning it," Sky added excitedly. "Yes, we could try that. Have you got any paper?"

"Sky!" She gestured at the mound before them.

"Not his. If the journal was a fake, we don't know what else is untrue here. You don't do rune magic on lies." He turned to their camp. "I haven't any paper. But you must have some in your bag?"

"I've got toilet paper. And that's it."

"What? No diary, notebook, nothing?"

"No. But . . ." She waved at the trees. "How about birch bark? Might be more . . . appropriate anyway. Part of the land."

Sky thought, Bark might work, except . . . what would he draw the runes with? A ballpoint pen? His own blood? He looked around . . . and saw it. Beyond the trees, over them. Everywhere. Another part of the land.

"Snow," he said.

"Snow?"

He turned to her, excited now. "I know what we'll do."

"What?"

"This."

Saying was one thing, doing another. He was no sculptor, his skill limited to slashing runes into stone. And the twilight played with his eyes, making it hard to define the white edges. But eventually three rough-hewn blocks of pure white, about knee-high and as wide, stood before the shed.

"Very Picasso." Kristin stood with her head at an angle, studying the snow runes.

Sky blew on his hands. He'd had to take off his gloves for the final shaping, and his chisel—the one he always used for carving, the quartz chisel from Corsica—had frozen his flesh. "They'll have to do."

"Oh, I think they'll do fine. But what now?"

"According to Norse myth, the world was formed from ice and fire." He smiled. "So now we burn!"

At the still-glowing fire pit, he snatched up three branches of the yew that had covered the wood supply, their needles rust-colored, dry. "Here," he said, offering one.

She didn't take it. "You want me to . . . I thought . . ." She jerked her head toward the snow runes.

"I had to carve them myself. I think there can be only one carver. But as I said before: all the way!"

He pushed the stick closer, and she took it, thrust it into the flame. It caught immediately, sweet smoke rising, yellow flame running up needle and branch. He did the same, and together they bore the brands back to the shed.

He didn't need to say anything. She knew what to do. And the All-Father had already been called upon. "*Ingwaz,*" she said softly. "Stored knowledge. Release it." Then she jabbed the stick's end into the top of the snow rune. Immediately, it began to melt.

Sky stepped up. "*Jera.* Harvest. Grant us our reward." He drove the wood into white.

For a moment they watched each transform, snow returning to liquid, the red-flamed fire sticks sizzling,

sinking into dissolving white. Then heat on his hand warned him. The last stick was being consumed fast. "I think I've been burned enough," he said, turning to Kristin. "Shall we?"

Her hand covered his, as his had covered hers over the runestones. Together they lifted, brought the brand down hard, driving it into white, chanting as they did.

"Yew to yew. To *Eihwaz.* A solution . . . no longer delayed."

They didn't know how they spoke as one, just that they did. And as they did, the first two snow runes collapsed, their still-flaming branches sinking into icy water, snuffing out in a flash of steam. Only *Eihwaz* burned a little longer, until that, too, fell.

Its spluttering ended; silence came, the silence of the forest and the night finally, fully fallen. A waning moon was out, that and starlight etching the trees in silver. And then, out of the silence, came a sound. The crack of something giving way.

They stepped back, startled, as before them the paper horde shifted, then collapsed. Pages spilled onto the snow.

"The water! It will ruin them." Kristin leapt forward, trying to snatch up what had slipped into the puddle left by the melted runes.

Sky hadn't moved. "I wouldn't worry too much," he said softly. "See?"

Kristin stopped, hands full, looked where he pointed.

It was as if the top of a mountain had sheared off, revealing its core. At it, perched there as if set on a ledge, was a roll of parchment. A red-ribbon bow held it together. The paper had not been squashed by the weight of paper above it. It was as if it had just sheltered within a cave all this while.

Waiting.

CHAPTER TEN

FARING FORTH

It was a family tree. And it began in the year 1066.

"See anyone familiar?" Kristin asked, craning over, pulling the sleeping bag up to her neck. They'd returned to the tent to study the paper and keep warm.

Sky cleared his throat. "There's . . . Thorkell Grimsson. There's Bjørn Thorkellsson and the other brothers. There's . . . their children. Look, Ingeborg Bjørnsdottir, Bjørn's daughter, see?"

He lifted the page to her. She peered. "That's a strange name, right next to Thorkell's at the top. " 'Henri de Barfleur,' " she read. "Why a French name?"

He was scanning the page ahead of her. "Speaking of strange . . . look at this—two English names suddenly amongst all these Norwegians: Matthew and Margaret Brakespeare."

" 'Died 1644,' " she read. Turning, she exclaimed, "If I remember my history lessons, mid-seventeenth century was a busy time for witches. She must be ours."

"Or he could be. There were male witches too. And Sigurd wasn't gender-specific when he mentioned it. All he did say was that he or she was English."

Kristin peered over his shoulder. "What are those marks beside Thorkell and Ingeborg?"

"They look like checks."

"What do you think they mean?"

He chewed his lip. "Remember, he wrote this paper before he died here in the burning hut—"

"Died . . . not entirely."

"Of course. But from my first travels back to Bjørn, I know he'd been Thorkell. And Ingeborg."

"So all the unticked ones are those he hasn't visited yet?"

"He may have by now. Some of them," Sky grunted. "I hope he hasn't visited Bjørn. He's not ticked but . . . I wouldn't want to share him."

Kristin laughed. "Oh, Sky! You're so sweet when you're jealous!" Then she tapped the page. "So, for now, we can forget about Henri de Barfleur and Ingvar—Bjørn's brother, yeah?—because they are not English?" He nodded, and she continued, "Which leaves Matt and Maggie as our prime suspects." She tapped the page. "They're unticked. But I'd bet he'd be able to tick them now. That one of them taught him how to possess another as . . . as easily as we saw him do." She bit on a nail. " 'Brakespeare'! It's got to be them."

"You're right." He'd been half hoping they wouldn't find anything. Wouldn't have to act. Now they had. And he did. "What did you say before? 'Knowledge is power.' " Sky sighed, "I suppose I have no choice. I've got to go."

"Not just you, buddy! Us!"

He looked at her, at the determined gleam in her eye. "Kristin . . ."

"All the way, you said."

"Yeah, but I didn't mean—"

"Twice, in fact!"

"I know. But I meant here, now, with the runes." Sky shook his head. "It's tough going back."

"Oh, and you think I'm not tough enough?" Kristin sat up, her sleeping bag falling off her shoulders, and thrust out an arm. "Want to wrestle?"

"No." He didn't—and not just because he wasn't sure he'd win. "It's not that kind of tough. I've told you before. Something gets switched on that can never be switched off."

"OK," she said, "I know there's a price. And I'm prepared to pay it."

"But we don't know how high it will be. From the way Sigurd talked about it, it was pretty damn high." He swallowed. "I think whatever it was tipped him over the edge. Literally sent him mad." He touched the hand she still had raised to him. "I don't want you to go mad, cousin."

She slapped his fingers. "I'm mad now. Furious!

Because you refuse to see the obvious. Sigurd probably cracked because he went back too often. Paid too many prices. You still might. But me—I'm a virgin."

"Somehow I doubt that."

She didn't even smile. "What I'm saying is—maybe I can handle it *better* than you . . . Wolf-boy!" She reached out, grabbed his wrist, twisted it up. "And this might be our only chance to go together. Two ancestors, ready and waiting."

He yelped, tried to slip her grip, failed. He could sense himself weakening, giving in to her certainty. So he used his last argument. "But how do *we* get back to *them*? I've sent myself back, but . . . it's strange, it's not like releasing one's Fetch here and now—"

"Which you still have to show me how to do, by the way."

"But time travel? I'm never quite sure *how* it's done. As we said before, it's to do with the question, the runes, and the need, but . . ." He shrugged. "I wouldn't have a clue how to send us both."

She released him, sat back. She knew she'd won, and smiled. "Well, maybe I know. Remember I told you that while you sat studying your belly button in that Corsican cave, I hadn't been exactly idle? Well, there's a branch of lore I've been getting into. Getting into a lot. Connected to the runes. Different. It's called Seidh magic."

" 'Seidh'?" He licked lips suddenly dry. "That's more . . . more 'woman's work,' isn't it?"

"Yes, Sky," she said, slipping out of her sleeping bag, pulling on a sweater, grabbing her jacket. "And in a later time, they'd call it . . . 'witchcraft'!" She smiled. "These Brakespeares are not the last witches in our family, trust me. Come!"

She unzipped the tent flaps, crawled out. Through the gap he could see the very last of the daylight, and he became aware of something else that had not been there before—the wind. It was strong, getting stronger.

A storm was coming.

It was bitter cold, the wind driving ice crystals into any exposed skin. Pulling up his hood, Sky put his back to it, tried to pierce the darkness. The waning moon was less help now, with tattered clouds being driven across it. He flicked on the lamp.

"Kristin?" he called. Faintly, as if from very far away, he heard her.

She wasn't that far. A little path from their clearing led deeper into the wood and, after thirty paces, opened into a circle of silver birch. She was standing at its center, her leather bag at her feet, eyes closed, head uncovered, arms reaching out to the side, bare hands gloveless.

"Aren't you cold?" he said.

"Not really." She opened her eyes, irises contracting in the light. "I need the stove, Sky. Can you grab it?"

"Can't we have supper back at the tent? It's a little more sheltered there."

"It's not for supper."

He felt a chill within the cold. "You're not planning on . . . not now!"

"No time like the present . . . for the past!" She smiled at him. "And certain spells are best woven at sunset. The 'faring forth,' for example."

"But we can't just . . ." He swallowed. "I mean, what about our bodies?"

"I know Norwegians are a tough bunch. But do you really think anyone's going to come all the way up here . . . with that coming?"

She nodded into the wind. Even in the little time they'd talked, its song had grown louder. "We have to make sure the tent's really secured," he grumbled, still seeking some delay. "We might be in it for a while."

"You do that. I'll prepare here. Do it, then bring the stove back." As she spoke, she bent to her bag. It was the same one he'd been inside as a hawk, so he knew it was roomy. But it was still a surprise to see how much stuff she had in there. Out came a knife, a corked bottle, a smoothed stick about the length of her forearm, a smaller leather bag, and what looked like an ashtray. Finally, incredibly, a small iron cooking pot.

"What, no Ouija board?"

She straightened. "I've gone a bit beyond that." She pointed. "Go!"

He turned, shrugging into the ice-heavy wind. But it wasn't the only thing that slowed him. All her . . . paraphernalia! It reminded him of Corsica, his great-aunt Pascaline, helping his Fetch leave his body so he could hunt as a Mazzeri, a Dream Hunter. It had been the first, necessary step to what he had achieved: freeing Kristin from Sigurd's possession. But he'd been so close to failing, and achievement had come with a heavy price—the legacy of a murderer, and a wolf forever lodged within him.

He knew Kristin was right—to fight Sigurd they had to learn how Sigurd fought. But he dreaded the necessity, and he knew the price demanded now was going to be the greatest yet.

He used the back of his ax to hammer pegs into every loop the tent had, brought some big fire logs over to weigh them down. Then he took down the

hanging tarp, which was bucking like a stallion, and shoved their packs and anything spare beneath it, folding the edges under, more rocks securing it. The work warmed him a little, but even on the short walk back down the path the chill returned.

And doubled when he saw what awaited him there.

Something else had come out of that bottomless bag. A dress, no more than a sleeveless sheath of white linen, covered his cousin now.

"Are you crazy?" he shouted above the wind.

She turned to him. Her face was as white as the snow on the trees around them, though her arms had a bluish tinge.

Her winter clothes were piled to the side, and

he went straight to them. "Put these on! You'll catch your death!"

"Uh-uh." She bent to the stove he'd dropped, set it up, pressed the starter button. Despite the wind, it caught. Immediately she put the iron pot on top of it. Uncorking the bottle with her teeth, she poured the contents in.

He watched, her down jacket in his hand. "Aren't you freezing?" he said.

"Yes, but it's not so bad. All ritual requires a bit of sacrifice, doesn't it? We both know that. This is mine." She waved at him. "Take your coat off."

"No way!"

"Sky!" she snapped, furious. Then she closed her eyes for a moment. When she opened them she was calmer. "Sky. This is going to be hard enough, more than I've ever attempted. We either do it, or we don't. But if you keep saying no to everything, it's not going to work." She took a step toward him. "So, do we do it or not?"

He stared at her, at her blond hair falling to her shoulders, into eyes that were now an almost iridescent blue in the frozen whiteness of her face. The dress clung to her—she was full-figured, not model-skinny—and it came to him that she looked like a Valkyrie, one of Odin's warrior-maidens, sent out to bear the best of all fallen warriors to the halls of Valhalla. There they would feast—until the day the trumpet summoned them to the last great battle, where gods, Valkyries, and warriors would fight against the fire demons, the giants, the frost lords. But they would lose. Ragnarók—the destruction of the Aesir gods, of the whole earth—would be upon them, the world sunk into darkness and ice.

Ice! Yet the Kristin who stood before him, this warrior-maiden, was not cold. Her courage warmed her. She knew his stories, knew the risks they were taking. And still she demanded that they take them.

Her courage could warm him too. "We do it," he said, reaching for his jacket zipper, running it down. But there was no moment to feel the cold, because she had run to him and slipped between his arms as he removed the coat.

"Good, Sky," she said. "Thank you. Thank you."

She held him for a moment—a strange moment, pressed against each other. He felt her tense . . . then she was gone, back to the flame, and the chill came. He shook his head twice, as if to clear it, and followed her.

She lifted the steaming pot from the stove by the wood grip in the middle of its handle. Now she placed a small metal tray onto the flame. From the little leather bag she pulled out what looked like dried moss and dropped it onto the metal. "Mugwort," she said, "gathered last Midsummer's Eve. It's the herb for helping to free the Fetch."

Sky remembered the plants Pascaline had heated.

She'd drugged him, and he shivered at the memory. "Isn't this all, you know, a bit black magicky?"

"That's from the movies. I don't believe in black or white. This is Seidh magic. It's from this land, as much a part of it as the runes." She frowned at him. "You remember your mythology, don't you?"

"Some." If he was honest with himself, it was the side of runelore that interested him the least. He preferred the practical stuff. "But I'll test you, if you like."

She sighed, a trace of a smile. "The runes are Odin's. But it was Freya, his wife, who taught him to shape-shift, change to bird or beast, travel through time. She was from a different race of gods, the Vanir. And they were more concerned with fertility, harvests. Love." She bent over the herb. It had begun to smoke. "Sniff!"

He knelt, did as he was told. It was a strange smell, sweet and acrid at the same time. And it seemed to drive away the cold. No, it *changed* the cold from something that chilled to something that exhilarated, like plunging into a freezing river on a hot day. "What do you need me to do?"

"A rune goes with the faring forth. Which one?"

"Raidho," he replied quickly. "Rune for journeys. To the living and the dead."

She unsheathed her knife, reversed it. "Cut it, Sky. Over there, into a birch branch. One facing the west, the departing sun. And as you cut, sing the rune."

"Sing it?"

She stood as he did. "It's another part of Seidh. The Galdr. The *sound* of the runes is almost as important as the sight of them. The sound is magic too. Energy. Release it!" She placed the knife in his hand.

The wind was blowing from the east. He turned the other way, checked the fading of light in the west, turned back to the birch. A branch faced the way he wanted. There was a strip of bark curling on the underside of it, and he pulled it away, revealing the wood beneath. Then he laid his knifepoint upon it, closed his eyes, took a breath, began to hum a note, a deep one, deep within him. Normally, he'd have been embarrassed about his singing voice, but he wasn't here. Maybe it was the mugwort, its scent still in his nostrils; maybe the echo from behind him, Kristin humming, too, a different note, higher, but in harmony. Maybe it was the concentration required to carve. For each rune had its own order of strokes.

"*Raidho* . . . ," they sang as one.

"Journey without
Within and on
Living to dead
Back and beyond
Time that is
Was, will be."

The song ended, just as the knife scored that last line up and to the center. Yet if it ended, it did not leave; notes clung to the branches, almost as clear to the eye as the sound was audible to the ear. He lowered the knife, aware that even as steel fell, wood rose. Kristin had an ash wand in her hand and now she turned in each direction, first north, then east, then south, finally toward the sunset. At each point, she chanted words Sky did not recognize, yet knew had been spoken in this land before, the tongue of the Old Norse. And as she spoke, the tip of her wand described a shape in the air, the same shape he'd placed into the tree. He saw the "R" of *Raidho* appear, curling as if made from smoke. But it was solid, and the wind could not scatter it.

She did that; breathed, sucking the symbol from the air on a huge inhalation. Sky knew what she had done—cleared the power, yes, you didn't leave power behind. But she had also taken the power into herself.

She turned to him and exhaled. But it was not mere breath that plumed in the air between them. A column of power linked them now. The wind gusted—but what bound them together could not be broken.

"What names do they call him?" She was shouting now, to be heard. "Wind Roarer! Tree Shaker!" She tipped her head back, eyes shut. "Odin rides at the head of the Wild Hunt. Listen to him come!"

She flung her arms wide as the storm roared down upon them like a living thing, doubling its force . . . and he swore that she rose from the ground!

"Kristin!" He had to bend to move forward, his

shoulders hunched against the ice the wind bore; not little crystals anymore . . . hailstones, striking, stinging. Yet he pushed against it now with a wild joy, with the song still in his throat . . . and found her along the thread of power that she had breathed out to him.

"We must . . . get inside . . . ," he shouted, though his face was only inches from hers. "This is not the worst!"

"This first," she yelled back, raising something between them. He squinted, saw that she held the pot, its sides cool enough now to touch. Yet the liquid within—wine, something else—was still hot enough to send fire down his throat, burning, intoxicating, as exhilarating as ice against the skin.

They drained it, he dropped it, turned her in the direction he hoped the tent was, bending to snatch up their discarded clothes—though he was moving beyond caring about anything so practical. Something was stirring within him, a pull of a different kind. Yet he knew: something more was needed. Something always was.

A last shove over the threshold.

He pushed her, both of them stumbling, laughing hard, into the teeth of the storm. Somehow they moved through the blasts. Somehow fingers found canvas. Metal teeth parted, rose up; he thrust her and their clothes in ahead of him. Then he turned back, offered himself for a last moment to the storm that only now was reaching its full force.

The Wild Hunt had found them, and a god flew at its head.

"Odin!" he cried. "All-Father! Guide us now."

The wind picked him up, threw him back, between the metal teeth, into the tent. The flaps leapt like living things; somehow he managed to slide the entrance shut.

The voice came soft from behind him. "You call upon Odin. All-Father. Summoner of storms. And it is right you do so."

"Kristin?" It was not her voice. It didn't *sound* like her voice!

The voice went on. "But Freya, his wife, is near as old a god. And she has different powers. Different needs. So *I* call upon her." The tone changed, dropped; the words that came next were breathed out like smoke, like runes carved into the air, hovering in the space between them.

"Come, Odin. Come . . . husband. Come."

Total darkness. But he didn't need to see, not when he could feel. The arms that reached for him. The body beyond.

Storm without. Storm within.

A last shove over the threshold.

CHAPTER ELEVEN

CIVIL WAR

Together. Then apart, because two bodies couldn't stay together when they were falling so fast, through darkness into deeper darkness.

Yet not completely apart. Sound linked them, something that he'd never experienced before when he'd traveled. Perhaps he'd just been deaf to his own screams. But here, for just a moment, he heard Kristin wailing, already starting to sound unlike Kristin, unlike anyone or even any*thing* human, dissolving into the rush of the fall, into wind that filled his ears like surf. A final glimpse, a flash of skin, fingers, stretching to what they'd been ripped from. Those gone too. Then it was just Sky, alone, falling through the total dark . . . toward the pinprick of light far below, which instantly expanded into a hole wide enough to plummet through.

He had experienced the joining before. Entered a body; once, a Fetch.

He had never entered a dream.

Now, he did.

It was a dream. She knew that, knew that the tugging came from beyond it. Yet, for the smallest moment, she was able to make even that a part of the dream. Not a summons back to the peril of the day. She knew who tugged her, who wanted her to stay; stay, and make the day last forever in the tall grass between the tombstones, the shadow never moving across the sundial they lay beneath; the sun never leaving their skin; and the river—just there, just down the path beyond the churchyard's gates—forever lulling them with the lap of water against pebbles.

And then came the sudden cold. She heard the storm hit, a season's change in a moment, chilling flesh. She felt them begin to fall through darkness, felt her hand slip from his. . . .

"No," she cried. "No!"

Another hand was pulling her. Not his. Another voice calling. Not his. "Mama? Mama?" the wail came.

"Hush now, child. Hush." Meg was as suddenly awake as she'd been completely asleep, pulling the small, trembling body of her son into her arms, immediately feeling, with a mother's total consciousness, the thinness of him, his bones pressed against hers.

"You were asleep, Mama, and you were laughing and you looked so happy and then you were sad and you were crying and I . . ." The words tumbled out on heaved breaths, and she smothered his face to her shoulder, whispering nonsense to him, lulling and rocking him until he settled into her, fell into the fitfulness that passed for his sleep. Carefully, she leaned forward, lifted the edge of sailcloth that covered the dogcart before her.

"Gudrun," she called, but her other child didn't stir. Rarely did when Meg tried to rouse her. She loved sleep as much as her mother was wont to before the troubles, would stay forever in that world of dreams. She was ever hard to lull. Once asleep, though, she would sleep a moon and a sun if she could.

A little smile came as Meg cradled her one, stared at her other. It lasted but the moment that it took her to look beyond them . . . to the street that curved from where she sat, down to the great wooden gates of the city at Mickelgate Bar. Hundreds of bodies lay between her and them—slumped over carts, jammed into doorways, leaning against walls, squatting on the cobbles, every space filled. Hundreds more packed the cobbled lanes that fed down to the street called Mickelgate, tributaries to its river, the flood held back by those twin slabs of wood. Those doors had denied entrance to Parliament's army for fifteen months, despite the savage hunger that had diminished all York's citizenry, pushed every child's belly out into a mockery of fullness.

She scarce believed the siege was soon to be over. York would still have held out for its king if half its garrison did not lie in bloody mounds upon the Moor of Marston, eight miles west. The army they'd marched out to join was meant to be their savior. Together they would scatter York's besiegers in one great battle. But the day had gone against them. It was the king's army that was scattered, leaving York to its pitiable remnants—more scarecrow than soldier.

Yet they had been offered warrior terms to yield the city: safe passage, under arms, to the nearest Royalist camp for any who desired it. Those who remained would make their own terms with the conquerors, most caring naught for victor or vanquished, caring only for bread.

Isaac moaned against her and she comforted him with soft words. She'd have stayed if she could have. This war, its reasons, were nothing to her. Her reasons were before her, fitfully asleep—Isaac, all of six, the fever pallor still upon him, mark of the sickness that had prevented them fleeing in a little more safety ten days before, when news of the defeat first came. And Gudrun, just four, sucking a shriveled thumb against her hunger, buried deep in a dream of plenty.

Her reasons. Leading them from one danger into another; a hard choice, yet none at all. Because *he* was coming. She could feel him as clearly as she had felt his hand in her dream, pressing her to stay. He waited now beyond those wooden gates. He would ride in with the conquerors. And he would take her reasons from her.

The leaving began when the iron cockerel atop the church of St. Martin-le-Grand was touched with dawn's light. It came in a drumroll, inexpertly played, that sent a ripple down Mickelgate as men and women stood, clutched what little they had, looked back. Somehow the thick mass parted, like the sea before Moses, allowing passage down the middle of the street, toward the great doors that finally opened.

The city's soldiers marched toward them; lurched more like, for the swaggering defenders were beaten men now, and many were drunk, though where they had found liquor in starving York amazed Meg. They came, half with eyes lowered in shame, half with them raised and challenging, pushing carts filled with wounded comrades, bloodied clouts on heads, legs and arms splinted, most giving off the same low moan as if from one tortured animal.

When half had passed, Meg bent to Isaac. She had her plan, such as it was.

"Here, love." She reached into the cart, pulled out the dress she'd cut down and shaped for him.

"No, Mother!" he protested, but not as hard as he had when she'd first told him what he must do. And he was too weak to resist her strength, urgent now as the soldiers' numbers began to thin and people gathered their belongings to follow them. She had positioned herself early on the street, so she could choose her place in the ranks. Not so tight to the armed men as to be among the first civilians; not toward their tail. Hidden in the middle of the mass.

Truly, the dress fitted ill. But clothes hang limp upon the famished. She draped a shawl over her son's head, wound it around his face. "You see that family ahead? With the chicken in the hutch?" He nodded. "Walk close to them. We will be here, just twenty paces behind you. Do not look back for us." She bit her lip, hesitating. "And remember what I told you: If you see your father, don't look at him. Don't call. Hide! It's a game, yes?" She looked hard at him. "Do you understand?"

He nodded. He was trying to be brave, she could see. But his chin was quivering, and moisture was in his eye. "All will be well, Isaac." She gripped his shoulder. "There's food aplenty in Uncle Torvald's house across the sea in Hareid. And he has dogs. Three spaniels to chase ducks with."

Dogs usually did it with Isaac. He swallowed, nodded, drew the head scarf tighter around his face. "Do not look back," she said firmly, pushing him off, turning fast so he would not see the tears she had caught from him. "Gudrun! Gudrun!" She bent to her other child, lying in the cart, shook her. But her daughter merely clamped her lips more firmly around her thumb, sucked harder. Meg straightened. Mayhap it is for the best, she thought. Doomsday would scarce trouble the girl if she had a mind to sleep. She would wake her when they were safe. *If* they were safe.

The last of the soldiers had passed under the stone archway. Citizens had filled the gap behind. Isaac had taken his place. The people began to move forward.

An older lady had sat beside them. She had played with Gudrun for a while just after midnight, had sung her the lullaby that had finally sent her to sleep. She shouldered her bag now, stepped into the road. "God's blessings upon you," she said.

The automatic response came: "And His Son's love." But the words almost caught in Meg's mouth. God and Savior had forsaken the land, in this year of the Lord 1644, and she found it hard to speak the words that once would have comforted. Though, even as she lifted the handles of the cart and started forward, she knew that the man who almost certainly waited on the road beyond believed exactly the opposite—that God and Son had brought a righteous flaming sword to cleanse England of all sin.

They passed under the tower, out of the gate. On the other side of it lay wasteland, a ruin of hovels destroyed by the enemy's bombardment to clear the ground for their assaults. The siege lines were a hundred paces farther on. They had been opened to let the vanquished out and the victors in.

Without a glance back, Meg left York, the city of her birth. Forever, she hoped, but didn't pray.

❧❧❧

She knew him long before she could distinguish his face. Recognized him in the way he sat his horse, as if he and the creature were one; centaur, not man and mount.

Matthew.

He was just to the side of the road, leaning forward, keenly studying all who passed, and she felt near faint with fear, knowing that stare would soon be upon her and hers. Yet she could not leave the studying of him, this man she had loved, the fruit of that love before her, asleep in the cart and twenty paces ahead.

He sat hatless under the already-hot July sun. For a keen moment she mourned the passing of the long black hair that she had teased, and pulled, and brushed so often. But long hair, he'd told her the last time she'd seen him, was a frivolity, a distraction to the Righteous, as was any adornment to the person. He was dressed, like all his Puritan brethren, in sober black, his white collar untrimmed with lace—he, who had loved lace as much as she had; more, laughing as they fought for the choicest pieces.

Look away! she screamed inside, pulling the wide-brimmed hat lower over her brow. She had lopped off the hair that he had so loved in his turn, hacked it to stubble, dyed that in cobbler's black, no trace of spun gold to betray her. And she was thin, and had traded a crust for a tight dress to show her thinness more. There were no curves now for him to remember. She was just another poor, sick townswoman, surely, even to that falcon gaze.

Fifty paces. Forty. Isaac would pass him in moments. She forced herself to breathe. "Look away," she muttered. "Look away now."

If he looked away, if they passed him, it was half a day, less, to the rendezvous at the abandoned church on the banks of the Ouse. Uncle Torval had promised in his letter: a boat would be sent down the river each day for a week in midmorning. It would take them to his warehouse in Whitby. Another of his fleet would then take them across the sea to Norway, to her mother's land. To safety.

And then, although she had not prayed, a miracle!

Just as Isaac drew level, Matthew did look away, pulled by sudden shouting. A soldier to his right was forcing his horse into the crowd behind her son. "Bartholomew Maggs," the man yelled.

"What's that, Sergeant?" Matthew moved his horse a pace forward.

"Maggs, Captain Brakespeare," the soldier replied. "Deserted the troop at Basing House this November past. Stole a pig when he went!"

He dismounted, began pulling a protesting man from the crowd by his collar. People moved past the obstruction quickly.

Twenty paces now, and closing. She looked up to see Matthew leaning down beside his horse's neck. The man was bleating, "Not Maggs! Not me!"

"Take him out, then, Wainwright. Let us get a good look at him."

"It's him, Cap'n. Damned bloody deserter, pardon the words!"

Ten paces now. Less. Nearly level, and everyone looking at the uproar, nowhere else, except Meg looking between her feet, pushing, pushing . . .

"Stop him!" came the cry. At the edge of her vision, someone was scrambling away, legs clearing a hedge, other legs hurdling it in pursuit. She was level with him now, knew he had to be looking the other way.

The shot exploded. Mayhem followed, horses whinnying, more shouting; cutting through everything, a high-pitched wail of agony. But Meg didn't even flinch. Not when she was so nearly free. So nearly . . .

"Father!" Even in the noise, the child's sharp cry pierced. Gudrun had thrown back the canvas that covered her, had looked up. . . .

Meg didn't, couldn't. She tried instead to build up some speed. . . .

"Gudrun!" His voice called her, full of wonder, of joy. Then the next word came. Hard. "Margaret."

She looked up then . . . into her husband's eyes, through the gunpowder smoke, as his pistol slowly lowered.

"Margaret," he said again, triumph in the tone, in those eyes, as he swung his legs off the horse.

CHAPTER TWELVE

THE WITCHFINDER

It was a cellar, rather than a cell. But it was still a gaol. The one window was set high up and barred; if that was to keep others out, it also kept her in. Not that she had the will to escape, were it even possible. She was back in York, and her reasons for fleeing were back there too.

It was evening before he came. Bread had been brought, which for the longest time she had not touched despite her hunger. Then she'd gobbled it down. Starving was no preparation for whatever lay ahead.

Which I'll learn now, she thought, rising from the stone floor as soon as she heard his tread in the passageway, his voice. But whomever he spoke to, he came in alone.

The evening sun slanted through the bars. He

raised a hand against it, found her. "The children?" she said, stepping forward.

"Well," he replied, not moving, "and well fed. They do not appear to have eaten for a long time."

"They have not. Thank you for feeding them." It came out formally, as awkward as it sounded, as if he were a kind stranger.

His reply was as strained. "They are my children. And I love them."

And me? she thought, but did not say. She had kept moving, halted now a pace away. Now she could see clearly all she had missed, in that one quick look on the road, before his men had bundled her away. Saw that if she had lost her curves, he had shed his softness. Lean as a wolf now; not stick-skinny, like the Matthew she'd first met when they were both seven. Not the reed-thin youth she realized she loved when she was just thirteen. Not even the gangling eighteen-year-old she'd married. This was a different sort of lean, a hardness of face as well as body; that hardness in his eyes—one of which was crossed by a fresh and livid scar that ran from beneath the close-cropped hair to the bridge of his nose.

"That's terrible," she whispered, reaching up to it. His hand caught hers, and they touched.

"It is nothing," he said softly.

"It was badly sewn. I could have—"

"You were not there." He did not say it as an

accusation, yet she felt it like one. He had asked her to go to war with him; many wives did. She had refused . . . for two reasons, well fed upstairs.

His hand on hers, shaking slightly. She looked, he withdrew it, and she remembered the opposite motion, him reaching, pulling her down. "I was dreaming of that churchyard this morning."

"Which one?" he murmured.

"The one by the river." She looked to the sunbeams. "It was a day much like this one. Hot. We'd gone there to escape our families. To be alone. Do you remember, Matt?"

"I . . . no . . ."

"How can you not?" She stepped closer. "We made our Isaac there that day."

His hands came up again, raised against her. He spoke, all softness gone. "I *do* remember. You luring me. To lie . . . in a churchyard!"

"Luring?" The word confused her. He was always the one who'd led, she who followed. Except—sometimes—at night. "It was long abandoned. A holy place once, yes. And there were ancient carvings there, from my mother's people. Runes—"

"More blasphemy. Sin atop sin."

"Sin?" Another confusing word.

"Naked? Between the tombstones?" The accusation in his voice was clear.

"We were so young. So in love."

"In heat. Like animals!"

She had tried to get closer to him as they talked. Now she stepped back, away from his anger, closed her eyes. "You did not think so then."

"I was blind then. But now the scales have fallen. Now I see." He leaned toward her. "I see your sin."

"My sin?"

"Your . . . *unbelief.*"

It was a word from one of his letters. An accusation he had made before. She'd thought it strange, because, before war pulled them apart, it was she who had always forced him, ever reluctant, through the church doors. "I believe, husband," she said softly. "I just do not believe as you do. That all is so . . . clear."

"And that is because of your sin," he said triumphantly. "There is no room in this world we are striving to create, our new Jerusalem upon earth, for such unbelief. We have learned that only unswerving faith in our God will bring us victory. And our enemies have learned the opposite—that their faithlessness will bring them only to hell."

They stared at each other; in his eyes she saw something and realized the difference between them.

She could leave him be. But he could not leave her. What he called her "unbelief" would not allow him to.

"But your sin," he continued as if there had been no pause, "is not my concern. Only God can judge you, and I must leave you to His mercy. But the Devil"—his voice dropped—"the Devil I can fight. *Must* fight. Here, now, upon this earth."

His eyes were afire, and seeing that fanatic gleam, Meg quailed. In the year since she'd last seen him, when he'd sneaked over the walls of Royalist York to visit them, what had been spark alone had grown incandescent. He had found God and justice in this same cause, Parliament's fight against the king. Many men had, and she could not begrudge him that. But when he ordered her to follow him, to bring their children where they could be brought up on God's true path, she did what she had never done before—she disobeyed him. Four smuggled-in letters had followed, each increasing in accusation, in fanaticism, finally in threats. Now that fire in his eyes told her that he was there to act upon them.

"The Devil?" she whispered.

Her fear made him calmer. "You know it, wife. And only by admitting it can you be saved."

She knew he was talking about her soul, not her life. Admit acquaintance with the Devil and you died. "It is not true." Her own voice grew stronger again. "I have had no dealings with Satan."

"Indeed?" She had retreated to the table, and he approached it now with slow steps. "Do you not cure with herbs?"

"Aye. Many do. Fevers, and the like. I've cured our son, oft."

"I would that you had not, if the price was his immortal soul." He did not pause for her cry. "And do you not chant over them?"

She frowned. "I pray for aid. As do you."

"Ah . . . but to whom?" Before she could speak, he went on, "And those carvings you read in that churchyard. Pagan words."

"I read the runes, years ago, yes. My mother taught me a little of the old writings of her land of Norway. But"—she shrugged helplessly—"it is like a fortune read by an old woman in the palm of one's hand. A diversion only."

"A diversion from God!" he roared. "Only God foretells. Only He decides!" His voice dropped as he reached her, bent to her. "And only those who suckle the Devil think otherwise."

She had never answered back to his anger. She couldn't now. "Is this all?" was the most she could manage.

He stared at her for a long moment. Then he went to the door, stopped before it, his back still to her. His voice came, quietly. "You know it is not all. For you know what else you do."

"What?"

"You fly." Her gasp turned him, and he raised a finger, pointed. "You leave your body at night, journey through this world. Sometimes as a woman. Sometimes . . . in the shape of a beast!"

From the moment that he spoke of the Devil, she

had feared that this might come. Yet how could it? Hadn't it just been another memory-turned-dream? For a summer, less, that one when she had first learned to love him. She was thirteen, just starting to grow from girl to woman, discovering other changes too. For once, *she* had led *him.* Out into the fields at night. Above them. Sharing her discoveries with the only one she trusted.

So long ago, such a brief, brief time. They had stopped, frightened by it, by the thought of anyone discovering them. In ten years, they had never talked about it. For ten years, she had flown only in her dreams.

She was startled by the rush of sweat flooding her skin, chilling there, a chill that closed like a fist about her heart. The betrayal did that, this last complete betrayal.

"But, Matthew," she said brokenly, "so did you."

He stamped his foot, the metaled heel a shriek upon the flagstones. "It is a lie," he hissed. "A lie! You came to me in a dream. Entranced me. Bewitched me!"

On his final words, he turned, rapped hard upon the door. Footsteps approached, a bolt was thrown. Two men entered. One small, bespectacled, carrying sheets of parchment, an inkwell, and quills. He went to the table ends, laid them down.

The other man was burly, in a soldier's buff coat and high boots. In one hand he held a length of rope; in the other, a small roll of canvas.

In their presence, Matthew's voice took on a different shade. All passion was gone, replaced by the steady tones of an officer. "I ask you now, Margaret Brakespeare, before these two good and honest men: will you confess your pact with the Devil?"

Somehow she stayed upright, though she felt her knees giving, had to steady herself against the table. "I will not. For I have made no such pact."

"Confess. Come to God. It will go easier with you."

Easier? There was only one penalty for such a confession: death. "I am not a witch. You, above all men, know this."

"I know nothing." He nodded to the soldier, who laid the canvas roll down next to the clerk, moved swiftly to her, shoved her into the chair, began uncoiling the rope. "But I will learn everything," Matthew continued. "For I have been appointed by my lord Fairfax, our commander; by Parliament, the only authority of this realm. And by God, whose majesty I humble myself before—"

"Amen," said the clerk.

"—to discover all those in compact with the Devil—"

" 'For all that do these things are an abomination unto the Lord,' " the clerk quoted, eyes raised to the ceiling.

"—in this county of Yorkshire."

Matthew had been standing upright as if reciting

an oath. Now he bent and began to unroll the canvas, just as the soldier stepped toward her with the rope. "You would put me to the torment?" she cried.

Matthew paused, looked up. His voice was calmer now, more normal. "We are not Spaniards, lady. There is no torment in our fair England." He bent again. "But that does not mean we do not have our own proven ways of finding out the truth."

She watched him unfold the canvas. "You did love me once," she whispered.

He looked at her—and she could see the tears start in his eyes. "Oh, and do still, Margaret!" he cried. "And how can I show my love more certainly than by wresting your soul from Satan?"

She did not know what hurt most: the ropes cruelly binding her wrists to the chair, the way the soldier roughly jerked her dress down to bare her shoulders, or the thought that the father of her children had become what she now named him. "You . . . a torturer?"

"I tell you, wife, I am not." As he spoke, he lifted something from the canvas roll. For a moment, she could not see it, it glistened so in the sun's dying beams. And then she did, just as he stepped forward. "What I *am* is the Witchfinder. And I will find the Devil in you . . . out!"

As he spoke, he bent and laid the tip of the needle against her skin.

CHAPTER THIRTEEN
THE SWIMMING

There was no comforting dream to waken from. No loving hand reached and sought hers. Sleep had come in brief snatches, pain-wracked, horror-strewn. And now she woke to more of both.

She tried to sit up . . . couldn't, cried out. It was as if they'd tied her to the bed. But it was blood, not rope, that bound her. When she forced her arm from the rough blanket, it gave with a little ripping sound. When she finally sat up, the filthy mattress she lay on rose with her—material stuck to her wherever he had . . . "pricked" her, he called it. At both upper arms, beneath the knee. At different points in her back.

Yet it was not the wounds where he'd driven the finger-length needles into her flesh that brought the tears now. It was the four places that had not bled, where she'd felt nothing. He'd found them, and they had transformed his tears—for he had wept, too, even as he drove the sharp steel in—into tears of joy.

"Praise be!" he had cried as he removed the last one, lifting it to heaven. "For the Lord has shown us where the Devil's creatures suckle upon you. Where the Evil One himself doth enter."

She had not understood how a needle plunged into flesh could loose no blood, bring no pain. But it was so—proof, Matthew said, that the Devil entered her there by these portals.

Weeping still, she lifted her dress, looked, still disbelieving. She could not see the two in her back—the one in the flesh above her hip, the other at the base of her neck—but she assumed they looked like this on her

thigh, a bruise now where the point had entered beneath a slight discoloration of skin. She ran her finger across it and . . . yes, it was raised, slightly, not even a mole. Yet raised enough, he'd told her, for the Devil's succubi to fasten their mouths upon the teat and feast.

She wiped her eyes, looked up. There was a lightening at the bars of her cell. And there was something else out there—a murmuring of voices. Yet these were not the usual sounds of a town waking. People were gathering. Why, she could not know . . . yet it made her shiver and draw the sodden blanket around her.

A little later, with dawn's pale light creeping into the cell and the voices growing ever louder, she heard the footsteps in the corridor and knew her answer approached in them. She wiped her face and stood.

The bolts were shot, the door opened, and there he was. She looked straightaway to his hands, clasped before his chest, dreading to see a roll of canvas there; but they were empty. "No needles?" She wanted to say it with defiance, but it came out as fear.

He came in slowly. "Alas, the time for them has passed."

" 'Alas'? Do you so desire to inflict more hurt upon me?"

He lowered his hands. "I never desired that. My only desire was to prove the Devil was within you. Having done so, I only want to drive him out." He sighed. "But the citizens of York have heard of your witchery. One of the men here yesterday must have talked in an alehouse. And many now see, in your alliance with Satan, a cause for the harm that has fallen upon them." He shook his head. "They are an ignorant rabble and do not accept the proof I established here yestere'en. They want their own proof."

The drone that had been building outside the house since before dawn began to be punctuated by shouts. She heard something called, repeated. It could have been her name. "What proof?" she said faintly.

He looked away. "They will swim you."

"*Swim* me?" The word did not make sense. She almost laughed. "But I cannot swim."

He nodded, eyes still averted. "I know."

He said something else, something about sending for his troop, encamped beyond the city walls. But his words were lost in the crashing of the door in the corridor beyond. Men, and some women, rushed now into the cell. At their head was the man who'd tied her down. When he came up to her now, she could smell the beer on his sour breath.

"This is her! Witch! Witch!"

"That we shall learn soon enough!" yelled another. "Bring her!"

She was seized, burly men pinning her on either side. She cried out as they gripped her wounded arms. She looked to Matthew, but still he would not look back.

She was picked up, borne from the house. Upside down, she could see the upper windows, see Isaac and Gudrun screaming something at her, their words lost in the ugly baying of the mob. She hated Matthew for leaving them to see her like this. But then she realized this might well be her last sight of them. So she took it.

They rushed her to a mill, close to the southern wall of the city, built to harness the River Ouse's race. Beyond the grinding wheels, the water formed a large pond. She was laid down beside it, and that same rope tyer swiftly trussed her—right thumb to left large toe, left to the right. A thicker rope was looped around her middle, its slack coiled and thrown across to men on the other side of the pond.

Matthew was above her, looking pale, and she called to him, "What will happen?"

He crouched. "Fools! They will not trust to the science of the Pricker. In their ignorance they believe that, in a swimming, the witch will float, the honest woman, sink."

She had heard tales of this. She had never believed them. Now she gasped. "So if I drown, I am innocent?"

He bent close, his head to hers, to whisper. "Try to sink. Expel all air. They will only swim you thrice." He touched the rope at her waist. "With God's mercy, these men will pull you up in time. I will be here."

He stepped away; others stepped in, picked her up, folded over as she was. The crowd screamed, "Witch!" as she was lifted over the pond's stone sides, screamed it again as she was hurled over them. They cried it a third time, but it came to her muffled, through water.

The cold shock of it! Yet after the press of sweaty bodies around her, the burning of the July sun, for a moment it was almost a relief. One small moment, though, gone when she knew that the green coolness was swallowing her and that she had no air.

She turned her face upward. Light was above her now, and she was rushing up to it, to sound building again on that one word.

"Witch!" they cried as she broke surface, sucking in air, and water, too, choking on that, spitting out what she could, sucking again . . . just in time, because she rolled facedown, her head went below; but not before she glimpsed the men on the far side of the bank, lowering themselves onto submerged stone ledges. She felt the tug at her waist as they forced the rope beneath the surface of the water.

As she shot down, she tried to remember what he'd said. Expel the air? It seemed madness, but this all *was* madness. He said they'd pull her out after a while, before it was too late. Maybe.

It was the only hope she had. So she breathed what was keeping her just alive out, watched the bubbles rise through green toward the light. Instantly her body convulsed, her head contracting in agony. And it was all worth nothing, because she couldn't stop herself rising; her body's need was greater than her will. Up she rose, to the light, to that word.

"Witch!"

She gasped, choked, sucked in air and water both, coughed it out. But she only had a moment of respite. A long pole was thrust down, thumped against her collarbone, slipped off, found flesh, sunk in. She sank faster now, deeper, pushed by wood, jerked by rope. Her ears felt as though they would explode.

And then it came—a stirring within, something shifting, separating. Something she had not felt in ten years.

Her Fetch began to leave her body.

Sometimes it had gone out as pure spirit. Sometimes as flesh. This felt like that, the way her skin, her very bones, seemed to push out, to expel something from her as she had once pushed to expel her babes.

And she realized, in a moment of terrible clarity, even as her body began to divide, that she did not need to rise up a third time to prove she was a witch. The sight of two of her emerging from the water would do that.

The thought made her smile, even as the last air was leaving her. Mild Meg, they'd always called her. Gentle Margaret. But now she remembered what it was she had both loved and feared about her Fetch.

She was Mad Meg. Rough Margaret. She could run across the fields naked under the moonlight. She could pull her lover down into the long grass among the tombstones. And she could rise up from the water, free from ropes, and laugh at her tormentors.

She almost did it, just to see their faces. And then she saw something else, other faces, behind the glass, their mouths wide, yelling in terror. Isaac and Gudrun, her children, her reasons for living, even just a little longer, for the hope of seeing them again. She opened her mouth . . . her *two* mouths to cry to them. Water poured in. . . .

Water pouring in. Air . . . gone. Yet something familiar to that, this point right now, just past the pain. A border crossed.

Fear fades. Because this has happened before. I have drowned before. It's not so bad after a while, remember? Give in to it. Surrender to the green darkness.

But . . .

"Nooooo!"

The scream muffled, lost in . . . in . . . not water! Cloth, a face full of cloth!

Where am I?

Lift your head!

When?

Lift it!!

Who?

"Uhhhhh!" Sky gasped, pulling his face up from the sleeping bag, his head out from under it. He flung his hand out, and it did not move slowly, as if through water. It smashed into a canvas wall, ice-heavy, solid as the wood of a coffin.

Their coffin! Weren't there two of them in it? Someone else . . .

Who?

"Kristin!" he yelled, reaching for her, yelping as he touched. If his body was freezing, hers was ice. Desperately, he flailed his hands around, hit plastic, grabbed, pushed.

Light from the flashlight, bright as the sun in York. Shining on Kristin, her bare arms purple with cold, her face twisted in terror. He knew why; for if he was still half Meg—and he felt that clearly, as clearly as he still felt the rope around his waist, pulling him—then she was wholly Matthew. Sky had been tortured—but it was Kristin who had done the torturing. Who right now was watching his own wife drown.

"Kristin," he said again, but no louder than a whisper. If she was not ready to return, could not return, he must not force her. The body must never be disturbed when the Fetch traveled. If it was, the Fetch might never return at all. He had learned that the hard way.

Yet her face, even as he watched it, twisted in another spasm of terror.

How could he leave her back there? The flash came . . . of them, as children, sneaking out at night, walking the neighborhood walls. "Are we walking or are we talking?" she'd say. They'd walk, and if one fell, if a neighbor caught either of them, the other always went back, never abandoned the other.

Besides, he hadn't learned what he'd gone back to learn.

Go back! He felt her still, Meg, the rope around both their waists, joining them, her Fetch sinking back into her, his Fetch still there. He was losing her . . . but he hadn't lost her yet. That told him Meg was still alive.

Snatching up the two sleeping bags, he pulled them around them, took Kristin's frozen body into his arms. He flicked off the flashlight. Darkness shrouded them once more.

"We're walking!" he shouted, reaching for the rope at his waist. . . .

He was back in the water. There was no air left in the body he shared. Meg had given up, sinking facedown into the darkness.

But he didn't want to drown! He couldn't leave

Kristin alone there. He had come back for her. And then he remembered! He was in those brief seconds when ancestor and Fetch were together. So he used one of them.

"Live now!" he cried.

He was almost gone. But as he slipped away, he felt his body—their body!—turning in the water, rising toward the light . . .

. . . something pulling around her middle, rolling her over in water that no longer seemed to be hurting her. Then she was in air, on stone, and someone was pushing on her chest. Water was vomited out, air sucked in.

"Meg? Meg?" Amongst the voices calling, one she knew.

Which one do you seek? she thought. Mild or Mad? For somewhere at the edge of consciousness, something . . . *someone* still lingered.

"Live now!" she cried, in a voice that was not her own.

"Jesu, protect me!" Matthew fell back. The people who'd pulled her from the water, who had surrounded Matthew as he worked on her, stepped back too.

"Hear her!" a woman shrieked, jabbing her finger down. "Hear the male demon within her speak! She is possessed!"

"Possessed!" The cry was taken up; the crowd surged forward, hands reaching for her. "Hang her for the witch she is! Hang her!"

Matthew bent, picked her up. "She is a prisoner of Parliament. She will be tried and given justice."

"Justice now! Hang her now!" The mob pushed in. Through glazed eyes, Meg could see the man who'd always tied the ropes coiling one now into a noose. Others in the mob reached, seizing Matthew's arms.

He clutched her tighter, bent against the storm, then roared, "Soldiers!"

Shouts came, the sound of blows, squeals of pain. The mob was driven against them by some force from the back. Then they pushed outward—away from the swords wielded by Matthew's troopers, the flats of them crashing into bodies like iron staves.

His men reached them, surrounded them, turned and formed a wedge driving into the crowd, who split into a gauntlet down which the soldiers marched. Hands grabbed at her, spit flew. "Give her to us!" came the cry. "Witch! Hang her! Hang her!"

The crowd, the stench, the burning sun, the hatred pouring upon her. Her breath was not easy, still water-wracked. And Matthew was squeezing her hard into his hard chest. She felt the darkness drawing her down again. This time, though, she sank into it gratefully.

CHAPTER FOURTEEN
POSSESSION

The old bell of York Minster began to sound midnight. She had lain there, waiting for it. Though she was exhausted, sleep was a distant memory, a fantasy of the rest she could not have. Not yet. At the second toll, she breathed out, stood up.

He had said he would come shortly after that hour. To pray with her, over her. To ask her once again to change her mind, before it was too late.

She faced the door, listened to the iron tongue she'd heard so often, knowing that it was the last time she would hear it strike the twelve. Whatever the new day brought, she would never listen to that deep voice again.

He came while the twelfth toll still echoed around the cellar. She closed her eyes, even as the bolts were shot. She had lost the habit of prayer lately. But she prayed then.

"Let there be another way, Lord. Merciful Father, let there be another way."

The door, her eyes, both opened, and she asked him the question she always asked him first. "The children?"

The words of his reply were the same, the sense of them different. "They are . . . well."

She took a step toward him. "They are not if you say it that way."

He closed the door behind him. Someone outside threw the bolt, locked them in together. "Isaac is . . ."

"Unwell?"

"Unhappy. He threw his supper at the servant girl, screamed and would not stop."

Meg looked away, to the dark night. "You are hanging his mother at sunrise, Matthew," she said softly. "Did you expect him to rest content?"

"I did not think he knew."

"I am sure there are many kind enough to tell him. The servant girl, for one."

He would not meet her eyes. "Nevertheless, it was necessary to quiet him. Punish him."

"You . . . beat him."

"The child would not hear. Kept screaming. Cursed me. Cursed God!" He flushed red. "As if he had one of your demons within him, like the one who spoke when you came out of the water." She stared at him, and her look turned his guilt to something else. "It is your fault, Margaret. While you have consorted with Satan, you have ignored your children. Or worse . . . sought to corrupt them. Well, I have them now."

"You have them now."

She said it quietly. And her quietness quieted him. "Have you thought more on what I said?"

"I have thought of little else."

He came toward her, hope in his eyes. "It is the only way, Margaret. Yesterday you were judged guilty in a court of law. If you had admitted that guilt, owned the Devil inside you, the court might have been lenient. But you did not. And the people of York have demanded justice."

"They have demanded vengeance. Vengeance for the horrors this war has inflicted upon them. They look for Satan in it. When they should look for men. Men like you."

He colored again, as if he would argue. Then he shook his head. "This matters not. What matters is your neck in a noose." He paused. "Or not, if you so choose."

"Choose? You say you can spirit"—she faltered on the word—"spirit me away from here—"

"I can, though I risk all to do it."

"—take me to another prison far away. Appeal to a higher court—"

"Yes! There is a little hope. A little time, at the least. As long as you admit your sin, renounce Satan, return to God."

"At the price that I must name others—"

"Those you consorted with, yes. For witches always gather in covens."

"And the final price"—she took a deep breath, fearing that even the words would make her faint—"that I must never see my children again."

He nodded, swallowed, looked away. "It is hard, I know. But Satan, once he has gripped you, will never let you go entirely. They would never be safe with you. Only a lifetime of prayer, of repentance in some faraway place, may free you."

I have them now! That was what he'd said. She looked at her husband, this man she had once so loved. At the hair cropped to the skull, because to let it grow would be frivolity. At his black garb that spoke to his purity. At the scar of war so livid even in this lamplight. At the scars within his eyes, which this war had also given him.

He took her silence as consideration. "That is your choice, wife. Your only choice. In the end it comes down to just one: God or the Devil."

She had thought to appeal to him one more time. On the heads of their children. On the love that once they'd had. But her study had told her—he would not bend. He preferred God, and His cause, to her and them.

Her prayer was unanswered. God had not helped her. Only she could help herself.

She moved toward him, her hands clasped before her. She could see the hope plainly within his scarred eyes. "But there is one more choice, husband."

Her words, the softness of them, the gentle rising of her hands to his chest, all lulled him. He spoke as softly as she. "What?"

"This."

Her hands touched him, pressing into his doublet, through his doublet. His hands rose then, sought to grab her wrists. But there was no flesh to grab. "No," he grunted, but she stopped the breath he needed to shout for help, trapping it in spirit fingers that pressed through to his spine. He sagged, yet she held him up, as he had held her at the mill pond, taking his weight, which was nothing to her now, as she sank into him, deep into him, her Double disappearing into him.

She had not been sure she'd remember the way of it. It had been so long ago when last she'd done this. And she had only gone into animals then—run as a fox, hunted as an owl. But midnight was the hour, "the witching time," it was called. When a witch was at her most powerful.

There had always been a struggle when possession was resisted. She was surprised to discover that a man's resistance was no stronger than a beast's.

She took the breath now that they both needed; staggered, his legs unfamiliar under her, reaching out to steady herself against a wall. She closed her eyes—his eyes—and somewhere from deep inside his body she heard a scream, trailing off, as if someone was falling into a void of nothingness.

"Hush," she whispered, in his voice. She felt him,

every part of him . . . and the delight in that. The strength of the man! The belief in himself! He had no doubts; nothing could stand between him and his certainty.

She felt *his* chest heave with *her* joy! She'd forgotten this—the pure exhilaration of possession! And a fox, a bird, the only things she'd inhabited before? They were nothing. A human, now! It was extraordinary. Why had she not done this before? Well, she'd never deny herself this . . . this *wonder* again!

She laughed out loud . . . and heard Mad Meg in the delight. Her Fetch, freed. She could run wild if she chose. Draw this sword at her side, use his skill with a blade to cut her way to her children, free them, ride from the city. . . .

No! She leaned against the wall, took a deep breath, another, to steady her thumping heart—his thumping heart. It was not the way. She had her plan. She knew what she must do. And Mad Meg, even with Matthew's strength, could not do it.

Gradually, her heart and breath steadied, and other feelings came from her possession. His memories flooding in, of her, of their children. Of the war. She felt his terrible hurts, all that he'd tried to heal in devotion to his cause.

"Oh, Matthew," she whispered, her pity in his voice.

She stood there for a long moment, till she knew what was her, what was him, till Mad Meg had stepped back. Then she crossed the room and threw back the blanket on the bed.

Meg's body lay there as she had left it, and she looked at herself for a long moment. Then, using his strength, she picked herself up. She was surprised by how light she felt.

"Sergeant," Matthew Brakespeare cried. "Praise be to God! She repents."

The bolts were thrown again, the door opened. The reed torch beyond showed her Matthew's man, the same whose discovery of the deserter on the road beyond York had exposed her. Wainwright was his name. Then his broad, swarthy face had been wrought in anger. Now it was lightened by joy. Heavenly joy.

"Hallelujah!" he shouted. "For our Savior has visited the prisoner and delivered her, like Peter from his chains." Then his eyes adjusted to the darkness of the cellar and he saw the woman in his officer's arms. "She *is* delivered, is she, Cap'n?"

"She's fainted, 'tis all. Overwhelmed by Jesu's presence."

"Praise Him!"

"Aye." She carried herself across to the door. "But now we must hasten, Sergeant. Is all prepared as I asked you, against this small hope?"

Wainwright stepped back into the corridor. "All, sir. There's a door into the yard hard by, the horses saddled. Come!"

He gestured, but Matthew's head flicked upward. "The children, first."

The man slapped his forehead. "How could I forget? I have prayed they would not be made orphans this day. Motherless, I mean. I can't help thinking of my own five in Bridport." He smiled, reached out his arms. "Shall I take her, sir, while you fetch 'em?"

She'd thought of leaving her body there while she went and got her children. But the sergeant had said "fetch." And she had never left her body with anyone, not even Matthew, when her Fetch had walked before. Just made sure it was safe, in an empty barn or unvisited copse. She could not leave it now. "See to the horses. Make sure none are about. I'll keep her by."

"Aye, Cap'n."

He stepped aside, and she moved to the narrow stairwell, went up. In the corridor of the merchant's house he had commandeered, she did not hesitate, took two more flights, up to the attic. She realized she knew the place as well as Matthew . . . no, *as* Matthew. She shuddered . . . and her thoughts moved again into his, to a churchyard hard by the river, a sunny day, the making of Isaac. . . .

She opened her eyes. She'd only ever been a fox, knowing its runs, the gaps it sought in hedgerows; a bird, and the best place to flush a mole or mouse. There was danger in this, to be so lost in another. She shook her head. Despite the power, the delight of it, she needed to be free of him as soon as she could be. She could get to like this too much.

Reaching out awkwardly beyond the body she held, she turned the doorknob.

Gudrun, as ever, was asleep in her cot. Isaac was standing, facing the door. He blinked as his parents came into the room, and spoke. "Have you hanged her already, sir?"

The cold way he said it! It nearly broke Meg's heart, the way he was holding himself, trying to be so brave. She nearly dropped the body she held, ran to sweep him up into her arms. Knew she couldn't. Matthew would not behave like that. She must behave like him.

"Wake your sister, boy," she said, as kindly as she could. Somehow it still came out hard. "Wake her, dress fast, and follow."

Gudrun protested but came awake swiftly enough. Their few clothes were flung on. Hand in hand, they followed their parents down the stairs.

"Is Mama sleeping?" she said.

"Hush, child! Yes. Yes, she sleeps."

They stepped into the perfect dark of the yard. "Sergeant?" he called.

"Here, sir."

The children held on to Matthew's long buff coat, making progress even harder. Then a light came, a gate on a lantern swung open. "Here," the sergeant called again.

Isaac had ridden soon after he could walk. Gudrun could sit a horse. The boy was swung up, given the reins, the girl placed before him. Though Meg hesitated for a moment, there was no other way. She handed her body over to the sergeant, mounted, then bent down.

For a moment, Wainwright did not pass her up, just stared into her sleeping face. "A miracle indeed, Cap'n," he murmured. "And it's good to cheat those jackals of a lynching."

He lifted her, and she grabbed herself, settling her between the strong arms, the reins either side. "Thank you, Jeremiah."

The sergeant laid his hand briefly upon his captain's. "I'll pray for you, Matthew," he said softly. "For all your deliverances."

She nodded, turned the horse's head. "God's blessings upon you," came the call from the darkness.

When she'd left York two days before, the customary reply had nearly choked in her throat. Now she declared it fervently. She needed all the help she could get.

"And His Son's love."

CHAPTER FIFTEEN
AWAKENINGS

It was more of his own troop guarding the gate and they did not question their commander. After that, it was not far. A few hours for a single rider even at night. But Isaac fell asleep, nearly toppled from his mount. She had to stop, to let them rest in an abandoned barn. She thought to stay awake and ward them. Yet she had not truly slept in days—and it seemed Matthew had not either. Light was in the sky when she awoke and urged them on, though the little rest did her more harm than good. Only desperation kept her eyelids open as they rode the last few miles.

The churchyard lay much as she remembered it. She had not been back since Isaac was a thought. The church's round tower, mark of a time before the Normans built their square ones, still stood at the end of the village. But few had lived in the village when she and Matthew had come there; now, it seemed, the war had driven even those few away. Most of the houses were roofless; many had collapsed, stones plundered for homes elsewhere. Gudrun clapped and pointed at a rabbit that scurried away in the grass that grew between the cobbles. She and Isaac ran off in pursuit.

Laying her own body down against the churchyard's crumbling outer wall, she climbed the grassy banks that rose steeply and ended in a cliff overlooking the river. To her right, a gap had been cut through the cliff, like a doorway that opened onto the water and the jetty. The old jetty was much as she remembered it, though the planks were ill-tended and one of the pillars had slipped. There was a small river skiff tied to its end—something else the last villagers must have abandoned. Miraculously, it was still afloat.

Beside the church lay what had been the village green, its cropped grass long grown wild. She searched for what she also remembered had been there. Matthew's toe found it, stubbed on wood. Bending to rip the grass away, she swiftly uncovered the village stocks.

"Praise be," she said, exploring, the phrase more familiar to the lips that shaped them than to hers. Though the machine was old and its thick, wooden blocks whitened by weather, it looked solid enough; the metal loops and the bolts that slid into them, though rusted, were still strong. They would still hold the ankles of the village's offenders against escape. She used all Matthew's strength and could not pry them from the wood.

She looked up to the sun, tried to gauge the hour. Her uncle's letter had said that, due to the tide, the boat would come every day between eight and nine. She did not think her uncle would be late. So how long did she have before she must do the last things to make herself, her children, safe?

And then she remembered how she could find out.

She walked past her body—would she ever get used to that sight?—and entered the churchyard. The grass grew high here, too, stone shapes thrust up to mark the headstones of those who had lived here once, died here once. One shape stood higher, and it was this she made for.

The sundial stood on a plinth that raised it from the grass sea. Its face was circular, its width about her forearm's length. A rusty metal triangle rose from it, like a spearhead driven into stone, and it was this that cast the shadow that told her the time. It fell upon the Latin numeral VIII. Eight of the morning. Just gone.

If her uncle held true, the boat would be here within the hour. If she did what she must, she and her children would be free. A new life called them, away from war, and hate, and the man she no longer knew, lost to both.

She was about to turn away when she glanced to

the top of the dial, saw what the metal had concealed before. The small, rough-carved letters that were also signs, neither English nor Latin. Her mother had taught her this language, from her native land, though these symbols were rarely used there now . . . except in some remote places, like the island of Hareid, where her mother was from. And if they were used, it was in darkness, beyond the sight and hearing of the village priest.

"Runes," she whispered, remembering that "rune" meant "whisper." And "secret." And she knew some of them.

There were three larger ones in a row; a fourth, smaller, set below, almost like a signature on a document. She laid a fingertip, Matthew's callused fingertip, upon that one. *"Uruz,"* she named it in her mother's tongue.

A twist inside, like someone poking metal into her gut! She doubled over, air sucked from lungs, breath as hard to find as underwater. And when it came, it felt almost . . . almost as if someone else had taken the breath. Someone else, within her and Matthew both!

With a cry, she wrenched her finger away from the cut stone, fell backward. She did not know what it was, just knew she had to get away from it.

And then she heard the shot. She rose, got more breath, staggered from the churchyard to the riverbank. The river twisted through the land, and many trees drooped their leaves into it. But several curves down, the still air of summer had not yet quite blown clear the smoke of a gun.

Her uncle, warning of his arrival? She could only hope. Turning, she stumbled back down the path. "Isaac? Gudrun?"

They ran to her, where she waited by her own body. They stared down at it. "Is Mama dead, Father?" Gudrun asked, as she had a dozen times that night.

She told them again, in their father's voice. "She sleeps only, children. She is ill. But she will wake soon . . . if you will help me."

They nodded, stared up at her . . . at him! Seizing a hand of each, she led them through the long grass of what had been the green, to what she had uncovered. How to explain this? She never could, when she could barely explain it to herself. But she did not need them to understand. She only needed them to . . . play!

She knelt, put their father's arms around each. "We are going to play a game."

"Which one, sir?" Isaac asked, already excited.

"It is like"—she thought—"like blindman's bluff. But there is no scarf for the eyes. Matthew is going to—*I* am going to put my legs in here. . . ." She swung the top block of the stocks up and pointed to the half circle in each block. "See? So when I lower them my feet will be held here." She lowered it, pointed to the complete circle that would trap his legs, as it had trapped the legs of any in the village who had offended.

"But how do we play?"

She pointed to the metal rod on the far side of the stocks. "When Mama—when *Father's* legs are caught, you push the bolt through and he—I—won't be able to escape."

"That's the game? It doesn't sound very good." Isaac sucked at his lip.

"Then the real game begins. Hide and find!" She could see them both brighten. "Mama wakes up, and she will come and look for you."

"But where shall we hide, Father?"

She leaned in, whispered it, pointing behind her to the gap in the riverbank. "There, Gudrun. That path leads to a magic boat. Get in the boat. Untie the rope, but hold the boat to the dock there. Mama will seek you there."

"She'll find us, won't she?"

The tears in both her children's eyes. They brought tears to her own. To Matthew's, and she felt how unused to them he was. "God willing, yes. She'll find you. If you do exactly what I have said."

She saw their hesitation, their uncertainty. Their father telling them this, the man who had thrashed Isaac only yesterday. And she knew there was so much that could go wrong yet. She had never been so tired. She had never done what she had done that night. What she still had to do.

But only in the doing of it would it be done.

She lay back, placed Matthew's legs in the half circle of the bottom block, then lowered the top block. Her ankles were caught, held snug. And she couldn't raise herself to reach over the stocks. He would not be able to escape them if . . .

"The bolt, Isaac." She tried to put a smile on Matthew's face. "The bolt and then . . . hide in the boat."

He looked at his father a long moment. For that moment Meg thought he was going to refuse. And then, he reached forward and thrust the bolt home. Without another word, he took his sister by the hand and ran.

Meg watched them vanish through the cut in the riverbank, an ache where her heart should be. Then she looked down at Matthew's legs disappearing into wood. She lay back . . . and it felt so good, the soft grass under her back, the cloudless sky above. She had lain on such a day here before. He had lain there too. They had made Isaac and then had slept in each other's arms. Slept . . .

No! She shook Matthew's head to clear it. She could not sleep, not yet. Maybe later and forever. But however tired she was, she had this last thing to do. Her children needed her. And even beyond that she knew: she could not hold Matthew prisoner much longer . . . or she might not want to let him go at all!

She lay back, but not for tiredness' sake now. Now

she had to seek that quiet, a moment of it, the same as she had sought and found before. It was on a breath, breathing out, stepping out. . . .

She opened her eyes. She was standing, looking down at the man in the stocks. For a moment, neither of them moved. Then he opened his eyes too. They rolled in his head as he sought sense. He tried to sit up. The wood of the stocks prevented him. He reached, felt what held him prisoner. Then he saw her, silhouetted against the sun. And confusion was driven from his eyes. Replaced by fury.

"Witch!" he screamed.

She fell back, her feet driving her away, away from the hands that reached for her, kicking the hand that caught a fold of dress. The hands grasped air—then began to lash at the wood that held him. Matthew was roaring like a beast, foam at his lips, pounding the stocks that held him, raking the wood with his nails. She could see skin break, see blood flecking the white.

She was up, staggering, bending over her body, breathing in. . . . Nothing! She still stood above, lay below. While behind her, a different sound came. She turned . . . to see Matthew raise his knife into the air! She cried out—she'd meant to remove the weapon from the sheath in his boot. Now she could only watch as he began gouging the wood near the iron hinges of the stocks.

Quickly! She breathed in, closed her eyes. . . . No! Still her above, her below.

What could she do? Race for the boat, leave her body? No! Something told her: a Fetch separated could not live. A body without a Fetch could only die.

With a roar, Matthew drove his thick blade under one of the hinges, levering it up. With a grunt, he bent to the two blocks, twisting, lifting it slowly, forcing metal from wood. He was nearly free.

There was nothing for her to do . . . but lead him away from her children, pray that her uncle arrived in time and would find them. So she rose, abandoned her body, ran into the graveyard.

He had left his roaring. The only sound coming now was the low shriek of wood yielding to metal and strength. She stumbled down to the end of the path, to the sundial. Fell against it . . .

Before, when she'd touched the smallest rune, the one that seemed to her a signature, it had taken her like a surprise kick in the guts. Now, when she touched it again, pain still came—yet within it she was able to feel . . . the rune cut in the stone. Feel the strokes that carved them. Hear the carver's name as if he stood beside her and whispered it into her ear.

"Bjørn's rune," she breathed.

Bending iron. Splintering wood. A man's frantic grunts. All beyond her now. For now there were only the runes before her and her Fetch's finger slipping into the grooves of the first one in the line.

"Laguuz," she sang, and other words came. Not on the stone. Released *from* the stone.

"Water at birth
Crossed at death
Secrets flow
Mother to child
Until their need
One is one."

Her finger slid to the second rune. Energy poured through it, into her. Her voice came and it was already starting not to sound like her.

"Thuuuuuriiisaaaz!" she called.

"The Thorn pricks
Blood gushes
Dissolve the stone
Shatter the walls
Body and spirit
One is one."

Far away, wood split, metal shrieked. Nearer, a finger moved, a voice sang.

"Ehhhwaaaz!
Horse and Fylgya
Faring forth
Riding the world lines
Along the bloodlines
Ancestor . . . us . . .
One is one!"

Meg looked up into cloudless blue, as if to hear the voice that sang in her, as if it came from above. Then she realized that was wrong. The voice hadn't come from the sky. The voice *was* . . . "Sky."

"I am here," he replied, in her head. Her Fetch's head.

He was. The shock of it! The joy! Once before he had entered an ancestor's Fetch—Tza, in Corsica, when she'd hunted as a Mazzeri. He'd experienced everything she did, as she did it. He'd learned the art of the Mazzeri Salvatore then. Learned to heal the dead.

But Tza had not been aware of him!

Meg was aware of him. Like the breath she'd just taken, like the shadow in the corner of her eye. Realized that somehow he'd been there ever since she'd nearly drowned. Inseparable from her, in the way she'd been inseparable from Matthew. . . .

Matthew, roaring now in triumph as the wood finally yielded to his fury.

"Quick!" Sky said. "Your body!"

And then they were moving, back down the path, through the gate. Even as she saw Matthew rise clear of the wreckage.

A Fetch going into a body. He'd done it often enough. More than Meg. So he could help her.

She stepped up to herself, closed her eyes. He steadied the heart that beat for them both, breathed . . . and it was done! She stood up and Matthew watched her rise. He was fifty paces from her, less. But she was closer to the river. She turned to it . . . as a second shot came.

"Run," Sky urged within.

She ran, and Matthew followed. Her legs felt as

stiff as wooden poles. Somehow they propelled her through the gap in the riverbank, him coming fast behind her, gaining.

Then she was on the jetty. It was long, about thirty feet, and the boat was at its end. Her children were in it . . . and it was still tied to its mooring. It would take a moment to loose the knots. A moment she did not have. For Matthew would be upon her.

"Untie it," she shrieked, and saw Isaac reach to obey; the last thing she saw before Matthew slammed into her body, hurled her onto the planking, knocking the wind from her.

"Witch!" he said again, not a scream this time, he didn't have the breath for that. Then he found some, turned to the boat, yelled, "Leave the rope, boy. Leave it!"

Isaac froze; Matthew turned back. "I did not know your power! I thought the Devil merely danced with you. I did not think he had made you his queen. To blind me. Bind me. Bring me here." He smiled, a terrible smile, lifting the knife he still carried. "But I have you now."

As she crabbed away from him, as he followed her out over the water, she could see the fury that held him—the triumph also. She saw with his mind, as she had seen with it for the night. How he had suffered for his faith. And how he had triumphed in the end. For he had proved her sin beyond all doubt now. He had caught his witch.

"You have me, Matthew. Take me. I will admit it all, confess to everything, place my neck into the rope." She kept backing away down the jetty as she spoke. "Just let my children go."

"Go? Where?"

"That gun that sounded? My uncle fired it. He has a ship; it will take them to Norway, to my mother's family. They can grow up there in peace."

He looked at her in wonder, stopped as she did, a half-dozen paces from the pier's end, out over the water. "That was your plan, witch? You *have* prepared." He shook his head. "But I do not think so. I do not know much about your mother's land. But I do know that what is in you has come from there, inherited in that blood." He shook his head. "I will not—cannot!—send my children to the Devil."

She bowed her head . . . and that voice came into it again.

"There is nothing left," Sky said.

"I know," she replied aloud, rising to a crouch, getting her feet under her.

Matthew was facing the dock end. Isaac was touching the rope again. "I warn you, boy . . . ," Matthew said, raising the knife.

"Now," said Sky.

"Yes."

She leapt. Matthew had not felt her hands at his chest in the cellar, but he felt them now as they slid round him. He staggered back . . . and for one single, endless moment, she thought that his great strength might keep them on the dock. But then she remembered that he was as exhausted as she was, and she felt him fall. Holding tight, she fell too.

Water closed over her again. Words came, the ones she'd spoken when he told her that they were going to "swim" her.

"I cannot swim," she'd said. She had never learned the way of it.

But then, of course, neither had he.

CHAPTER SIXTEEN
REVELATION

Tight in each other's arms, sinking down into the freezing dark, mouths stretched wide to breathe the unbreathable . . . until, somewhere far above, a bubble of air, the faintest gleam of light. Drawing them up, pushing to it, faster now, falling in reverse, rushing toward . . .

"Aaaah!" Sucking the air in, great gulps of it, their mouths so close it was as if they were competing for it; realizing that—feeling the limbs that joined them—their flesh like sheets of ice fused together. Realizing, thrusting apart . . .

"What . . . ?"

"Where . . . ?"

Sky's hand, wrenched free of hers, flailed back, struck hardness. Not the wood of a jetty; a flashlight, a switch on it.

"Kristin!"

He screamed it . . . because a headless body was before him, a draug with arms spread wide.

"Wh-wh-what?" she said, teeth chattering, as her head emerged from the sweater she was pulling on. Immediately she reached for more of her scattered clothes. Suddenly conscious of his own bare and frigid skin, he began to reach, too, pull on, zip, and button.

The frenzy warmed them a little; not enough. When every item was on, Sky reached out, touched the tent wall. It was frozen solid. Their breaths, still being heaved out, passed through the light before them to catch and glisten in moisture on the canvas walls, freezing in an instant.

He looked at her—at her knees drawn up, her chin resting upon them, arms wrapped around. At both the horror and the question in her eyes. He wasn't ready to deal with either. Not when he was this cold.

"Ouuut!" He began fumbling at the flaps. But his fingers were solid lumps and the zipper was frozen shut. Reaching into a pocket, he found his Corsican grandfather's lighter. Somehow he managed to get it to strike; somehow he didn't set fire to the tent. Grasping the zipper's metal tongue, he jerked it open.

To a snow wall! He stared at it, horrified, until he felt the tap on his shoulder. "Here," Kristin said, handing him gloves. She already had hers on. Together, they began to dig their way out.

It took a while; they had to scrape the snow back into the tent. But the wall was only about a foot deep and suddenly collapsed. They fell through . . . to dazzling sun reflecting off pure white. They squinted up into the clearest of blue skies.

The exercise had warmed him enough to speak without chattering. But not enough to think. "Fire," he muttered.

She nodded. "And tea! For pity's sake, give me tea!"

It was, of course, the English answer for everything. As they sat by the fire they swiftly built, drinking it strong and supersweet, it was even answer enough for a short while.

But not for long. They'd only spoken a few words. They'd checked the time and found they'd been gone two nights and the day in between them—time lived in the present as usual bearing no relation to time spent in the past. They hadn't discussed anything that mattered.

Then Kristin began. "Look, we have to talk about what happened."

He wanted to avoid it still, make a joke. "What? The fact that you stuck needles into me and tried to drown me? Or the fact that I possessed you and *did* drown you?"

She waved a hand impatiently. "All that, sure. But before that . . . how we went back." When he didn't react, she put down her tea mug and looked straight at him. "Did we?"

He wanted to say "Did we what?" Joke some more. But he didn't want to appear too lame. So he said simply, "I don't remember."

She made the joke. "Just what every girl wants to hear the morning after!"

He shrugged. "Well, you did get me drunk!"

The joke had gone. "Do you *really* not remember?"

He looked straight back at her now. "Do you?"

Silence as each studied the other. Then she shook her head. "I remember you coming into the tent. I remember saying . . . something. But it didn't sound like me."

"Well, your Fetch is a *different* you, remember. . . ."

"Oh, convenient!" she said sarcastically. "It wasn't me, officer, it was my Fetch."

"It's always worked for me!"

She smiled briefly before she frowned again. "It was something to do with the Seidh magic. Freya's the goddess of that. Of . . . of love too. In *all* its aspects." She blushed, went on. "Like with runes, the journey begins with finding a way into a trance, often a sacrifice but sometimes an offering of some kind. . . ." She trailed off, then leaned forward. "Sky, do you *really* not remember?"

He sighed, put down his empty tea mug. "My memories are all blurred with the actual going back."

"Blurred," she echoed, nodding. "Exactly. Me too. So . . . we'll just leave it like that, yeah?"

He felt two different things, equally and at once. Relief . . . and a twitch of disappointment. But truly, he couldn't remember . . . much. "Sure."

"Right."

"Good." There was a long moment of silence. Then he was up, headed to the log pile, grabbing a few, returning to feed them into the flame, while she scraped up more snow for the kettle, dropped it again onto the gas stove. When they'd settled, he said in a matter-of-fact voice, "So what *do* you remember? About Matthew?"

She closed her eyes. "Everything, of course," she whispered. "I know you warned me, that it would always . . . he would always be there. Inside me. His life. His . . . hates! Boy, could he hate!" She shuddered. "But I didn't think . . . I didn't realize. . . ."

"No." He poked a stick into the fire. He was sorry for her, of course, that her time back had been so horrible. Yet a part of him was glad too. Welcome to Sky World, he thought bitterly. But he said, "So you learned what you needed?"

"Oh, yeah. I know all about possession now. Before, when . . . Sigurd came into me . . ."

"You screamed."

"I'm sure I did. But I couldn't remember the horror afterward. Sigurd saw to that. He needed me . . . ignorant. Unaware." She shivered. "But that moment you came into me—Meg into Matthew—I felt it all right." She shivered. "It was horrible. Disgusting!"

"Serves you right. Torturing bastard!"

She didn't smile. "But you don't believe that, do you, Sky? No one—no one!—deserves that. Every part of me . . . slithered into. Occupied. It was like someone groping me, worse. . . ."

He felt a pulse of anger at the description. Then guilt, because she was right. Wasn't she? But he managed to say, "I know! At least, I know from the other side. Because I did . . . the slithering in, remember? Oh, and thanks for putting it like that, by the way."

"Sorry! Of course!" She came across, and he made room for her on the log he sat on. "If the knowledge of possession lives in me, the knowledge of possessing must live in you." She squeezed his forearm. "How awful that must be!"

"It is!"

He said it fervently enough, he thought. But was she looking at him funny? He asked his next question, fast. "So you think you can resist it? I mean, that was the point, wasn't it, why we went back? To learn about possession so we could stop Sigurd possessing you? Us?"

"I . . . I think so." Her brow wrinkled in thought. "Because there is that moment, isn't there? When the hands reach, when the other's . . . Fetch, I suppose, starts to delve into you?" She leaned forward. "Like with you in the church hall, right? Sigurd didn't just plunge into you."

"I think he was taking his time, prolonging it, but . . . yeah, you're right, there are a few moments. . . ."

"And those moments are when you *could* stop it. Matthew didn't realize what was happening until it was too late to stop Meg. But I'm pretty sure that if I had those moments"—she nodded, determination clear in her eyes—"Sigurd wouldn't find me so easy. Because I'd be ready for him." She looked at him. "What about you?"

"Ditto." He threw another log on the fire. "I mean, I haven't had your experience, exactly. I haven't actually *been* possessed. The berserker. The wolf. They were both aspects of me. But"—he looked back at her—"what was it we said before? 'It takes a thief to catch a thief'? Well, I'm that thief now. And, yeah"—he nodded—"I think it would be pretty hard to steal from me."

Something cracked and exploded in the fire, shooting out some sparks. They both ducked, laughed. "Hey," Kristin said excitedly, "maybe we should practice?"

"What?"

"You know . . . I'll try to get a hold on you. You resist. You put a move on me, I slip your grip. 'Possession wrestling.' A whole new Olympic sport!"

She laughed again but he winced. "I don't think I'm quite up for that now," he said.

"No, not now, of course. When we get our strength back." She whistled. "Takes it out of you, this time-travel stuff, doesn't it?"

He smiled. "I warned you." The smile faded and he leaned forward, took her hand. "But I don't think possession is something we want to dabble in. It's dangerous. There's always going to be a part of one's Fetch that's . . . uncontrollable. Believe me, I know," he sighed. "No, I think we should take all that we've learned . . . and be ready."

She pressed his hand, then let go. "All right."

For a moment of silence, each stared into the flames. "Poor them," Kristin said at last. "Poor Meg and Matt. And those children!" Sadness replaced laughter; tears came into her eyes and she reached up to wipe them away. "They watched their parents drown."

"Yeah." Sky used a stick to shove a log into the center of the fire.

"But her uncle must have found Isaac and Gudrun, right? Taken them back to Norway?"

"I suppose so. Otherwise we wouldn't be here, would we?"

Another silence, only broken by the crackling of burning wood. Sky's eyes sought among the embers. He had so much to tell her still. And one thing he couldn't. "Listen," he said softly. "Something else happened back there. . . ."

He told her about the runes on the sundial and everything that had happened afterward. Almost everything. She had been through a lot, experienced extraordinary things. But this news stopped even Kristin's brain. "Wha . . ." was all she could come up with.

He shook his head. "Trust me, I know."

Finally, full words came to her. "How can you be certain Bjørn carved it?"

"Because I have carved as Bjørn, remember? Cut that same symbol—his symbol, *Uruz*—into the blade of his ax, Death Claw. And he cut *Uruz* into that sundial, marking it as his."

"He tagged it? Viking graffiti? 'Bjørn was here.' "

"Exactly."

"But why those other runes?"

"I don't know exactly. I don't know what situation he was in. He didn't carve them when I was in him as a young man. I'd remember. But he was near York then, so maybe sometime after I left him he carved a rune-spell to summon his Fetch."

"And in 1644, it was there to summon yours?" Kristin sat back. "I'm sorry, but that is just too bloody weird!"

Sky laughed bitterly. "Yup. It's right up there with the werewolf."

Kristin didn't smile. "But it was you, Sky, who came alive in Meg? And not just for that one moment of entry? For longer?"

"Much longer. And here's the scariest part." It wasn't . . . but it was scary enough. He licked his lips. "I wasn't just along for the ride. I . . . affected what she did. I made her do things." His voice quavered. "Kristin, I altered something in time."

She came up onto her knees. "You can't know that. Everything you described, Meg could . . . would have done herself. Reentered her body after reciting the runespell. Fought to save her children. Killed herself and Matthew for them."

"I know. She could have done all that on her own. Probably did. But I . . . I know I had control too. I just know it." Sky ran his hand over his head. "I was alive then, in her. Me, Sky. And I could have changed . . . history."

"But you didn't!" Her voice was gentle, obviously concerned. "And you won't! If we ever need to go back again—which I half want to, I admit, just to have a better experience than I had with that . . . torturer!—well, I can't think of a set of circumstances when that runespell would be recited again. And until it is, you'll be safe. Time will be safe."

"Sure . . . ," he murmured.

She leaned over, reached for him. For a moment, she held him. Then she came off her knees, onto her feet. "And speaking of going back," she said, "I think we better cut our holiday short and head home. We've learned what we needed to learn. Maybe it will be enough to stop Sigurd in whatever he's up to now." She smiled. "And I, for one, can't wait to find out what that is."

She walked away, down the path toward their tent, and he breathed out, feeling her as if she still held him.

Feeling her also inside him, where Meg was inside him still, Matthew inside her, Kristin inside him. Layer upon layer, like one of those wooden Russian dolls, another one inside, then another.

He turned back to the fire, ignored her call to come help break camp. There was one other thing he needed to think about first. That one thing he'd been unable to tell her. Couldn't tell her, though it was a part of all he had told her. It had been there, underneath all the fears he'd spoken of, all his protestations.

It was the true cost of his new knowledge. What Sky had known as a hawk, as a wolf. But never as a human. Never until now. Until Mad Meg, who he knew felt exactly the same.

Kristin had obviously thought he was upset, telling his tale of coming alive in his ancestor. But he wasn't. Concerned, yes. Figuring it all out, of course. But the main feeling wasn't concern or fear. Not at all.

It was longing.

Oh, the joy of it! The sheer, unparalleled wonder of living another human's life. Not as them, not dissolved in Tza or Bjørn or Meg. As himself.

That was the true cost of this trip. And he was so happy to have paid it. Yet what would Kristin think of him if she knew what he wanted most now?

"Sky, come on, aren't you going to help?"

She was calling again through the trees, from their tent. She couldn't see him, which was just as well. Couldn't see the smile on his face.

Sigurd had said something the moment before he possessed Dirk in that boathouse. Sky hadn't understood it then. He did now.

"If you've paid for something," Sky whispered, rising, "you may as well use it."

CHAPTER SEVENTEEN

TWELFTH NIGHT

"It's easy enough to lose a draug," Sky said, pulling back the curtain in his father's den, seeking the deeper darkness within the garden below. It was not hard to find.

"Really?" said Kristin, distracted, her eyes fixed on the screen before her, her forefinger clicking the mouse.

"Sure. I mean, you could lead 'em across rooftops. They've got no head for heights."

"Hmm?"

"Or you could confuse 'em. Give 'em, like, a math test. They've got no head for figures."

On the table beside Kristin, the printer began to spit out paper. She sat back, rolled her shoulders, turned. "What are you doing?"

"Well, you asked me how we could lose our shadows. I'm suggesting ways."

"No. You're standing there thinking up bad jokes about headless spirits."

"I told you before, they're not a problem." He let the curtain fall, crossed to her. "Sigurd's not in telepathic conversation with them. He just leaves them there to show his power. We'll just get in the car, go. They've got no head for—"

"OK! OK!" She reached to the printer, pulled a sheet out. "So we're booked. I think it was the last room in the place." She lifted the sheet, read. " 'Hotel Excelsior: City Luxury in the heart of the Country. All your conference needs catered to.' "

He squinted. "Double bed. Cozy."

"Shut up. We won't be doing any sleeping."

"Promise?"

She hit him. "What's with you? We're about to go take Sigurd on again. We don't know what he's got planned except that he's holding a conference for would-be Fetches and draugs, the climax of all these local meetings. Planning something huge . . . and you're just cracking jokes. Aren't you scared?"

"Terrified." He yawned, smiled at her look. "This is me being terrified."

She shook her head, turned to collect more papers. "You've been weird ever since we got back from Norway. Are you sure you're ready for this?"

"Oh, yeah."

She stood, gathering papers. "Shut that down, will

you? I'll just go and say bye-bye to your folks, tell 'em we're off to that club."

"Sure." She left and he bent, used the mouse to click off the screens she'd opened. Paused at the last one, the one that announced the conference. " 'The Church of the Freed Spirit invites you to Twelfth Night,' " he read to himself. " 'The end of the Yuletide feast. Come and join the Wild Hunt for its last ride!' " There was more, the delights that awaited. Most importantly, it promised enlightenment. A blinding moment of transcendence.

Sky speed-read, his gaze falling fast to the bottom of the page. To the line that was the slogan for the cult of Sigurd.

"Freedom is yours."

"Bring it on," he said, clicking off the screen.

"There!"

The fog lay heavy on the roads, getting ever thicker the closer they got. So thick that Sky's face was pressed to the windshield as he tried to see the sign they must have driven past before. The headlights lit it now, through fingers of gray mist.

"The Excelsior." Kristin swung the car off the paved road, tires crackling over gravel. Beyond the arrow with the one name was a larger sign, blue with gold lettering in copperplate, detailing what the hotel had to offer: Modern facilities in eighteenth-century surroundings. Hi-tech meeting hall. Spa. Gym. Pool. Guided walks in the Malvern Hills.

"So what is this place?"

Kristin spoke as she stared. "Conference hotel. There's lots around. Firms take their employees off for weekend workshops, bonding, that sort of thing. My mum's company does it all the time."

"Does your mum go to those?"

Sky pointed. Below the main board was another, hung from hooks. "The Excelsior welcomes the Church of the Freed Spirit."

"Not so much."

They sat for a moment, only the low throb of the engine disturbing the silence. "Uh, why aren't we moving?" asked Sky.

She turned to him. "Isn't he going to be waiting for us?"

"Sigurd?"

"No, Sky, Santa Claus."

"Probably. But . . . well, maybe he'll be too distracted by all this. Plus we have left it till the last night. And last time he saw us, remember, he bloody nearly possessed me. And he already had you. He's got to figure we're terrified. Any sane person would run a mile."

She bit her lip. "Maybe we should."

He shook his head. "We can't. You know we can't. Besides, he's got a lot to distract him. I mean, all this . . ." He waved at the hotel, unseen in the fog beyond them. "This is his big night, right? He's promised everyone something . . . spectacular tonight. Nothing less than enlightenment." He grinned. "I think he's got other things to focus on than two scared grandkids."

He wasn't sure he believed it himself. And Kristin still didn't look convinced. "Besides," he added, "look at our brilliant disguises." He gestured at himself, the suit he was wearing, the tie that half strangled him. He'd shaved his beard and head, taken out his earrings. She was wearing a dress, her hair bobbed and dyed black. He leaned over, tapped her leg. "It's just a very dark section of wall, cousin. Are we walking, or are we talking?"

She sighed. "Walking." She slipped the car into gear, and he gave a little grunt of relief. For a moment he'd thought she might actually want to turn back. And he didn't, not at all. The closer he got, the . . . hungrier he felt.

The car had barely moved forward when the spiked iron gates slowly swung open. "Creepy," she muttered.

"Electronics," he replied, pointing up. "Smile for the camera."

She drove forward. The gates closed behind them, the lens swiveling as they went through.

They passed down an avenue of elm toward a glow of light in the foggy distance. It grew brighter as they approached. The lane ended in a wide, graveled semicircle before a huge brick manor house. Four columns supported a portico over massive wood-and-glass doors. On either side of the main house, large wings glowed with lights. High above, ranks of chimneys added smoke to the fog.

A sign directed them to a parking lot, hidden by poplars, to the right. It was packed tight, and they just squeezed into a space between two trees.

"Conference attendees: Hutchinson and Weird."

"*Weird,* madam?" The tall desk clerk peered over his glasses.

"Weir, sorry!" Kristin giggled nervously. "We're very late!" she added, as if that explained it.

"You are indeed, madam." The man, who was probably in his fifties, with gray hair and moustache, reminded Sky of a particularly patronizing math teacher he'd once had. "The late-afternoon session's nearly concluded. They will break soon for supper, before the evening party."

"Ah, well! At least we're in time for the party, eh? Ow!"

Since she'd begun to giggle again, Sky pinched her hard, stepped forward. "Two keys, please, uh . . ." He peered at the name tag. "Scott."

"Sir," the man replied, as if the word was hard to get through his throat. He then began punching numbers into a machine, swiping the key cards.

Sky pulled Kristin back, whispered, "What's up with you?"

"Nervous," she said. "I mean, look at this place!"

"I know. Shhh!" Sky turned back to the desk, reached out his hands for the key cards.

The clerk looked as if he was reluctant to hand them over. "The current session ends in twenty minutes. And they are most scrupulous about not letting people in or out during it. You'll have to wait for the Twelfth Night celebrations proper to commence. But you can watch proceedings on channel 51 on your television." He pointed to an archway. "The conference center is at the back of the house. There's a lift or stairs down three floors—"

"The conference center is underground?"

The clerk looked witheringly at Sky for the interruption. "This is a heritage building . . . sir! Home to the Lords of Swithycombe for five centuries. One can't just construct a modern facility anywhere." With a sigh, he finally passed the keys across. "Your room is the opposite way. Up. High up!" he said with satisfaction. "You may take the lift or the stairs, as you choose. May one summon help to carry your, uh, bags?"

He was looking at the backpacks at their feet. "Oh, no," said Kristin, adopting the same tone. "One can manage quite well oneself."

"So pleased." The man shot them a final glare, turned away. They were dismissed.

Scott had been right about the room being high up. There was a top floor, three stories up, and then there was a narrow attic stair beyond. "There's oxygen at the next camp," Kristin called down from the tiny landing.

When Sky had struggled up the last flight, he fell through the door Kristin had opened. "Could it be smaller?" he said, looking around. The roof sloped and he could only stand fully in the center of the room. The bed was a double . . . for hobbits. And what looked like a narrow closet was actually a shower cubicle and a tiny sink.

Kristin was standing in the only other place that could take her height—where the window was cut into the roof. "It's like a sauna too. Shall I open this?" Sky nodded and she lifted the window, set it on its arm. A man-sized gap let in lots of air. "And now . . . ah!"

She picked up a remote. There was a TV set mounted on the wall opposite the bed. The first click brought up an entrance screen detailing the various options, from kid flicks to "adult" entertainment. She went to "Channels," scrolled down through various news and quiz shows. Then she clicked again, and . . . a man was talking into a microphone. The camera was close on his face, and though there was no sound, Sky could immediately see the passion with which the man was speaking.

"Now where . . . ah!" said Kristin. She pressed and held a button, and a voice grew to fill the tiny room.

". . . understand? I've spent my working life as a physicist. I have dealt only in what can be observed, proven to my eyes, concluded in my calculations. . . ."

The camera panned back, and both could see that the man was sitting in a wheelchair. Behind him, he also appeared on a huge screen—a screen that had a jagged "S" shape soaring up through clouds. It looked like a lightning bolt piercing the purple-tinged darkness, but they both knew it was something else.

"*Sowilo.* The Sun."

"Shh!"

The physicist was still speaking. "The disease took my legs years ago. And science told me I would never walk again. I am a man of science; I believed I'd been told the truth. And I would never, normally, have gone anywhere near a place that had 'Church' in its title. But something drew me to the Church of the Freed Spirit. Someone. And there I learned that everything I had always believed to be true wasn't."

Sky gasped.

"What?"

"Didn't you see it?"

"See what?"

A different camera angle showed them the crowd now. Sky stared at the faces, all looking up with almost the same expression—a yearning. Most were applauding. "On the screen behind the speaker. Don't look at it directly," Sky said. "Choose a corner. Defocus your eyes."

"O . . . kay."

The camera cut back to the wide shot, the man against his own image on the rune-marked screen. "Wow!" whistled Kristin.

"See it?"

"Yeah! For, like, a nanosecond." She turned to him excitedly. "It's what you said he did before, at the other meeting. He's putting in flashes you can't really see."

Sky nodded. "He's planting an idea. A rune."

They said it together. "*Ehwaz*—rune of the Fetch."

The man had paused, staring down at the clapping crowd. Now he began to speak again. "Truth, friends. For so long we have been fed lies—by our priests, by our governments"—the sound of more applause—"even, I have to own, by our scientists. We have been told what society wants us to believe. What will make us behave like everyone else. Accept what everyone says is our reality. I accepted the reality of this wheelchair." He thumped the arms. "And then I met a man. A young man, wise beyond his years."

Music had begun to play. Soft, stirring, a pulse to it like a heartbeat.

"And that young man came into my dream. And in my dream, he lifted me from this chair. I walked again, ran. In the end, I flew like a hawk, soared above this world into another."

The lights on the stage were narrowing to a pool around him. The music had grown in volume, in sweetness, yet with a core to it, an inspiring strength. The man's voice strengthened with it, rose above it.

"And I learned something else from this wonderful man. Do not believe what they tell you. Believe instead in your own truth. Believe in the Church of the Freed Spirit. Believe that . . . freedom is yours."

His hands were still clutching the arms of his wheelchair. Now, he began to push up. The music built, underlying the applause. Behind him, *Sowilo* turned a crimson red.

He stood, stepped away from his chair. The applause grew thunderous. But someone had raised the volume in his microphone to cope with it. Lifting his hands above him, the man shouted, "Friends! Will you rise and welcome that young man? A truth-seeker. A leader." He turned around, stretched out a hand, beckoned. "May I even say . . . a Messiah!"

A figure had appeared from behind the screen at the back. Maybe he'd been there all along, in the shadows. A light was growing on him, slowly, slowly. His head was lowered, and it looked as if the jagged lightning bolt on the screen had struck him . . . or was rising from his back.

The light warmed, bathing him in gold. He lifted his head. And even though they both knew who they were about to see, they didn't know which body he'd appear in.

"Dirk," Kristin whispered, at the same time that Sky said, "Sigurd!"

On the screen, in tight close-up, Dirk van Straaten smiled.

He held the position for a long while, let them see his handsome face, his perfect teeth parted in a smile. Then slowly he moved forward to the microphone. The other man had gone, vanished, by wheelchair or foot, no one had seen.

"He's quite the showman, isn't he?" Sky said, transfixed.

"You should have seen his Macbeth at Cambridge last year," Kristin muttered.

"He's got them, hasn't he? They've had two days of this, locked in that room. Building to—"

"Shh! He's going to speak."

The camera, which had been playing over the ecstatic crowd, cut back to Dirk. He gently motioned for quiet, and immediately, they quieted. "Friends," he said softly. "Truth-seekers."

"He's toned down the South African accent, hasn't he?"

She gestured him to silence again.

"This is Twelfth Night. A time for celebration, for liberation. Our ancestors used these twelve days to feast, to commune, to set aside the darkness of winter, to gather around their hearths, drink ale and mead, listen to the old stories. To make new stories . . . and new additions to the tribe."

"Clever. He's promising them sex, booze—"

"Will you shut up!"

"And we will celebrate just as our ancestors did. They call us to the feast that is even now being prepared. You have listened enough, striven enough, witnessed enough in these two days, in this sacred space. You have all worked so hard." He raised his arms high. "But now Twelfth Night is upon us and we will play!"

A great cheer greeted the declaration. He motioned again for a silence that instantly came. "Go, and ready yourselves. We meet again in one hour. And then, after we have gathered around our own hearth, here, in this room—when we have feasted, when we have drunk of the communal cup—I will tell you one last tale. A myth, some would call it. A miracle to others. But to me—to you!—it will simply be the truth you seek."

Another cheer. This time he waited for it to subside. When silence came, he spoke softly. "A final thing. Do you remember when you arrived? How each and every one of you was greeted and welcomed by your name into the sacred circle we have created? Well, now we must greet some latecomers to our feast. They may have missed all we have witnessed, all we have shared. But they are seekers for truth, too, and freedom can still be theirs. Join with me then, friends, and welcome . . ."

Dirk had been staring out, talking to the crowd. Now he paused, then looked straight into the camera—and so, straight out of the TV screen. Straight at them.

"Welcome, Sky and Kristin," he said. "Welcome to Twelfth Night."

The shot changed. The entire crowd was on their feet. "Welcome, Sky and Kristin," they shouted. "Welcome to Twelfth Night."

The echo had not yet faded when the three men came through the door.

CHAPTER EIGHTEEN

DUNCAN

They came in a shouting rush, smashing the door against the inner wall. Kristin was nearest them, too stunned to do much more than slap at the huge biker who lunged at her. But the room was tiny, and the other two got stuck behind the first one's grab. It gave Sky a moment to recover from the shock, another to reach for a weapon. Any weapon.

It wasn't much—a lamp snatched off the bedside table, the plug wrenched from the wall socket. Its base was a solid wooden block and he brought it down hard onto the second biker's head.

"Out the way!" The third intruder tried to dodge past his stricken buddy. He went one way, Sky went the other, over the bed, bending under the sloping roof. The man chased, shoving the bleeding man aside. Sky raised the lamp-club again . . . and a hand shot out and gripped his throat.

"Gotcha," yelled the first man, the one who Sky, twisting around, now saw had Kristin's throat locked in the crook of an elbow. But he also saw her bend her head down, grab flesh with teeth . . .

"Aiee!" the man shouted, forced to ease both grips. Kristin dropped to the floor, rolled away. Sky, coughing, staggered back . . . and arms the size and strength of steel cables shot round his chest, lifting him into the air.

"Get 'er," came the bellow in Sky's ear as he flailed, lashing out with his legs. A few kicks connected; he could feel heel strike bone, hear the grunt of pain. But the man just squeezed tighter, and the air he used to kick he could not replace.

Through eyes fast misting, he saw Kristin dodge for the door, nearly make it, slip on a rucked-up edge of rug. The man stooped, grabbed, had her again. This time he twisted her arm up behind her back.

She cried in agony. And this brought Sky back, cleared his eyes enough to focus on her pain. And on something else . . . the insignia on the back of the biker's leather vest. It probably once held the spread wings of the Hell's Angels. He could even see a faded pattern where those stitches had been. But something had been stitched over it. These men had a new allegiance now.

On the biker's back was the lightning bolt of the Church of the Freed Spirit.

But to Sky, head swimming with lack of air, eyes

beginning to mist again, it had an older meaning. It was *Sowilo.* The rising sun. Also the rune of return, the one he'd used to send his ancestor Bjørn back to his rest. Sky had been Bjørn, twice now. Somewhere inside, he was Bjørn still. And his ancestor had . . . special powers. Particular appetites.

Eyes misted, air nearly gone, like drowning, which he'd also done twice now. But in drowning, there was always a moment of peace, of clarity. Perhaps of choice. To live or die. To act or not.

That moment came. Brought the thought of Bjørn again, then the feeling of him. Not just as he was; as he could be. When the mist in his eyes turned blood-red.

"Bjørn!" He did not need to yell it, had no air to yell it with. He only had to lower his head all the way forward, then jerk it sharply back.

A crack, a cry, the arms that held him loosened. Sky fell forward, gasping in air, taking what he'd need, fueling himself . . . for the man throwing Kristin into the corner of the room, clearing his hands, then filling one with a knife. Bjørn-Sky saw it, wanted it, wanted him to come, needed him to come. . . .

"Alive, 'e wants 'em," came a warning shout from behind Sky, a voice gurgling with blood. A glance told him the man he'd butted was rising; the other was coming forward, knife still out. The third man, the first he'd hit, was standing again too.

Good.

"Sky! Go!"

He could take them all, all three, then look for more! But a voice was calling him back, out of the redness.

"Go, Sky!" Kristin yelled. He saw her throw herself forward, saw the knifeman wobble as she hit his legs, start to fall.

"Where?" he wanted to yell. Then he looked up. Air was coming in from above. Cold air. Night air.

He didn't want to leave her. But with one of them free there was hope. So he leapt, grabbed the sill, hoisted himself half out. Enough to support him so that when one leg was grabbed, he was able to use the other to kick, kick hard. A yelp and he was free . . . but he'd been leaning too far, and the kick launched him. The roof sloped and he began to build up speed, rolling down it. . . .

His hands, desperately reaching, grabbed a clay chimney pot. It crumbled under his velocity, was wrenched from its mount, but it slowed him. He grabbed another, just as his legs fell over the drop . . . and this one held. Panting with terror, he got one leg onto the gutters and hauled himself back onto the fog-slick tiles.

He only had a moment to breathe before a shout made him look up to the window . . . just as a man climbed out of it. But as soon as the man's feet touched the roof, he slipped, and the chimneys he hit did nothing to slow him. Sky rolled to the side, out of the way, desperately clinging to the clay chimney pot.

But even as the man tumbled past him, instinct kicked in. He shot one hand out, an attempt to save another human's life. But the biker's speed, his bulk, could not be slowed. Something brushed Sky's hand, he grabbed it . . . and then the man was gone, pitched into darkness. Strangely, in his falling, he made no sound. A long time later, it seemed, Sky heard a dull crump.

He clung there as if his fingers were welded to the chimney pot. Then there was movement above; another man leaned out the window, calling. "Dean? Dean? You got 'im?"

Sky forced himself to move, to crab across the slate roof. Eventually, he came to a level part, a flat roof with a ledge and a door at one end. He sat down, eased limbs that were all cramped . . . and noticed that there was something in one of his hands.

It was what he'd grabbed in his pathetic attempt to save the falling biker. At first, he didn't know what it was. Then he did, and the confusion of the sight drove away the last shreds of his terror.

"A gas mask? Why would a biker have one of those?" he wondered out loud.

Music, from far below, distracted him, the whine of fiddles and pipes. Twelfth Night was starting.

But how will it end? he thought. There was a clip on the back of the mask. Attaching it to his belt, Sky moved to the door. It was unlocked, and he went through it into the house.

◆◆◆

The attic was a series of interconnected spaces under sloping roofs. It was lit by a single bulb every fifty feet or so, the areas in between cast into shadows. The jumble of centuries snagged Sky's legs as he stumbled along, from modern castoffs such as broken printers to old trunks that had to be Victorian at least. At what he thought was about halfway along, wedged right into the angle of the roof, Sky ran into one of these—literally. Rubbing his bruised shin, squinting, he saw that it was almost like the one he'd explored in another attic what seemed like a hundred years ago: Sigurd's sea chest. It had contained his runestones. The beginning of all Sky's journeys.

Sky had been seeking a quiet place, somewhere he'd be safe. The chest looked perfect—empty, deep, and with a hole the size of a fist in its lid, so it wasn't totally airless. But the memory of that other chest, all that had come from it, nearly made him move on, seek again.

Then he stopped. "No," he said out loud, defiantly, "if I'm going to beat him, I can't start out by being afraid of him."

He folded himself into the trunk, knees raised. It took a while, his heart still not settled after his escape, his mind still full of all he had to do. Far below, he heard music again, a heavy, almost tribal beat now, pulsing through the old house's bones. He breathed deep, again and again, his mind gradually clearing, his body sinking back. When the moment came, as ever it was like that one when consciousness transforms to sleep. Unknowable.

He rose up. Looked down at himself, nodded once as if in farewell, then lowered the lid.

Licking his lips, he headed for the trapdoor. He didn't knock his knees on any obstacles now. It was the big advantage of the spirit Fetch that Meg had introduced him to, just before she took possession of Matthew. He could touch, move objects if he wanted to. But nothing could touch him. Nothing and no one.

The corridor ran the length of the top floor of the hotel. Quarters for servants once, but their garrets were extra guest rooms now. The one he'd escaped from was only a few doors along.

Hanging his head through the trap, whose door he'd quietly lifted up into the attic, Sky saw the whole length of the house. All the fire doors, which were meant to be kept shut, were propped open by extinguishers. No doubt so that the two bikers who were patrolling—one was one of the attackers, one wasn't—could see anyone who appeared. Anyone who had to come down from the roof.

Luckily for Sky, there were several trapdoors, a stair at each end, and windows like the one he'd escaped through. So the bikers kept separating, moving, looking up, around. Sometimes one would move fast to a door that opened . . . where a guest would appear and be startled by the man running up.

Sky waited, listened. When he heard a conversation at the far end of the corridor, he stuck his head through. Both bikers had their backs to him. Swinging down, Sky stepped into a doorway that was set a little back. The frame hid him. Reaching, he found the door was open. He knew a biker would be coming his way soon enough, so he slipped into the room.

Someone was in there. He heard a man singing in the shower. Leaving the door open a crack, Sky listened to the footsteps approaching down the corridor. When they were nearly there, he opened the door more, stepping behind it.

"Hey!" he said softly.

"Someone there?" called the man from the shower.

"Who's that?" the biker said, stepping in. He had his back to Sky. The jagged "S" was an arm's reach away.

Sky reached. He'd thought that maybe this first time it would be hard. But just as he'd felt Bjørn stir in the fight before, so now he felt Meg. Located that part that was her within him, that would always be her now. The switch that had been thrown. The switch he threw now.

Sinking through the rising sun, for the first time in his life, Sky possessed a man.

There was no resistance. Just a long wail like she'd heard—*he'd* heard—Matthew give, someone falling off a cliff into a bottomless black pit. It trailed off, vanished into eternity. And Sky was in him . . . no! Sky *was* him, this man. Duncan Smee. His life, side by side with Sky's, accessible like a twin hard drive, all of the data, all of the lived experience, there, enmeshed. Sky felt his large belly wobble before him and immediately craved a beer. Felt the right knee, smashed in a motorbike crash, never completely healed, which accounted for the way Duncan stood, favoring the left leg. Ran his finger down the scar on his cheek—a knife had done that, a gang fight, a back alley in Brighton, outnumbered three to one.

Something about the name. It wasn't the one he'd been born with, never knew his dad, hated his mum. He'd changed it.

"Duncan Smee." He spoke it aloud, lips and throat shaping the words in a rough, working-class accent. And then he saw it, what it was about the name.

"Duncan Smee," he said again. "Duncan's *me*! And I'm *him*!"

"What's so funny, Dunk?"

Sky turned. The other biker, one of the ones Sky had fought, stood behind him in the corridor.

"This bloke's singing, Pete. Dreadful!"

The door to the shower room opened. A middle-aged man stood there in a towel, spectacles misted. "Oh! Can I . . . help you?"

Before Sky could speak, Pete did. He tapped his walkie-talkie. "We've had word, friend. Party's starting early." The phone began ringing. Pete pointed. "That'll be them to tell you."

As they were leaving, Sky turned back. Said the phrase they'd been repeating all weekend, all the time. "Be free!"

"Freedom is yours," came the reply.

The two bikers stood in the corridor. "The man says to get downstairs. Schedule's brought forward."

"What? Because of this kid?" Sky said contemptuously about himself.

"Forget him. We've got the girl and the man reckons he won't go far without her. Plus hotel security's hunting and they've got cameras everywhere, except up here. They'll spot him when he comes down, or if he gets anywhere near the conference." He headed for the stairs. "Let's go."

Sky found it hard to just walk. He wanted to run, to leap, bad knee and all. The body wasn't as good as his own—older, not very fit, that belly—but it had all these other ways of being. And all these other memories, experiences to be played through. He'd have liked to have taken his time, doing that.

Then he looked down . . . and knew he had no time. Because at the other man's hip hung a gas mask. There was one at his own. There was another attached to Sky's belt upstairs.

Something was about to happen. Something that Sigurd-in-Dirk was now rushing toward.

CHAPTER NINETEEN

FREEDOM IS YOURS

Someone had been busy. When they'd seen the conference hall on the screen, the chairs had been in rows. Now they were arranged around tables, twelve to each one. Every table had a flag, each flag a different rune. People circled them, seeking their names on the cards placed before each seat. But as he walked toward the stage, Sky noticed that the four tables in the center all had *Sowilo.* The Sun. Which, Sky remembered, was not only what banished the darkness. It was the journey *through* darkness to light. To the freedom that light brings. "Be free," he muttered.

Pete, walking beside him, nodded. "Freedom is yours," he replied.

And then they were walking up the stairs onto the stage, crossing to a huddle of men in leather jackets who parted as they approached . . . and there, at the center, was Sigurd. Dirk, of course, in body. But Sigurd in the eyes.

These swept over him, and Sky held his breath. Would Sigurd know him? But the eyes focused on another. "Well?" he snapped.

Pete shook his head. "Nothing. Probably still in that rats' nest they call an attic. I could take a few of the boys, go end to end—"

Sigurd cut him off with a gesture. "No. He doesn't matter. Anyway, we have her!" He jerked his thumb into the wings off the stage. Sky looked, and his heart lurched. He could see part of an ornately carved couch. A large black curtain, hanging from rails above, obscured most of it. But not its end, where two ankle boots showed, ropes bound around them.

He saw them twitch, push out against the bonds. He had to resist the urge to step toward them. Then Pete said, "Mask for her, Mr. van Straaten?"

"I'll deal with that." He turned back. "You all know your jobs, your positions?" There was a murmur of assent. "Then go to them. Be free!"

"Freedom is yours," came the group reply.

They broke from the huddle. Sky, watching Sigurd disappear behind the black curtain, resisted the urge to follow him to Kristin. He couldn't betray himself, not yet. Duncan had a job to do. He was to take up position by the shutter mechanism. He was to close the shutters on command. And then? Closing his eyes for a moment, Sky searched inside Smee. It was like a combination of computer and film, data and images, running behind his eyelids. No. He hadn't been told what was going to happen next. Sky had known straightaway that Smee wasn't very smart. He was a foot soldier, recruited for his strength, a mean temper, and, once it was won, his loyalty. Pete, who seemed to be top biker, would give him orders that would be instantly obeyed.

But in searching within, Sky suddenly gasped, stopped where he was between two tables. He'd . . . touched something with his mind, a hidden place within, like a . . . a box that was locked, that just needed the right key. And in that instant he knew that the man had not just been chosen because he was strong, vicious, and would obey orders unthinkingly. He'd been chosen because his Fetch was right there, within that closed box, yearning for release. Awaiting some action that would set it free.

"Freedom's mine," he whispered.

He began to move through the crowd again. The drinking was accelerating. Heated wine gave off the scent of strange herbs, similar to what Pascaline had fed him in Corsica before she helped him leave his body and go to the hunt—some kind of relaxant. With Duncan's eye—and thirst—he noted pints of beer being poured from kegs. They'd brewed a special ale for this feast. On the side of each keg was stamped *Laguz*—rune of the sea, of all things liquid. And Sky, remembering the last time he'd seen *Laguz,* in a churchyard, shivered.

He took up his position. He couldn't think of anything else to do, not yet. He knew his job was to close the shutters in the ceiling—which were only at ground level above, because the conference hall was underground. But why? There were five screens hanging from the ceiling. Perhaps Sigurd was going to project another film onto them. But it was night outside, and the windows didn't let in a lot of light. Maybe it was to stop people—the hotel staff—from looking in? That made more sense. Whatever ritual Sigurd was about to enact, he wouldn't want witnesses.

One of the men who'd been on the stage was crossing the room. He was the only one who wasn't a biker—a small, skinny man with a wispy mustache, glasses, and a headset. He climbed a short flight of stairs, went into a glass-paneled booth. Sky saw him sit, lean forward, then heard the man's voice crackle in his walkie-talkie.

"Stand by, everyone."

Another biker, Jim, stood on the opposite side of the hall's only doors. He hadn't been on the stage, had been standing there the whole time, using a clicker, counting the people. As a couple rushed in, laughing, Jim clicked, then turned toward the glass booth, waved, before stepping outside. The doors swung closed. There was the clunk of solid locks.

"We're a go, gentlemen. Stand by, shutters!"

That was him! Duncan! The buttons were beside him, an old-fashioned crank handle beside them for backup.

The lights began to dim. What could he do? He still didn't know what was happening. He couldn't betray himself by not acting. And he couldn't take them all on, not even if Bjørn came and helped him with his ax. He had to wait for his moment, had to hope that one would come.

"Shutters . . . go!"

What could he do? He pressed the buttons. Immediately, he heard a faint grinding sound, looked up to see metal slats unfolding over the glass above. He didn't need the backup handle. Electricity was sealing the room, as snug as any coffin's lid. And at the exact same moment as the blinds began to close, the music, a pulse underneath the hubbub till then, increased in volume. Conversations hushed as people began to listen to the ancient drums, knucklebones ghosting across tightened hide. A flute blended in, serene, lonely. At the moment its first notes sounded, projectors began to beam images onto the five screens. And Sky realized that they weren't just in the corners of the hall, they were at the cardinal points—north and south, east and west—while the last one hung straight above the middle. But it was the sixth image, projected by a laser around the entire room—a thin belt, encircling all the others, encircling everyone—that confirmed for Sky what Duncan couldn't know.

The images were runes, in a cast, which Duncan had never seen before.

But Sky had.

He had carved them at midnight on the floor of a hut in the mountains of Norway. Kristin had chanted them—his cuts, her voice, bringing them into being. And a voice began to chant them now, a man's voice, soft but strong, to the beat of that drum, the call of that flute.

"Othala," he sang out joyously. *"Thurisaz. Ansuz. Raidho. Pertho."* The runes on the hanging cloths were named, one by one.

A man emerged from between the black drapes at the back of the stage and began to walk slowly toward the front. He had a microphone in his hand. And Sky knew that that man had been there, too, in the high mountains of Norway, at the cutting and the chanting. He had been there in another body, a weary, old one, fast failing; and he had used these same runes to help kill a man. Used the force of his sudden dying and the power of darkest magic to shed his failing flesh and possess another's soul.

Sky stood, unable to move, barely able to breathe, watching his grandfather walking slowly forward. He was in Dirk's body, had used Dirk's mind to go past the old ways of cutting and carving, tradition blended with these modern techniques. Sigurd and Dirk both had created this new sacred space. They'd bound it with runes. And then they'd invited Death to call. And

Sky knew it was not one death this time. Hundreds. Hundreds who, in the explosion of their murder, would unleash untold power. Power enough to free the Fetches of his disciples, the ones who had proved themselves over this weekend, over the months of selection. The ones who had the "S" of *Sowilo* stitched on their backs . . . and gas masks hanging from their hips.

Suddenly, Sky knew! And he remembered what Sigurd had said to him once long ago. "Come! A little suffering at the beginning so that humanity can live forever!"

Sigurd had reached the front of the stage. He stared out for a long moment before he lifted the microphone to his lips and breathed the name of the final rune. *"Hagalaz,"* he whispered.

The hailstorm that encircled them in laser light was about to descend on them all.

And there was nothing that Sky could do to prevent it.

The word was a cue. "Masks on," came the voice from the walkie-talkie.

There was nothing he could do . . . except reach down, unclip the mask from his belt, slip the straps over his head, tighten them. . . .

The lights in the room darkened. People murmured in joy, in wonder, as the runes above them, the one around them, began to glow flame-red.

The voice again. "Ten. Nine. Eight. Seven. . . ."

Sky looked to the glass booth. The man was signaling the counts with his hand as he spoke them. "Six. Five. . . ."

And it was then Sky remembered. "Kristin!" he screamed, his voice tinny and trapped behind the mask. He took a step forward.

"Three. . . ."

He'd never make it! He froze, watched the man in the booth make the last two beats silently with his hands. He couldn't help it. He counted it down.

"Two. One."

Nothing happened. People gazed up, pointing, laughing. At the nearest table, three arm spans away, Sky found he was staring at a young woman in a bright blue dress. She had a wineglass raised to her lips, was gripping it by the stem. He was so close he could see the red runes reflecting in her eyes. Then something changed in them. And the wine stem snapped in her fingers. She slumped down, slipping to the floor. The man next to her reached for her . . . then fell over her, his head hitting the table as he did.

No one cried out. There was no sound save for the smashing of glass, the splintering of wood as someone's chair gave under sudden dropped weight. Everyone who'd been up was down, anyone who'd sat at a table was now sprawled over it. At the nearest one, a wine bottle had been knocked over, its contents slowly leaking out over the table's edge, dripping onto the carpet like a run of blood.

It had taken only moments to kill close to two hundred people! To kill Kristin perhaps, up there bound and gagged beside the stage. Yet, even as tears started into his eyes, Sky sensed something was wrong with it all. He'd felt no stirring in Duncan. That box with his Fetch remained locked inside him. Death had released nothing.

Then the walkie-talkie crackled. "Everyone to the front of the stage," came the voice, muffled now inside a mask.

Sky obeyed, powerless to do anything else. From various parts of the hall, the bikers moved forward. Two of them dragged boxes from behind the curtains that hung over the front of the stage. As Sky approached he saw that Dirk had come down. He bent now, opened a box, reached inside.

"Here," he said, and gave Sky a handful of masks. "Quickly now. Put them on everyone at these tables." He gestured to the ones in the middle, each marked by the *Sowilo* flag.

Sky stepped away, watched. The bikers had spread out, were lifting slumped heads, pulling masks over faces. And he realized what was happening. Those in the center had to be the chosen ones, selected from the meetings up and down the country, finally narrowed down over the course of this weekend. They had to possess special skills, connections, wealth perhaps—not to mention an accessible Fetch. They'd made the cut. Sigurd wasn't going to rest content with just a dozen bikers as his disciples. He'd need a mass movement, a major cult. These men and women were to be its officers—and Sigurd's beginning.

Then Sky remembered something else, something he'd read. In countries where they still executed people, you gave one drug to lull them, a different one to kill them.

Everyone in the hall was still alive!

"You!"

He turned. Sigurd-Dirk was bent over a body, slipping a mask over the face. "What are you standing there for?" he snarled. "The gas's effect only lasts five minutes. Move!"

For a second, the two men stared at each other. It was a second that held, and Sky thought he saw the beginnings of a suspicion grow in the South African's dark eyes. He turned swiftly, carrying his masks to one of the tables. Glancing back, he saw that Sigurd had returned to his task. So he quickly darted left and slipped up the side of the stage.

She was still there. And with an extra twist of horror, Sky saw that she had no mask. Perhaps Sigurd planned to save her before the second drug came. Perhaps he was sacrificing her, too, one more surge of power for his ambitions.

"Kristin? Kristin!" He jerked her shoulder, and she stirred, muttered something, did not wake. Swiftly, Sky put a mask on her face. She had handcuffs on, her arms behind her, and there was nothing he could do about that. But he had a knife on his belt and he used it to cut the ropes at Kristin's ankles. "Good luck," he whispered. Then he turned back to the hall.

The job was nearly complete. Sky joined Pete in securing the last masks. Then Sigurd was shouting from the center of the room. "Come! Come!"

They gathered in a cleared space between the tables, surrounded by the unconscious masked forms. They were right under the great screen, the one that bore the giant, jagged "R." *Raidho,* rune of the journey. Rune of the descent into the Underworld. Into the realm of the Dead.

They stood in a rough circle. "Come!" shouted Sigurd, as best as he was able through the mask, to the man in the booth. Instantly, he emerged, rushed down to join them. "All well?" Sigurd asked him.

"The computer will take it from here." Even as he spoke, the lights in the hall dimmed further. Music came again, but no longer a gentle whisper of a beat, a soft flute. This was war music, trumpets and cymbals, with drums beating out a march, a call to arms. On the track, too, thunder rolled following the dip and flicker of simulated lightning.

"Let us begin!" said Sigurd.

He stretched out his arms, wrapped them around the shoulders of the man to either side. It spread; Sky was seized, pulled in tight. And then, as the feverish music built, the circle began to move . . . widdershins, against the clock, the direction always used for magic of the blackest kind. And as they moved, the chanting began. Duncan had been taught the words. But Sky would have known them anyway. Because they were nearly the same words Sigurd had chanted in the mountains when he'd sacrificed Olav and, for the first time, stolen a soul. The same words that would be used to kill and steal now. So many dead, so that the chosen ones' Fetches would be freed . . . freed to do Sigurd's bidding.

Odin
All-Father
Shape-shifter
Come
Change them
Shape them
Blood for blood
Come

They moved in their circle, stamping as they went. The chant, though muffled behind the masks, was loud enough.

Thor
Thunder God
Bringer of storms
Come
Change them
Shape them
Blood for blood
Come

Sky could feel it building as it had built that other

night. No matter that the runes were projections, the lightning recorded. Something was stirring, in the blood, within the circle, beyond it. He felt it coming, felt, as he had that night, the desire to just give in to it, to let the dark forces take him over. Duncan wanted it so badly, he could feel the surge inside him, the terrible craving.

The verses repeated, the circle sweeping around, him with it, wanting it. . . .

Then he glanced across the circle. Saw Dirk—and the triumph in his, in Sigurd's, eye.

No! He kept the scream inside his mask. Slipped from the arms on either side of him, which sought and re-formed above him, the men too lost to notice him drop to the floor. He rolled away as boots trampled past.

Change them
Shape them
Blood for blood

He ran for the stairs of the booth, tripped, missing them because lights had begun to strobe on and off. He lay on his back a moment, watched the circle there, and gone, and there again. As he rose, lasers shot lightning bolts across the room.

Change them
Shape them
Blood for blood

He fell into the booth. For a moment he did not have a clue where to look because everything was panels and meters and slider switches. Lights pulsed, dials glowed . . . and then he saw the computer. It was built into a solid wood console, no cables showing to jerk free. On its screen, a giant, jagged "S" was moving.

He grabbed the mouse. The main screen appeared, a bewildering array of icons . . . and a clock, in the top-right corner. It was counting down, and as Sky looked, it went from one minute to fifty-nine seconds.

He clicked on a patch of blue. A box came up, the user name there. But the box underneath was blank.

Password? What bloody password?

He clicked Enter, clicked again. Nothing! In the corner, the counter moved into the forties.

He couldn't sit there and crack a password! Not in forty-five seconds. There had to be . . .

Desperately, he looked around the booth. Beside the banks of dials, there was one small table. It had a thermos on it, a half-eaten cheese sandwich . . . and a magazine. He turned away, then turned back. The magazine was for supporters of the soccer team Leicester City. There was a player in the club uniform on the front, blue shirt, white shorts.

Wait! Duncan had talked soccer with this man . . . Malcolm was his name. He was a fanatic for . . .

He tapped "Leicester" in. Failed. "Leicester city." Failed. "Leicestercity." Failed. He hesitated. He didn't want to try again. He could get locked out.

The clock turned to thirty seconds. Through the glass, he could see the circle appear and disappear in the strobe lights, whirling ever faster. He could hear the muffled words:

Change them

Shape them

Blood for blood

He could see something else, too, in the room; other movement. People were beginning to stir, the stronger ones, the narcotic that had held them just starting to wear off. But they wouldn't wake in time to help him. And he couldn't help them unless he could remember . . .

Leicester! What was their nickname? He'd known them all once, when his walls had been covered in team posters and fact sheets. Arsenal were the Gunners. Manchester United were the Red Devils. He'd moved around so much he'd supported lots.

Twenty seconds! He looked around again for something to smash. But it was all a sealed unit. He was not going to do it. In a moment, most of the people in the hall were going to be gassed to death. Fifty Fetches would step forth . . . and no doubt offer their gratitude to the man who had freed them. Fifty, and the twelve bikers. He had to get ready, get back to Kristin and his own body. Sigurd, who'd come to him as a fox, as a lynx, was about to transform into a god with the power of life and death. And there was nothing Sky could do about it. . . .

"Fox!" Sky blurted out. "Leicester's nickname was the . . ."

He typed the name in the box: "Foxes."

The box vanished. He was in.

Ten seconds. The chanting below was building to a frenzy, the lights strobing so fast they blinded; laser lightning bolts seared into his sight, transferred to the screen before him, rolling down it . . .

His hands were shaking so much he almost couldn't get three fingers to work. Control. Alt. Delete.

A box came up. "Pressing again will end this program."

He pressed again.

Seven seconds. Frozen on the dial. And in the hall, the lightning stopped, the music stopped. The strobing ceased. Only the whirling figures whirled on, and then only for one more turn.

Change them

Shape them

Blood for . . .

The bikers leaned on each other, their chests heaving. Then a head rose clear. "What . . . ," said Sigurd-Dirk. "What has happened?"

He looked up at the booth. And even though it was dark and the glass was frosted, Sky could feel their eyes meet.

"You!" came the cry from the hall.

The circle broke apart. "Get him!" screeched Sigurd, pointing. Men began to run up the stairs. Sky reached, slammed the door shut. There was a lock, and he turned it. But the door didn't look too solid under the attack of steel-toed boots. It began to splinter. . . .

The siren was an ear-splitting roar. Someone had found the fire alarm. Sky smiled. He bet he knew who.

Emergency lights had come on in the hall. The red exit signs were blinking. People on the floor below, at the tables, began to stir. He saw a woman raise her head and vomit. A man tried to stand, fell.

The pounding had stopped at his door; he saw the leather jackets streaming away. And Sky could see panic had replaced anger on their faces. They all ran for the doors. When they flung them open, there were already hotel staff outside.

Sky slumped back. It was over! The doors were opened, he could hear the faint grind of the shutters he'd closed rolling back. The main lights came on. On the floor, at tables, people were waking up.

Then Sky shot forward, seeking through the glass. Sigurd was no longer where he'd been, leading the circle. Sky searched the hall . . . and spotted him. He was standing center stage. And at his feet lay Kristin.

CHAPTER TWENTY

THE DYING

Desperate people reached for him, coughing, silently pleading for help. He had to ignore them, keep moving toward the stage, toward the tall, dark-haired young man who was watching a biker limp across the hall.

Kristin lay at Dirk's feet, her hands still held behind her in handcuffs, a mask still over her mouth, so she couldn't speak. But he could see her eyes, see both the fear and the fury in them.

Sky took his own mask off. Dirk didn't have one, so the hall had to be clear.

"Grandson." It was his grandfather's voice—older, Norwegian-accented—that came out of Dirk's mouth now, all need for concealment gone.

"Sigurd." He nodded, stopped five paces away, looked at Kristin. "Is she all right?"

"Yes." Sigurd looked down. "I think so. But I don't *know.* I tried to see for myself. Thought I might . . . live in her again for a while. She was always so smart, so capable." He frowned. "But she . . . resisted me! She's learned how." He looked up at Sky. "Matthew?"

"Maybe." Sky took a pace forward. He didn't know what Sigurd intended. Nor what he could do. Dirk was huge, strong, while Duncan . . .

"And you, Sky," said Sigurd, looking Duncan's body up and down. "You've visited Meg, haven't you?"

Sky nodded. There seemed no point in lying.

"Lucky you. Poor you. How *was* that for you, Sky?"

"I think you know."

"Oh, I do." Sigurd nodded. "Isn't it wonderful that we've . . . shared that experience? And what a ride Mad Meg gave us!" He leaned in, staring through Duncan's eyes, into Sky. "Now you know me a little better, Grandson. Now you understand." He smiled. "For there's nothing quite like possessing someone, is there?"

Sky grunted. "For you, maybe. Not for me."

"Oh, for you too. I can see the hunger in your eyes. Some people would say that the hunger is the price you've paid for the knowledge. Just because it's insatiable." He ran his tongue over his lips. "And I say: fools! They just don't know that it's the best thing ever! Better even than a hawk, eh? Another human's life . . . yours. I bet you can't wait to"—he eyed Duncan's body—"trade up, perhaps? Who will you be next? Shall I tell you?" He leaned closer to whisper, "Anyone you desire."

"No! No one!" Sky shouted. "I am not like you."

Sigurd laughed, that laugh that shook his whole body. "Oh, blood of my blood! We are so alike and always have been. In our passions. In our quests. Now in our desire for . . . this!" He spread his fingers over Dirk's chest. "And the more lives we share, we are only going to come closer, closer, till we are . . . inseparable." He reached out a hand. "I'll be you, and you'll be me. And then what will we do? What wonderful things will we do?" He spread his arms wide. "For ourselves. For the world!"

Sky wanted to yell his denials, fight the feeling rising in his chest, building as he struggled with Sigurd's words. But he felt himself weakening. Weakening . . . and at the same time growing stronger.

"Sigurd . . . ," he began.

A male member of the hotel staff rushed up to them, leaned on the front of the stage. "Are you all right up there? How's that young woman?"

Kristin's eyes bulged in anger. She tried to speak beyond the mask. "Do not worry, my friend," Sigurd said calmly, in Dirk's South African tones. "I am a doctor. I am giving her some oxygen. Help the others."

The man turned back, moved away to lift a crying woman from the floor. In the distance, sirens were wailing. Sky looked at others weeping, puking. And the sight took away his hunger, brought back his anger. "We won't do anything together, Sigurd. I don't know exactly what you *were* doing here." He waved at the hall. "I know you were gathering disciples, freeing people's Fetches so they could help you to . . . What was it you said on the fire escape, before you severed my Fetch from my body? 'Bring immortality to humanity'?" Sky's voice got quieter, harder. "Well, we've bollocksed that for now, haven't we? Stopped you in your tracks. What your next move is, I can't begin to guess. All I do know is that whatever it is, the cost will be too high—for me. For Kristin too. So together, blood of your blood, we'll be ready to fight you again. Stop you again."

They stared at each other for a long moment. Then Sigurd's face—Dirk's face—hardened. "Sad. But predictable. You're always so predictable, Grandson. But then young people always are. It's what always makes you easy to defeat."

Sky felt the anger sweep through him, through Duncan. He tipped his head to the wail of sirens getting louder. "Oh, yes? You want to talk to me about defeat? That's defeat, heading your way."

"That?" Sigurd laughed. "That's just the sound of one option closing down. It wasn't even the best one. Not after what happened with Meg. *In* Meg. The other lesson learned."

Sky stiffened. "What do you mean?"

"You know." Sigurd stepped closer. "After Bjørn's runes were recited—and the story of how they got there is one you'll want to hear, Grandson—after we came alive inside of her, as ourselves, well . . ." His voice dropped to a caressing whisper. "Weren't you tempted, Sky? To do things differently? I suspect neither of us did, it was too sudden, too shocking. But we could have, couldn't we? Helped Meg survive, get her children back to Norway, live happily ever after." He laughed softly. "To alter Time itself, Sky? What would we become if we did that?"

There were shouts from the end of the hall. More men and women were rushing through the doors, some in white coats, some in blue. The first of the paramedics and police.

"Time," said Sigurd, differently. Reaching behind him, he unclipped something from his belt, lifted it. Sky saw that it was a small steel cylinder. "Sarin," his grandfather announced. "A deadly poison derived from rice. I've enough in this hall to kill all these people, and more besides. The power of their deaths releasing the Fetches in the chosen ones I went to such lengths to find. All those meetings. All those . . . pathetic, yearning people." He shuddered. "But in here . . ." He flicked the lid off the tank. Beneath it, Sky saw a small mouthpiece. "Just enough for one."

Sky took a step forward. He was still five paces away. Too far. "She's your granddaughter, Sigurd."

He looked down, as if he'd forgotten she was there. "Kill Kristin? Are you crazy? I love her. And Dirk loved her even more. How we share our possession's feelings, eh, Sky? The joy of that! And poor Dirk. How can I leave him here to . . . what is the English phrase?

'To face the music'?" He nodded again at the sounds of more sirens.

Sky took another pace forward. Four away now. Maybe even Duncan could make it from there. "What are you doing, Sigurd?" he said softly.

"I've somewhere to go. And I need a sacrifice to take me there." He lifted the cylinder, smiled. "See you . . . *sometime*!"

"No!" screamed Sky, leaping. But Duncan's knee betrayed him. The bigger man took a pace backward and fired the gas into his mouth. His body began to convulse, froth foaming from the lips. He staggered, fell backward, smashed onto the stage.

Sky bent over him, gagging at the whiff of acrid gas that hovered in the air. He reached for the man's throat, felt a pulse, one flickering beat. Then it was gone.

Sky stared, too stunned to move . . . until, behind him, he heard a scrabbling, a moan. He turned—to Kristin, eyes bulging her question. He pulled the mask from her face.

"He's . . . ," she gasped.

Sky nodded. "Murder and suicide, both at once."

"Dirk!" Tears misted her eyes.

Sky looked into the hall. More staff were pouring in. More police. He reached for her shoulder. "We've got to get out of here," he said, gently pulling. "Where are the keys for the handcuffs?"

"In his pocket," she replied, her voice a monotone, her gaze still on the body.

Sky found them, released her. With a huge sigh, her eyes cleared. She stood, looked him over as if for the first time. "Sky, you've got to . . . where's your body?"

"In the attic."

"Get it. I'll get the car. Meet you there!"

Sky found he couldn't stand. And it wasn't Duncan's knee. Kristin bent to him. "Hurry, Sky. We can't get caught here. Too many questions we couldn't answer." Still, he couldn't move. She shook his shoulder now, a little more gently. "He's dead, Sky. Dirk and Sigurd both."

Finally, Sky rose. "Not entirely," he said softly.

"What do you mean?"

The crackle of a walkie-talkie turned them. Another policeman ran into the hall.

"Later," said Sky. "Is there a way out the back there?"

"Yes. It's where I kicked in the fire alarm."

"Let's go."

He left Duncan dazed and confused beside the trunk. He'd thought that getting back into himself might be hard after all he'd been through. But his need drove him, and it was quick. Once inside his own body, though, Sky felt shattered. It was hard to drag himself, first to their room to grab their bags, then to the car park, where Kristin flashed her lights to draw him.

They drove in silence, headlamps off, bumping and lurching over the rough ground just inside the wood, parallel to the hotel driveway. When they could see the gate, they waited, concealed by a tree. Police cars and ambulances were coming through it at regular intervals, lights flashing. They could hear more coming. They had to wait for their chance.

With the engine off and the fog licking at the windows, the car was a cold shell. Kristin looked across. "Are you all right?"

"Not really."

"You're shaking. There's a coat back there. . . ."

"It's not the cold. It's . . ." He scrunched down. "I miss Duncan."

"What? The fat biker? You're joking!"

"OK, not him exactly. But I already miss . . . the possession of him."

Her voice came on a cold whisper. "You what?"

It was time he told her. "You heard what Sigurd and I were saying?"

"Yes. He was talking about a . . . a hunger for possession. You were denying it."

"I was. Because I don't want to believe it. But . . ." He shut his eyes. "It's what I couldn't tell you in Norway, after Meg and Matthew. That she *loved* possession. More, she craved it."

"A bit like an addiction."

"Exactly like it. Better than any drug, I'm sure." He opened his eyes, looked across at her. "Kristin, I think I am addicted to possession."

A fire engine flashed through the gate, horn sounding. They listened. Another was coming, getting closer. Kristin reached, took his hand. "But it's OK now, Sky," she said gently. "I'll help you. You won't have to do it anymore. Sigurd's beaten. Gone."

"He's gone all right. He's gone back."

"In time?" He nodded. "Well, then he's definitely beaten."

An ambulance came through. Its wail passed up toward the house, stopped; nothing filled the silence. "Go!" said Sky.

She started the car, slipped it into gear, steered slowly between the trees, headed for the gate. "Because I watched him . . . them," she said. "Nothing emerged. No seagull, fox. Nothing. Sigurd did not transfer. He's gone . . . but he didn't leave a body behind. Do you know what that means?" She thumped the steering wheel. "He can't come back. We've won."

"Not . . . necessarily."

"What do you mean?" she snapped at him. "If he's in the past, he's not Sigurd anymore. He's whoever he is. And with no body to come back to, he's stuck there. He'll live that life. Die that death. He won't know he's Sigurd. He can't try his stuff there. I mean, he can't change things, back then."

Sky scrunched down farther into his seat. He felt very cold. "Can you turn the heat on now, please?"

She made no move. "Well, he can't, can he? *Can* he? Unless . . ." She gripped the steering wheel, her knuckles whitening. "Oh my God!"

"Exactly." He finished for her. "Unless he's found a way to retain himself—his consciousness—back there. Come alive in an ancestor—as himself." Sky was shivering uncontrollably now. "I told you, that happened to me in Meg. It happened to him too. I could have done something then. Changed time."

"You didn't."

"I know. And I don't think Sigurd did either. But if he goes back, finds a way of coming alive then, through Bjørn's runes . . . through . . ." Sky shot up. "Crap! He mentioned Bjørn, what happened to Bjørn, how I should hear *that* story. What if he's been into him? What if he's gone back to his need—when Bjørn carved those runes, runes of *awakening,* to bring out his Fetch. It would bring out Sigurd. He'd be alive then, as Sigurd, inside Bjørn. He'd have learned how to be . . . aware back then. And with the powers we've seen he has . . . well, he could hop into whatever body was most useful. And then he *could* alter time itself!"

The enormity of it stunned them both. The car had been creeping forward. But as soon as Kristin reached the gravel of the driveway, she flicked on the lights and gunned the engine. They shot out of the gates, accelerated away.

"Hey! Slow down, will you? You'll get us killed."

Grudgingly, she eased up a touch on the pedal. But they were still shooting down the narrow, misty roads at close to fifty. "Look," she said, "aware or not, it doesn't mean Sigurd could alter time. According to particle physics—"

"Oh, please! You study ancient Norse at university!"

"I also attend a series of lectures called 'Time Travel: A Physical Possibility?' " She gave a brief grin. "A Cambridge education. It's very rounded. And, obviously, the subject interested me. . . . And Sigurd in me too, I suppose."

"So . . . is it possible?"

"Well, some people think so. Various theories, various ways to travel. Mostly linked to surpassing the speed of light. But we go back through bloodlines, so that's different." She swerved to avoid some roadkill. "But there's a lot of debate about what we could do if we did get back. One of the theories is actually called 'The Grandfather Paradox.' "

"Get out!"

"Truth. If you went back and met and killed your grandfather, would you immediately, like, snuff out of existence yourself?"

"It's a tempting option. But would I?"

"Ah, depends if you subscribe to relativity theory. There's something called a 'CTC'—a Closed Timelike Curve—"

"Whoa! Slow down! Both ways!" he said, staring at the speedometer, which had crept above sixty again. "Remember, brainiac, I didn't even graduate yet. I've been busy. So keep it simple, will you?"

"OK." She dropped a gear for a tight bend, thought. "Some people believe in an infinite number of parallel universes. You can alter time in one—kill your grandfather—but in a gazillion others, other things happened. Your grandfather killed you. You sat down together and ate pancakes."

Sky snorted. "What a load of bollocks!"

"Brilliant, Sky. You've just dismissed quantum mechanics in one pithy statement."

"I just don't buy it. What's another theory?"

"That you can't actually erase what's written. You can only . . . affect it in some way. So you try to shoot your grandfather, you miss, he ducks into an alley . . . and meets your grandmother there. It's a sort of self-tidying universe."

Sky was about to condemn that one, too, when suddenly an idea hit him. "But that's wyrd," he said.

"You're telling me. And it gets weirder. There's this stuff about photons—"

"Not w-e-i-r-d," he spelled. "W-y-r-d."

"You mean, like, Norse Fate?"

"Yeah, but remember it's not fate as we know it—something that's *bound* to happen because of actions taken in the past. The Norse didn't believe in a simple past, present, future, right? They only had 'Time that is . . .' "

". . . 'and Time that is becoming.' So?"

"So, all Time is just the continuous flow of wyrd. No past to set things absolutely, just flow. Wyrd that can be rewritten. . . ."

"Yes!" The speedometer was creeping up again along with Kristin's enthusiasm. "There's that story of the gods rewriting a famous warrior's wyrd. Odin liked him, so he said he would always be victorious in battle. Thor didn't like him, so he said he might win but would always be badly wounded. . . ."

"You know what," Sky said, seeing it. "This is exactly what we do with the runes. They are the tools of wyrd. Symbols of life's forces and energies cut into stone. We read someone's destiny—like Odin's ever-victorious warrior. But with different runes, we can rewrite that destiny. Not change it entirely. He'll still win his battles. But Thor's runes reshape his wyrd, so he's always hurt. Making victory less sweet."

Behind him on the backseat was his rucksack. Reaching into it, he pulled out the soft wool bag that contained his runestones. "We see what is, what might be if nothing changes—then we see what we must do to change it."

He reached into the bag. A stone fell into his hand. He lifted it out, squinted. "Of course. *Uruz.* Bjørn's rune."

"May I?"

For a moment, Sky thought of pulling the bag away. But this was Kristin. And they'd been through too much for him to start denying her now. "Help yourself."

Steering round a bend with one hand, she reached with the other. "What is it?" she said, holding it out to him.

"What would you think?" He smiled. "*Eihwaz.* One of the runes I carved in snow. It led us to the family tree. So it's a rune that helped us rewrite our wyrd. You'd been possessed, nothing you could do about that . . . except learn to resist possession. *Eihwaz* helped send us back."

"OK. . . ." She handed Sky the stone, and he took it in the same hand that held Bjørn's rune. "So you're saying that if we did go back in time, and became, like, *aware* back there, that we *wouldn't* alter time?"

Sky bit his lip. "*Maybe.* The self-tidying universe sounds great in theory. But how can we be sure?" Something had been growing in Sky, an awareness, a thought just out of reach. Then he had it, and it made him gasp so loudly that Kristin swerved to the center of the road, swerved back.

"What?"

"Oh my God, I've just seen it. . . ." His voice came in a whisper. "We're worrying about not changing the course of history, but maybe that's what Sigurd *wants.* He doesn't care about the world as it is, or the people in it. He only cares about what he thinks is his destiny." He closed his eyes. "Maybe he's found a way to *stop* the universe from compensating. He wants to rip up the fabric of wyrd." He looked out the window, at a world speeding ever-faster past. "Bloody hell, Kristin. He wants to bring about Ragnarók!"

Her voice also came in a whisper. "The last battle of the gods?"

"It's a battle, but it's worse than that. Because it's a battle that ends in the destruction of . . . everything. Of everyone. And then a rebirth into who knows what."

The fog was thickening. Kristin was hunching ever-farther forward over the wheel. But he saw, in the dashboard light, that her face was grim yet determined. "So how do we stop him?"

"There's only one way. We have to follow him back." He swallowed. "Maybe that's *our* destiny—our role in that self-tidying universe you were talking about. To repair the fabric of wyrd that Sigurd slashes."

"But we don't even know where—when!—he's gone."

"I think I do." Sky closed his eyes. "A time when history really *did* hang on a knife's edge. When you could actually say that a little shove one way or another might have changed the world, and everything in it."

"A tipping point."

"Exactly. In Germany . . . well, what would have

happened if someone had assassinated Hitler in 1920? In the U.S.—what if the South had won the Battle of Gettysburg?"

She nodded. "So where do you think he's gone?"

Sky took a deep breath. "I know where I'd go. Where the travels began."

"Ten sixty-six," she whispered.

"The Battle of Hastings. Yes. When the Anglo-Saxons, who believed in the runes and all that went with them, were conquered by the Normans—French essentially—a people who didn't. They changed England . . . forever. And England, let's face it, changed the world."

It even silenced Kristin for a while. Not for long.

"So you reckon Sigurd's gone there? Then? To give that little shove?"

Sky nodded grimly. "It all fits. It's the era he's obssessed with. It's when Bjørn was in England, when those runes of . . . of *awakening* must have been carved in that churchyard."

"So . . . do you think he's Bjørn? Who else was on the family tree we found?"

Sky reached back into another pocket of the rucksack. Quickly, he unfolded the roll. Kristin flicked on the interior light. "Can you still see?" Sky asked.

"Sure. Enough," she said impatiently. "So, who's there?"

Sky's finger ran up the list of names. "There's

Thorkell, but he dies. There's Bjørn and Ingvar, and . . . oh, yeah, that French name. Henri de Barfleur."

"How did we get a French ancestor?"

"Wait!" Sky looked up, staring at the world speeding past, focusing on nothing but his own hurtling thoughts. "The Normans were French but . . . only just. 'Norman' was short for 'North-man.' About a century before, that part of France was conquered by Vikings."

"So another of our ancestors was one of those conquerors?" Kristin whistled. "They certainly got around!" She looked across. "So you think Sigurd's gone into *him*?"

"We've got to hope so. Because if he's gone into Bjørn or Ingvar, it could get crowded. We'll be wanting them."

Kristin's eyes glimmered in the car's interior light. "So we go. But how?"

Sky shrugged helplessly. "You know, I think we'll have to trust the runes and our need."

Without him willing it, his hand had dug into the bag again. Once more, another stone chose itself and pressed into his palm. He drew it out . . . and sighed. "Of course," he whispered.

She glanced across. "Which is it?"

"Raidho," he said simply. "The journey." He intoned it, and it sounded like a bell tolling in the car. "Across worlds. Across time. Over the border between life and death."

He was looking into his hand. She was looking at him. Neither was looking at the road, at its sudden bend and its glimmering black ice.

Wheels slipped, failing to grip; a steep slope, brakes useless against it; metal shrieking, buckling with the first roll; the smashing beginning. Yet it wasn't the noise or the pain, not even the sudden sheet of blood, that fell with Sky into the darkness. It was the three runestones, searing their lines into his flesh. *Uruz, Eihwaz, Raidho.*

Wyrd.

CHAPTER TWENTY-ONE

BJØRN

Wyrd.

This was his then, its final turn—Bjørn, son of Thorkell, drowned in an English river. Such a fate would have irked him once; he'd always dreamed of a long life, of all the great things he would do with it. Yet as the last of the air fled his lungs, acceptance came. There was nothing left to him; the ability to affect his wyrd had ended when the waters closed over his head. Though he was sinking into darkness, into the soft river mud, neither was so bad. And something of him would go on. Had he fought well enough to earn a place in the hall of Valhalla, there to feast with the other heroes until Ragnarók, the final destruction of the world? He would know soon enough. Just beyond that last glimpse of light, perhaps, the Valkyrie waited to bear him away.

Agony! Shooting through every sinew, filling him

like water did, like darkness, coming in a shriek of steel, metal buckling like an ill-forged blade. Something thumping into his chest. He reached down, felt it, his . . . *hamr*! His birth skin, ripped from his face when he first slid into the world, so he could take his first breath. It had been saved, placed in a leather sack, for it marked him as a traveler between worlds. Now the sack's neck cord, like the cord that linked mother and child at birth, was grabbed, tugged, and he was rising up through the water, away from the darkness, back to the light. . . .

"Gaaaah!"

The first breath hurt as much as the first water had! But beyond the pain, Bjørn had another chance to rewrite his wyrd, and he seized it.

He was kicking now; but he was also being pulled by that same neck cord toward the river's bank, the leather threatening to do what the water had not. He reached up, grasped a wrist. "Leave be," he coughed, water and words. Instantly the pressure slackened at his neck, returned in his armpits, the grip transferred.

"Easy, bear cub, easy," said Ingvar, his brother. "And quiet too."

Almost immediately they were into the reeds at the water's edge, their feet seeking purchase in the sloping mud. Bjørn slipped Ingvar's grip, turned, scrabbled up behind him to firmer ground. Falling onto it, Bjørn lay there, shaking, coughing, aware of little save the pain of life returning.

Then death came too . . . into his ears, in the wail and shriek of men dying. Many men. Despite his brother's restraining arm, Bjørn crawled a little higher up the bank, parted the reeds. . . .

It was as if he'd thrown a door open onto Hel's own hearth. Not fifty paces from him, the remnants of the Norse army were making their final stand. Just after he'd been knocked into the water, Bjørn had glimpsed a tall Viking holding the narrow bridge. But the English must have swept him aside, because they were now on the far bank in force, their numbers ever increasing, their opponents' diminishing. The Norsemen had ferocity, but they had little armor. Their king had waited outside York for tribute, not sword thrusts, and most of his men had sent their chain mail back to their longships.

"Do we go to him?"

Ingvar had slid up beside him. Both saw King Harald Hardrada. Few could miss him, for he was taller than most men by a head and a half. And the noise he made in his berserk fury, under his raven banner! They watched him cut down one warrior, another, any that broke through the gaps in his housecarls' weakening shield wall.

"Our father's dead," Bjørn said softly.

"Aye. And Thorolf?"

"Dead." Bjørn's eyes closed as he remembered his huge brother, cleaved almost in two by an ax. "Eirik?"

A shake of the head. "An English sword took him."

Bjørn opened his eyes. He knew his had tears in them, and he could see more than river water in his brother's too. "Then I think the House of Thorkell has given the king enough blood this day, don't you?"

Before Ingvar could reply, a great shout drew them. The shield wall had fallen. With a roar, Harald Hardrada lifted his sword high and charged into the ranks of his enemies. For a moment, it looked like they might give before him, lucky men scrambling aside, men whose wyrd was inescapable falling to the huge blade. But then Bjørn and Ingvar, bowmen both, saw an English archer crouch and shoot. The arrow flew up, straight into the throat of the king of Norway.

For a moment, almost a silence came. Men held their blows to gaze, to hope, to disbelieve. For a moment, the king still held his sword high, as if to give more strokes . . . until it fell from his hand, plunging point-first into the ground. Then Harald Hardrada fell, his enormous body thumping onto the earth.

The silence was shattered by two shouts—of triumph from the Englishmen; of despair from every Norse throat. To a man, the Norsemen turned and fled.

"Come," Ingvar said, starting to rise.

But Bjørn clutched his brother's arm, pulled him back down. "Not that way," he said. "Look back!"

Ingvar followed Bjørn's finger. Across the river, which was only as wide there as a Viking ship was long, men also lay hidden in the reeds. On that bank, the men of Hareid had fought to hold the bridge. The few who had survived were crouched there now.

"The hunters all seek a share of the hunt. And they have the killing rage on them," Bjørn said, pointing at the bridge where the last of the English army was running across. "We'd have a better chance that side, to my mind."

Ingvar smiled briefly. "Are you so keen on another swim, brother? But you are right. Let us go."

Once more, Thorkell's sons lowered themselves into the chilly water. Though Bjørn was still bleeding at arm and thigh, they were not deep cuts. It was the spear haft to the head that had knocked him into the river before, that had nearly sent him down.

Hands reached soon enough, gripped, pulled him ashore again. He looked up to see some twenty men crouching amongst the reeds. "Is this all?" said Bjørn.

"You see them, Bjørn Thorkellsson. All that live from the host of Hareid." It was Gray Arnstein who spoke, the smith from the village, a bloodied clout around his head hiding one eye. The other glimmered. "But is it the Bjørn we know or the bear that is before us now?"

Bjørn saw the same question on each face. They had witnessed him in the battle, seen the berserk rage take him, feared the beast in him just as he had once feared Black Ulf, whose severed head was food for fishes now. The old berserker had gotten the death he craved. Bjørn, though, now the rage was past, wanted life.

"The man, Arnstein. One you have always known for his cunning. Will you all trust him to lead you back to the ship and then home?"

He was the youngest there. But they had seen him come of age. He was known as a rune reader, a seer of visions. And now he was also a warrior of the most fearsome kind, equally gifted and cursed by the gods. Each of them, even Ingvar, his elder, nodded.

"Then come," he said. "Every man who can, help another who moves slower. For this I vow—not one more woman will turn widow in Hareid this night."

He rose; and as he did, Gray Arnstein reached out, delaying him. "Here," he said. "We may yet need to fight. So the bear will need his claws."

And the smith handed Bjørn his ax.

Bjørn looked at the weapon he thought he'd lost forever when he was knocked into the river. He had not called it by the name he had chosen for it; could not before battle, before it had tasted first blood. Now it had, and somewhere in its rune-marked planes, a trace of the souls it had dispatched yet lingered.

He named it now. For what it brought. For the beast within the man who wielded it.

"Death Claw," he said, lifting it high. "Lead us home."

Dusk light glimmered on metal as the men of Hareid slipped silently away.

⁂

"Anything?"

Ingvar shook his head, fell down beside his brother, leaning his back against the churchyard's wall. Around them, those of the Hareid men who were conscious sank back too.

"What is holding them? Honir returned an age ago!" Bjørn grumbled.

They had sent Honir ahead. He was the best hunter in the village, due to his skill at concealment, his fleetness of foot. He was also one of the few unwounded, which many of his comrades put down to his noted skills. He had found their longship at the anchorage, told the crew left with it to loose its tethers and make for this rendezvous, chosen by their father against an unlikely defeat. It was a church on a riverbank, downstream, and so closer to the open sea.

Ingvar chuckled. "You've only been in a longship once, bear cub. They require some handling, and we left only five men to do it. They will be here soon."

Soon enough? Bjørn thought but didn't say. To the east, a glimmer showed the coming of day. With its light, the English patrols that had passed in the distance, looking for fleeing Norsemen to spear, would come closer. Or the villagers who had fled their houses would return and betray them.

Somewhere in the distance, someone gave out a terrible cry, a rising shriek of agony, suddenly cut off. Everyone stirred at that. Some made the cross of the

White Christ before them, others traced the lines of Thor's hammer in the air. And everyone felt what followed it—a drumming in the earth. It did not take Honir, running in from the land side, where he'd been keeping watch, to tell them what was coming.

"Horsemen," he panted.

"How many?" asked Bjørn, rising.

"Many."

"Perhaps they will ride past, like all the others."

Gray Arnstein called up from the river. "The ship comes."

Keeping low, those who could slid to the top of the bank. *Ravager* was indeed there, upstream, its sail hoisted to catch what little wind was offered; two oars were out, two men at each, helping to push the boat forward. But wind and oar counted for very little. It was the tide of the river that did most, and it was sluggish at best. *Ravager* came, but slowly.

"Too slowly," Bjørn muttered. He turned back to the land, to the horsemen, more than a sound now, dawn's first light glimmering on their spearheads. Honir had been right; there were many. Fifty at the least, all armored, helmed. Approaching fast.

Faster than the ship, which seemed, even as Bjørn looked back at it, to get caught in an eddy that turned its prow to the side, taking all the efforts of the man at the tiller and his four comrades on the oars to swing it around again.

Bjørn looked down. The bank was steep everywhere, a slide of scree and mud to the water's edge. In only one place was it passable, and the villagers had cut steps into the earth there, leading down to a small jetty, where one fishing skiff was tied. The path to those steps was a narrow channel carved through the grassy bank. No wider than a man.

One man. "Arnstein," Bjørn called softly, and the smith turned. "Get everyone down to the jetty."

The man's eyes went past him. "Will we have time?" he said uneasily.

"Perhaps I can find us the time. Go!"

Those who could helped those who struggled through the gap, down the steps. "Ingvar," Bjørn called again, and his brother came. "Remember the man on Stamford Bridge? The Viking who held off the English for so long?" Ingvar nodded. "Well, that gap's no wider than the bridge."

"What are you thinking?"

"If these English soldiers do not pass us by . . . one man could hold them off long enough for *Ravager* to get here, for all to get aboard."

Ingvar sucked at his lip. "Could?" he echoed. "But what man would do it for . . ." He broke off when he saw his brother's eyes. "No! You cannot be the one, Bjørn. If it is our only choice . . . well, then I am the elder. I will stay."

Bjørn laid a hand on Ingvar's arm. "You heard my

vow. Not one more widow to be made in Hareid. You have a wife, a child, another coming—"

"It makes no difference—"

"And I have no one."

"What of Sweet Gudrun?"

For just a moment, Bjørn's breath caught in his throat as he thought of the girl back in the valley, Gudrun of Heimdall, the scent of blossom about her that gave her the nickname. Then he shook his head. "A dream only. A boy's dream."

Still Ingvar looked at him stubbornly. "I cannot let you fight alone."

"But I will not be alone. I will have my friend here"—he reached up and touched Death Claw, once more in its sling on his back—"and something else."

Despite himself, his brother took a step back. "You think your . . . your bear will just come at your call? You are exhausted."

Bjørn nodded. "I am. But there are ways to summon the spirits, other than the ways of battle. With runes. With the singing of them. With the help of the gods. You know this."

"I know. I have walked a little, aye. But not like you." He shivered. "And I am not a rune carver."

"Then leave that to me. And help me with the rest."

"Help you to die?"

"We all die, brother. And a berserker *must* die.

Would you rather have me turn into Black Ulf? To eat raw flesh on the high fells and become the night monster to terrify your twelve children?" He forced a smile. "Come. You know I believe in the old gods. This end would see me feasting in Valhalla, sure. Would you deny me that?"

For a long moment, Ingvar still looked like he would refuse. Then he shrugged. "What must I do?"

"There are no stones here. I need something to carve on." Bjørn had been looking around. Now he squinted, lifted an arm. "What's that?"

Together, they crouched low, ran into the churchyard, as the sound of hoofbeats died. Swiftly, Bjørn raised his head. Three hundred paces away, at the crossroads near the village, the soldiers had halted. It was light enough now for Bjørn to see a man standing before them, waving, pointing. Their way.

He looked down. Before them, on top of a waist-high column of stone, was what he'd spotted—a shaped circle of granite. It was a forearm's width across, a hand's depth. And it already had some marks scored into it. "Help me," he said.

The brothers bent and together rolled the circle of stone through the gates toward the cleft in the bank. "What is it?" Ingvar asked.

Bjørn looked at the half-finished carvings on the stone surface. "A sundial. Do you remember the finished one Father brought back from one of his raids? These figures are the hours of the day. Whoever was carving it must have fled when our fleet came by, because he dropped these." Bjørn hefted the chisel and small wooden hammer he'd picked up, then bent to the stone.

Ingvar was staring over his head. "Do not carve yet. They still may not come."

Bjørn laid metal to stone. "Then I will carve against the misfortune that they do. But I will only sing them into life if I have to." He gestured with his head. "The ship?"

Ingvar crawled up the bank, crawled back. "Not far. An arrow's reach."

"Good." He bent, laid metal edge to stone, said, "Odin. All-Father. Guide me now."

He began. First, to claim the stone, he carved three simple lines, the same symbol he'd scored into his ax blade—*Uruz,* Bjørn's rune. Then closed his eyes. Clouds swirled behind them, then parted. He began to cut what he saw.

He had brought forth runes before, to see the way of things in the world. Love runes he'd carved on a tree trunk . . . and Gudrun had decided to take a longer way home that day. When he'd wanted to learn to free his Fetch, he had gone alone to the fells, lived in a cave for a week, cut marks upon its walls, held his caul tight to his heart. He had flown beyond himself, as both beast and man. And he had dreamed . . . not usually of the warrior's life, of battle and plunder, but of a life in the valley, and the time, especially when the long winters shut him inside, to fare forth in fur or feather, learn the patterns of wyrd, those that were unalterable, those he could reshape.

"Perhaps." Bending low, he blew dust away from the last cut line. "If the horsemen do not come."

And then they did. Ingvar looked but Bjørn didn't, just watched them start out from the crossroads in his brother's eyes. Arnstein appeared through the gap. "*Ravager* is one bend away," he puffed. "But we'll never get her afloat again if we beach her. We have to ferry the wounded men out to her in that one skiff." He bit his lip. "It will take time."

Bjørn smiled. What else could one do when wyrd showed itself? "Then I will have to see if I can find you some." He rose, put his hand on Arnstein's shoulder. "See them aboard."

The big smith nodded. "May the gods watch over you, bear cub."

"And over you." Bjørn watched the man disappear again down the bank, then turned.

"Bjørn—"

"Enough, brother. It is written. Now all you can do is help me."

They could both hear the jingle of harnesses, the snorts of horses drawing nearer. Still, Ingvar hesitated. Bjørn grabbed an arm. "Help me!"

The other man shrugged. "What must be done?" he said.

"First, this." Bjørn scooped the chisel up, turned

his hand up, laid the edge of the blade upon it. Sharp enough to gouge stone, it sliced easily through flesh, opening a jagged line down the center of his palm. Wordlessly, Ingvar offered his, didn't flinch when the iron bit. Then they wove their fingers, not over as if they were to wrestle, but together, slotting through. "We call upon the gods. . . ."

Ingvar still followed the old ways too. With his other hand he made the sign of the hammer in the air. Then he joined in the invocation.

"Odin. All-Father. Guide us now."

They crouched down over the stone that lay between them, then Bjørn pushed their conjoined fingers into the runes. Blood from their slit palms flowed into

the channels, turning them instantly red. And in that moment of flooding, the sundial's surface seemed to dissolve, no longer stone to their eyes; all liquid, but not like the surface of a still pond. This was a turbulent sea, swirling and turning. And shapes danced in its depths.

"Sing the names with me. Sing the runes to life. Awaken the spirit within," Bjørn cried.

They both knew the names. *"LAAGUUUZ!"* they chanted, drawing it out, their breath upon the blood—the word itself—causing the liquid surface below them to surge. Then Bjørn sang on, alone,

"Laguz
Water at birth
Crossed at death

Secrets flow
Mother to child
Until their need
One is one."

He had always read *Laguz* as a rune of change, of the life-sustaining liquids, blood and water, moving him on. Now he saw the danger in it, too, the storm in an ocean's depths, that storm within him, savage forces surging up, about to burst forth, needing something, needing . . .

Fingers shifted their pressure, new lines pressed.

"Thuuuuuriiisaaaz!" they called, and Bjørn sang on alone.

"The thorn pricks
Blood gushes
Dissolve the stone
Shatter the walls
Body and spirit
One is one."

Ingvar joined him in his shout, both staring at this rune of attack, of challenge, yes, but of something much more. It was the rune that smashed down opposition, toppled the walls between flesh and Fetch, allowed the storm within *Laguz* to rise. It was the berserker's rune, frothing in the liquid surface of the living stone, dissolving the boundaries between rock and air. Bjørn felt himself fill with the force of it, growled to greet the spirit waking within.

Maybe he would have stopped then, seized Death

Claw, begun the killing he now craved. But there was a last rune cut, and it was Ingvar who pulled his fingers onto it, Ingvar who cried its name, Bjørn who joined him, then took it on.

"Ehhhwaaaz!
Horse and Fylgya
Faring forth
Riding the world lines
Along the bloodlines
Ancestor . . . us . . .
One is one!"

Something shaped from stone-cut, word and blood. Red-coated, shaggy-maned, wild and unbroken, channeling the energies of *Laguz,* flooding

through the walls that *Thurisaz* had shattered. And in its bursting forth, wyrd was reshaped, rewritten. Fetches surged along the bloodlines and poured through the gap of Time.

Fingers were ripped from the sundial as if lightning had struck it. Bjørn falling . . .

. . . Sky falling.

CHAPTER TWENTY-TWO

1066

Falling into mist, into nothing, onto nothing. Always before, there had been that tiny moment when the Fetch sees who he's becoming, just before he becomes. When the one who receives feels a presence, a second before that presence is absorbed.

A tiny moment. A second, no more.

Until now.

In the mist stands Sky, stands Bjørn. Each reaches. And pulls the other close.

Bjørn says: *But I know you. I saw you in my shield boss, the day we reached this land.*

Sky hesitates. *What can I tell him?*

He has not spoken. But Bjørn does not need words to hear. *You can tell me the truth,* he says. *What are you?*

The truth? Sky replies. *I am . . . a part of you. The same. And different.*

Ah! You are my Fylgya.

In a way, Sky says. *Or perhaps we share the same Fylgya—though I call it my Fetch. But I come from another place, another time.*

Bjørn studies him. *We have something in my land: Vardogr. The going out. I do this. I have slipped into the skin of an animal. But I have never gone into another person. And never before have I met . . . a part of myself.*

Sky smiles. *Both happen.*

Bjørn does not smile. *But why does it happen now? I summoned another . . . Fetch, you call it? One I need desperately. Why did you come?*

Because I was there to be called. And because my need is desperate too. Even more than yours, I fear.

Their gazes locking, eyes the same blue-green. A moment of judging; how long, neither knows.

Bjørn speaks. *What is your need?*

Sky replies, *I pursue another Fetch through time. His name is Sigurd. He is . . . blood of our blood. And he is evil.*

How so?

He has come to tear apart the fabric of wyrd.

How? Wyrd can only be reshaped, not destroyed.

He thinks he has found a way to destroy it.

Only the gods can do that. At Ragnarók.

Perhaps he thinks he is a god. And he would welcome Ragnarók.

You can stop him?

I do not know. All I know is that I must try.

And you need me to do this?

I cannot do it without you. I need to be you and myself

at once. And where . . . when I come from, something has befallen my body. I cannot return there now. Anyway, if Sigurd succeeds, there may be no "now" to return to.

What will happen to you?

Sky shudders. *I'm not certain. But I already know what it's like when someone cuts my Fetch from my body.*

Bjørn studies him. *He did this?*

Sky nods. *He tried to turn me into a draug.*

The worst of fates!

Yes. And it has been your fate once. Because the man I pursue ripped you from your rest once. Will rip you from it. For a time, you will be a draug.

Bjørn's turn to shudder. *You can stop this?*

No. It has happened. Will happen. It is in my past. It is in your future. Sky sighs. *I don't know if you can understand how it can be both.*

Bjørn stares for a long moment, speaks. *What is there to understand? There is no past, no future. There is only time that is, and time that is becoming. That is the flow of wyrd.*

*And I am just beginning to understand that. But when you became a draug, what I did do—will do—is release you. I will use the runes—*Algiz, Tiwaz, Sowilo. . . .

Bjørn gasps. *You are a rune reader.*

I am.

And you saved me with runes?

I released you, yes.

Silence again. In the fraying mist, other shapes soundlessly shift. A car rolls down a slope, smashes into a tree. Horsemen unsheath their swords as they ride toward a churchyard.

Bjørn speaks. *Then I will release myself to you . . . for a time. But know this—I will not be gone entirely. I will aid you as I can.*

I will need the aid.

Then let us begin.

Sky leans forward, reaches out. Bjørn raises a hand, halting him. *But first you must aid me.*

How?

I made a vow: not one more widow to be made in Hareid this day. You must honor it. Even unto death.

Sky nods. *When we are one, your vows are mine.*

Bjørn reaches. It is like reaching into a mirror. He

clasps Sky's hand. Eyes seek, confirm the promise.

But how do we do this? Bjørn asks.

Sky hesitates. Then he places his other hand against Bjørn's chest, tapping the shape that hangs there. Not what contains it. What's within. *This is your hamr, yes?*

Yes. It covered my face at birth. . . .

As mine was covered. It marked me—as a walker, a seer. Through it I am joined to my mother and through her to all who have gone before, on and on, back. Sky smiles. *It joins me to you.*

Bjørn smiles. *Then come,* he says. *Join me now.*

He reaches his other hand, too, grasps the caul that hangs from his descendant's neck, as his is grasped. In the mist, shapes move again. And . . . memories! Memories of both, playing in each other's minds.

Bjørn gasps. *You have lived as me before!*

Yes. And died as you as well. As an old man.

Bjørn laughs. *Old seems good right now . . . I think! If my life was all I dreamed it would be. If my death was . . . fitting.*

Sky laughs too. *If your dream was adventure and love and glory, then, yes. And in the end . . .*

A vision comes. In both their minds, a longship burns in the night.

. . . In the end, you will be the last of the Vikings.

Well, now! Bjørn sighs. *That's not such a bad thing to be.*

They lean toward each other. Flesh dissolves into flesh, mind into mind. Falling . . .

"Sky!"

That name—his from another time. The voice whispering it, from then too. They open their eyes. . . .

"Sky . . . is it . . . are you . . . ?"

He sat up, rubbed his eyes. "Yeah. I think. That was . . . so weird." He looked at the Norseman opposite. "Kristin, did you . . . did you talk to Ingvar? Like, negotiate to, you know . . . take over?"

"Why would I?" Ingvar's bearded face frowned. "No, I just heard the runes being chanted, the runes of awakening. So I chanted too. There was a moment, a cry, and then . . . then I was here." She lifted a huge, bloodied hand. "Wow!"

"I think Ingvar hasn't traveled much, unlike Bjørn. . . . Whoa!" He had tried to stand, but went down on one knee.

"Are you all right?"

"Don't know," Sky muttered. "Give me a minute."

Kristin leaned down, laying one of Ingvar's big hands on his brother's shoulder. "I don't think we have a minute. Listen!"

Sky heard the soft fall of hoofbeats on the dry earth. For a moment it made no sense, a sound from a different world. Then he remembered. "The English!" He gripped Ingvar's hand, used it to pull himself to his feet, didn't let go until the ground ceased moving. "I have to fight them," he said groggily.

"What? Of course you don't!"

"*Ravager,*" he slurred. "Men need time to get aboard."

"Sky . . . you're not Bjørn! Listen. . . ." Hands grabbed at him again, shook him hard. "What's the point of being here if we're going to die now? Let's get the hell out of here!"

Sky shook his head, trying to clear it. It didn't help much. "I . . . we didn't. Bjørn and Sky . . . can't die here. We know they . . . they didn't."

Ingvar's gaze went to the sundial. "We were trying to summon Bjørn's berserk Fetch, weren't we? But our

Fetches came instead." He looked up. "And the berserker didn't, did he?"

"No." Sky looked at Kristin, seeing her despite the beard, the long, dark hair, the broken nose. "And this isn't like any of the other times. You see, I . . . I did talk to Bjørn."

"You *what*?"

"He's still here." He tapped his chest, the caul hanging there. "Not just his body either. He's, like, my instincts."

She stared at him, then shook Ingvar's head. "Well then, you both had better come up with something fast because . . ." A gesture with the chin.

He looked. The first horsemen were just riding around the edge of the church wall. Sky bent and picked up a bow, notched an arrow to the string.

"What the hell are you doing?" she hissed.

"Dunno. Just feel better with a weapon in my hands." He turned to her. Bizarrely, a smile came. "Goin' with the flow."

"Oh, great," said Kristin, "I'm in 1066 and I'm listening to hippie-speak."

He had to do something. For both of him. "Go and see what's happening with the ship."

With a grunt, Kristin slipped through the gap in the banks. Then Sky stood up.

The horses shied. Getting control, one of the men lifted his shield around to protect himself, then shouted something. It was strange, because it sounded like English, but Sky couldn't make any of it out. But he found he could speak Norwegian.

"I do not understand you," he called back.

"He asks you if you cower here alone, Norseman," came another voice, in his own tongue, spoken by the man who led the rest of the horsemen around the corner of the church. He wore no helmet, golden hair falling to his chain-mailed shoulders. And Sky realized he had seen him before, had heard his voice, as Bjørn. This leader had called for the men of Hareid to surrender before the battle at the bridge. Just before a bear was born.

"I do not cower here at all, King Harold Godwineson," he replied, the words coming easily, from some calm place inside. "For you see me in plain sight. And yes, I am quite alone."

They looked at each other for a moment, the king stroking his long mustache. Then his gaze went past Sky. "Apart from your friend the dragon, I venture."

Sky glanced back. *Ravager*'s prow had just come into view. "Oh, yes," he nodded, "apart from him."

The king laughed, turned. A command was given. The horsemen flowed around, up the steep slopes. Bjørn had been right—none ventured down them, and from his glancing he could not see any bows. The only way to capture or kill his countrymen was through the gap. Through him.

Harold had ridden forward a few paces. "You know me, youth. But do I know you?"

"My name is Bjørn Thorkellsson, King. I was with the men of Hareid, who held you before the bridge."

"Ah! That old man, that berserker, was one of you. Took poor Edwin's arm." He shook his head in wonder. "Have you any more berserkers amongst you?"

"That you will have to see if you do not let us leave."

"Ah, Vikings! No odds too great, eh? I appreciate it because . . . I am half one of you. My mother was Danish."

"Well, the Danes were Vikings once, though mostly farmers now."

Sky-in-Bjørn gasped at his rudeness. But he found he could not help what he was saying. This was Norse turf. He had to let his ancestor defend it.

Yet Harold took no insult, laughed again, and Bjørn could see it was something that came easy to him, for all his cares. He leaned forward in his saddle. "Have you not had enough of killing, my young friend? And of dying? Your countrymen lie thick upon the ground."

"With many of yours." He swallowed. "But since we are talking, and you are not killing, you must have an offer?"

The king smiled. "I have. The same one as before. You will be our prisoners. After Stamford Bridge, there's many an English household will need a man to work the fields this year. Maybe, after a time—"

Bjørn's hand went up. "You offer what we refused before—slavery."

"I offer life. And hope. Instead of death."

"Others will die too."

"Are you that good with the bow?"

"I could put an arrow into your eye from here, King."

"Well, I wouldn't want that." Harold leaned forward, picked his helmet off his saddle bow, put it on. Two metal rings reached down from the front of it, protecting his eyes. "Do you want to reconsider my offer?"

The humor was gone now. Sky saw the men about him stir, hands reaching for sword grip and shield strap. Fear swept through him . . . yet he knew only some of Bjørn's people would be aboard. Fear would not help them. They needed time.

"May I ask my men?"

The king nodded. "You have a few moments. To choose between life and death."

Is that the choice? Sky moved through the gap, stared down at the little river jetty. The skiff had made a couple of journeys, but it could only take three at a time. Men still jostled below. Ingvar-Kristin looked up and shrugged in despair.

What do I do, Sky thought desperately. What is the choice here? I know Bjørn is not meant to die in England. I died as him, an old man in Norway. But the rest? Do the men of Hareid become slaves? They would not die . . . yet. No more widows would be made in Hareid this day, so his vow would be kept. But it irked him, almost as much as it irked Bjørn.

Slowly, undecided, he climbed back up the slope. But the king and his men were not staring at the gap in the bank, waiting for him to emerge. They were watching a single rider, galloping along the river road. One of Harold's men had been dispatched to intercept him. Along with everyone else, Sky watched the two meet, then gallop over. In the dawn light Sky could see this man was filthy with road muck and exhausted, too, barely clinging to his saddle.

Words followed, some of which Sky understood. It should be Kristin standing there, he thought, because she'd told him that she'd studied Old English at Cambridge. But all Sky could do was watch the king wearily remove his helmet and slump farther into his saddle as if all the weight of the world pressed him into it.

A silence came. Then Harold roused himself. Orders followed, and single riders began to gallop off in all directions. The king himself turned his horse's head away from the river, and only a word from one of his men turned him back.

"Norseman," he called, and Sky stepped forward. "You may return to your homes. No one here will stop you. Tell any of your countrymen you meet: they have

Harold's leave to go home. I cannot now afford to lose one more man. I will need them all if—" He broke off, began to turn away again.

"King!" If Bjørn had guided for a while, it was Sky who stepped him forward now, his own need prodding him; Sky thought he knew what word the Englishman had just received. "Do you go to fight another enemy?"

Harold jerked back on his reins. Around him, several of his men muttered oaths and made the sign of the White Christ. "How could you know that, when I only just have learned it?"

Sky reached for the only explanation that might pass. Not untrue either. "I read runes, my lord," he replied. "And in them I saw this—that the tally of blood in this realm has not yet been reached."

He raised the bow, sighted, shot his arrow. Though men flinched, it went nowhere near them but instead glanced off the tail of the weathercock atop the church spire. The bird spun around and around, metal squealing, until it settled.

"A reader of wyrd." Harold nodded and a brief smile came. "My mother was one such." He looked down at the bow in Bjørn's hands. "Are you as good when your target is a man?"

Sky felt his heart beating ever faster. "Just as good, Lord. But my brother is even better."

One of his men leaned in, whispered urgently. But Harold raised his hand to him. Nudging his horse a little toward Sky, he said, "Then let me make you a different offer. My army is short of bowmen. It is one advantage the invader will have over us when we meet. He will have bought most of his. How if I do the same?"

Sky wanted to roar his delight. But Bjørn within him was the cunning one. "I'd consider it. How much gold are you offering?"

"A piece of it a day, to any of you who will join me. With as much of the foes' armor as you can carry away when we conquer. Does that sound fair?"

"It does to me. Let me speak to the others."

"Be swift!"

Sky ran to the top of the slope. "Ingvar!" he called, but she was obviously having a Kristin moment, because the smith had to nudge Bjørn's brother before he turned. Sky could see that half the men had got across to *Ravager;* others stood on the dock still, uneasily holding their weapons.

Sky ran down, and the offer was quickly put to them all. But only Ingvar immediately stepped to Bjørn's side. "Do you not think we have lost enough men in this land?" Gray Arnstein ventured.

"I think it will be a long winter, with only scars to keep us warm." Sky smiled. "My brother and I will throw the dice again. Anyone else?"

It was a Viking's explanation, not to return home without booty. It was accepted with barely a grunt, and fortunately, no one else stepped forward to join them. "We will tell your mother you will return with the spring, sons of Thorkell," Arnstein said, stooping to pick up the rope and pull the skiff to the jetty. Three men immediately got in and began to pole toward their ship. Only six remained.

"Kiss her for us," Kristin said. "And my wife and child." With that, the two brothers turned and walked up the bank. "Do you know what you're doing?" she whispered.

"Not really. But I think Bjørn does," Sky replied. "Nice Norwegian, by the way."

She snorted, bending to pick up the shield, bow, and arrows Ingvar had put aside to help cut runes. "Well, I don't think it would be too clever to speak modern English, do you?"

"No. Our new friends already think I am a little . . . spooky!"

On the far side of the churchyard, Harold had dismounted and was again surrounded by his men, who were listening to his commands. For a moment, Sky and Kristin studied them. Most were taking off their mail coats, rolling and securing them above their mount's rump. Long swords were at their sides, axes hung in slings along one of each of their horses' shaggy flanks, a shield slung across the other. Drinking horns were passed; hunks of rough bread were being chewed. Despite the gravity of the news, several men, Harold included, were laughing, tossing back their heads, their fair locks shaking.

"They love war, don't they?" Kristin muttered.

"It's what men did," replied Sky. "Do," he added, feeling a little surge within, as if Bjørn had shifted inside him.

"But what the hell are *we* going to do?" She turned to him then, eyes terrified. "I mean, we are back in time! What if we kill someone who wasn't meant to die then? Now!"

Sky shrugged. "I think it's what we talked about before—wyrd's not as fragile as all that. If I give a man my cold in 1066, the Second World War might not happen? I think that's nonsense!"

A smile came through her fear. "You've got a cold?"

He sniffed, smiled too. "All that swimming and drowning." He shook his head. "No. I'd say, try to tread as lightly as possible. Try not to kill anyone. But most importantly—"

King Harold had seen them. "Are you joining us then, Norsemen?"

"We two, my lord."

As they walked forward, Kristin whispered from the side of her mouth. " 'Most importantly' what?"

"Don't get killed yourself."

Before she could reply, Harold called from his horse. "You may each double up with one of my men."

Two men signaled. The Vikings mounted behind them. Sky was nearest the king. "Do you not wish to know who you ride to fight, Norseman?"

Sky nearly blurted it out. Careful, he thought. "My king, I will kill anyone you pay me to kill. But if it pleases you to name your enemy, I shall be pleased to hear him named."

Harold raised his voice so all could hear. "We ride to fight Duke William of Normandy. He has landed in the south of my kingdom, bringing an army of Norman scum and French mercenaries. We've a hard road to travel, and a hard fight at its end. But God is with us, and my realm unites against the foe." He rose up in his stirrups. "For England!"

"Godwineson!" came the shouted reply, the horses surging forward. But it was another name that came to Sky's lips. Another enemy he feared—and hoped—was waiting at the road's end.

"Sigurd."

CHAPTER TWENTY-THREE

A TALE FOR BATTLE'S EVE

"It was the season of the ax. The season of the sword. The hour of the tempest. The hour of the wolf. It was Ragnarók, the last battle, and it shattered the earth."

Sky paused, taking a deep breath, leaning forward, framing his face in flame light. In his own life, he had never been a storyteller. But Bjørn was.

He had already told of the three-year winter, the famine in the land, all bonds of kinship shattered as mothers snatched crusts from daughters' mouths, as father slew son, and son, father. But Bjørn knew the part of the tale his listeners truly wanted to hear—of the fall of the gods, before their most terrible foes. And now Sky gave it to them.

"Dawn came, and the gods' golden rooster crowed in Asgard. Yet now, for the first time, a rival challenged him, from the depths of the world—a cockerel, soot-black, calling from the gates of Hel itself. And in that instant, the earth was split in two. Yggdrasil, the tree of life, was gnawed through at the roots by the dragon Niddhog. And as the Life Tree toppled, the Norns, who had spun the threads of wyrd from the beginning of time, ceased their spinning. In that moment, every barrier that separated the nine worlds crumbled."

Sky had a hand on a stick. Now he thrust it deep into the fire. "Surt," he cried as sparks flew high and men jumped back from them, "ruler of the realm of flame, led his fire demons screaming down upon the world. From frozen Jotunheim, the Frost Giants blasted forth hail and storm, unleashing trolls and ice monsters to ravage the land. Deep down, far beneath the crust of the world, Hel's gates split asunder, and all the evil that they had held back from the world now burst in." He lowered his voice to a hiss. "While in the North a dreadful longship set sail. It was made entirely from the fingernails of the dead, and Loki, the Trickster God, was at its helm. He steered straight for Asgard, vengeance pumping the black heart he clutched between his teeth . . . his own!"

"Holy Father protect us!"

It was the abbot who cried out. The churchman had mocked the tale, when it was first begun, as nothing but pagan nonsense, a story to frighten children alone. But Sky could see he was as caught as any, as frightened. And the look of terror on his face made some others laugh.

"Peace, Leofric." The king reached over and pushed the cleric's jaw up. "And put your own heart back in its rightful place."

More laughter. Sky smiled, rode it out. He was quite pleased with his new addition of the black heart to an old tale. And he had learned—Bjørn knew—laughter was rarely a bad thing. It relaxed the listeners—for the true horrors to come! He waited a moment—not all Harold's court, gathered round his fire, spoke Norwegian, and someone was translating Bjørn's tale as he went. When the murmuring stopped, he spoke again.

"As the earth was broken, so were all the fetters that had ever bound monster. And of these monsters, the worst, the most terrible, were the wolf Fenrir and his brother, the dragon Jormungand. Both had waited a thousand years to take revenge upon those who had chained them. Now, with slavering jaws spread wide, they bounded toward their enemies."

Sky had dropped his voice, and people leaned closer in to him. It was time for the heroes.

"But from Asgard's gates, Odin, the All-Father, burst, leading the Aesir gods and the vast host of the greatest warriors who had ever lived; who, since their deaths in battle, had feasted by night and fought by day in Valhalla, awaiting the trumpet that would summon them at this hour of need. Each was armed with spear or sword or blood-ax according to his will. Each had a helm of impenetrable iron, each a coat of mail forged in the fires of Darkalfheim. And on each warrior's back was a shield edged in iron, blazoned with their marks—Dragon! Stag! Bear!"

Sky named the insignia of the leaders—Harold's Dragon of Wessex, his two brothers' beasts. Noted the recognition in men's eyes before he went on. "Odin, riding his eight-footed stallion, charged straight at Fenrir the Wolf, whose jaws were so vast they stretched from the vault of heaven to the flattest plain and still had not opened to their full. The All-Father bent back, hurled his spear, Gungnir—the spear that never misses its mark—but it just vanished down the throat of the terrible beast and did not slow him. In the next moment, with one snap of his jaws, Fenrir swallowed horse and god and all!"

"All-Father!" came a shocked whisper. And the scowl the abbot gave made Sky smile. These English had been followers of the White Christ for ten generations. More. But not everyone had forgotten the old gods, it seemed.

He raised his voice again. "Odin's son, Thor, could not help him. All alone he strove against the flame-belching dragon, crashing blow upon blow on its scaly head. No creature had survived even one strike of his mighty hammer, Mjolnir, before. On and on he smote, a giant smith at a fiery anvil. In the end the monster perished. Yet as it exhaled, its dying breath carried all the pestilent gases that had brewed in its hundred stomachs. Nine steps Thor stumbled back—and on the ninth, the terrible poison choked him, and he fell."

"Thunder God!" came from several voices, and Sky was not sure that the abbot was not one of them.

His voice deepened. "On the Plain of Vigrid—a hundred miles broad and long and every inch filled with warrior or monster—the armies stood toe to toe, shield to shield, and fought. The corpse mound grew, rising to flesh mountains, and still the fight went on. But then, at the last, two Frost Giants dressed in the skins of wolves reached up and plucked from the sky both the blood-red sun and the sword-slashed moon. The darkness was infinite." His voice dropped to a whisper. "The world was no more. Ragnarók had come."

"But what then?" It was definitely the priest who gasped his appeal, but no one laughed at the irony now. They were too intent on Bjørn's face.

"Then?" Sky looked around at the faces of the Englishmen, the king and his brothers, his nobles and guards. Each bore the same rapture, the same question. "Then, Ragnarók was gone, taking with it the rule of the Aesir gods. The dark held the world . . . for an age and a day. Until there came the smallest glimmer of light within the infinite black. And the sun rose again." A sigh came, which he topped. "Seeds sprouted, trees bore leaves, eagles flew over the world and spied on rivers once more filled with fish. And from the twisted roots of fallen Yggdrasil, two creatures who had sheltered there from the terrible storm emerged. Lif and Lifthrasir—'Life' and 'Will to Live.' Golden-haired, strong of limb, he was shaped like a hunter, she like the fairest of milkmaids. And their children would fill the world."

If Sky had been telling such a story in his own time, he'd have said, "The end." But Bjørn knew better. He simply bowed and stepped back.

The priest, recovered now, could contain himself no more. "You see, my king and nobles. It becomes the story of creation as told by our holy book. Adam and Eve and the Garden. The pagans just stole our story."

Harold took his time to speak. Sky knew he was the leader of a Christian land and fought under the White Christ's cross, that he prayed each night and day. But Sky could also see that the king's eyes shone with his story, and he was proud. "Undoubtedly, Leofric. God's word is the only true one." He nodded at the amens that followed. "Still, what a battle that was! I'd almost trade a day in paradise for a blade in my hand on Vigrid field."

"My lord king—"

A raised hand stilled the abbot's further protest. "But we have our own battle to fight tomorrow, and only a few hours left to pay our debts to God and sleep both. So God's night to you all."

Slowly, reluctantly, the men in the circle dispersed

to find what rough bed they could make. But as Sky turned to go, Harold called him. "Your fee, skald," he said, and pulled a large silver bracelet from his arm.

Sky raised his hands. "Tomorrow, my king, is when payment falls due."

Harold smiled. "That will be for your arrows. This is for your words."

Sky bent forward, grasped the silver ring. But Harold didn't release it. For a moment the night diminished to just the two of them, joined across the circle, and the king's voice came in a whisper. "You've seen something, haven't you, rune reader? About tomorrow."

Startled, Sky took a step back. But he found he couldn't let go of the bracelet. Silver still bound them as Harold bent his head closer to hear. He had to speak. "Lord King, I . . . I have seen nothing . . . clearly, I . . ."

It was true. Sky knew the history—Harold fell, some said to an arrow in the eye, at the end of a long and bloody day. But he also knew Sigurd was there to change that history. If he succeeded, this man, whom Sky had grown to like and admire in the two-week march from the North, would live and rule. This man, who believed in the power of the runes and the walking of Fetches, would be king and shape his land in his own image. But if Sky could stop his grandfather, as he must strive to do . . . this man would die.

"Will you read the runes for me a last time, Bjørn Thorkellsson?"

Sky-Bjørn had cast the stones he'd carved on the journey down a few times for the king. He'd predicted a successful hunt for provisions, another son to be born to Harold's mistress. Now there was only one thing the king wanted to know. And Sky-Bjørn could not tell him. "Forgive me, Lord," he whispered, "but I cannot."

It seemed an age that Harold held him there—with silver, with the power in his eyes. "Well," he said softly, finally. "We shall know what you have not seen clearly soon enough, Norseman. Till then, we must put our trust in God." He smiled slightly. "And accept whatever wyrd has written for us both this day."

He let go of the bracelet. Sky stumbled back, bowed. The king turned and, without another look, disappeared into the darkness beyond the firelight.

Sky turned the other way . . . and ran into Kristin. Bjørn's brother had sat in the shadows behind him, listening. Now she spoke. "Why did you do that?"

"What?"

"Tell that story." She fell into step beside him. They had found a small yew tree whose branches gave some shelter and had left their meager goods beneath them.

"The king asked me for a tale."

"You could have refused."

"Maybe. But Bjørn couldn't."

Kristin stopped, held his arm. "You are not the same. I feel like Ingvar, sure, but—"

"I *am* the same." They were beyond the range of

any fires and the waxing moon was hidden behind clouds. He could barely see Ingvar's tall shape. "I don't know how it is for you. But I've . . . melded with Bjørn in some way now. I haven't displaced him entirely. I'm never sure which of us is speaking, acting. I've become him—and he's become me." He closed his eyes. "And I'm not sure what we'll do now. What terrible things we'll do."

"Terrible?"

He reached for her, turned her so they both could gaze at other, distant fires. "There," he said. "There, in the Norman camp, Sigurd waits. We don't know exactly how . . . but he's planning on changing the course of history tomorrow. And part of me—Bjørn in me—wants him to. And Sky in me too. I want Harold to win! And yet I can't let him! Alter history on a scale like that and what will happen to the world we know?"

"It will be changed. Utterly. Totally." She bit Ingvar's lip. "But have you wondered if it might change it for the better?"

"Every moment of every day." Sky shivered. "But we can't take on the gods' role. It's not up to us to bring about Ragnarók, just because Sigurd thinks we should. But he's grown so powerful. He seems to always have powers we haven't even dreamed of yet. I'm . . . I'm not sure we *can* stop him. All I know is that we have to try—and that the price is going to be the highest we've ever paid." He closed his eyes. "We don't need the runestones to tell us that."

" 'We,' " she echoed. "Is that you and me or you and Bjørn?"

"Both. You and Ingvar too. All four of us. Confusing, isn't it?" He squeezed the shoulder he still held. "Will you help me do the right thing?"

"Which is?"

Sky sighed. "I wish to God I knew. To gods!"

After a moment's silence, she spoke. "I'm with you, Cousin Sky. Brother Bjørn. We said it before in the mountains. 'All the way.' Whatever the cost." He could see her hand rise up, gesturing to the enemy's firelight. "And Sigurd's not the only one who's grown powerful. Remember that. Tomorrow . . . he's going to have to watch out for us!"

CHAPTER TWENTY-FOUR

THE BATTLE OF HASTINGS

It was not the cold that made Sky shiver.

In the three hours since dawn, the sunshine, strong for mid-October, had dried out his dew-soaked tunic, while the press of bodies, as the hill gradually filled with the hosts of England, brought its own heat—and some pretty funky smells! He reckoned that the ridge was about eight soccer fields long, before it dropped steeply at either end. So once the front line was established by shields, the thousands of men who marched up could only form a mob behind. They went back in at least ten rough ranks. At about a square yard per man, what was that? A thousand men per soccer pitch?

"But do they even play soccer in 1066?" Sky muttered to himself. "Maybe I can get a game going! France versus England. Settle it all that way!"

He almost laughed . . . and shivered again instead.

Not because of the cold. Because of the men who were marching and riding into the valley below.

The enemy came in their thousands, too, though Sky found it hard to tell if these Normans and their allies outnumbered the English, because so many of them were on horseback and that made their force look bigger. He seemed to remember, from his schoolboy history—he still found it incredible that he had studied this battle at school!—that the numbers were about even. About eight thousand a side, then. It didn't seem so much when he recalled other history lessons. The Second World War had armies of millions! But as he saw the sunlight flicker on lance point, sword, and mace, he remembered something from Bjørn's recent experiences.

It took just one man to kill another.

When he shivered for the third time, a voice came. "Do you need to borrow a cloak, Norseman?"

Sky looked up. He was standing just below the very highest point of the ridge. And at that point, at the very center of his line, stood Harold, king of England, looking down at him. "No, my lord," he replied. "I have a touch of nose sickness, that's all." It wasn't a lie. In the two weeks since he'd been forced to swim in the river outside York, he'd never been dry or warm enough to shake a cold. And a sneeze confirmed his words.

"God's health," Harold commented dryly. "I hope it will not affect your eye?"

"It will not, my lord."

"That pleases me."

A man ran up to the king, and low-voiced words were exchanged—to Sky's relief, because it took the attention off him. Many others were already looking at him curiously, this Viking their chieftain kept close. And Sky was puzzled too—though he thought it might have something to do with their last conversation, on the spinning of wyrd. Perhaps Harold would try to persuade him to cast runes for him one last time before the battle? To seek a better answer than the one he'd read in the young man's eyes the night before?

A nudge turned him. Kristin pointed down the hill. "So, do you see him yet?" she asked, as she had close to twenty times before.

Sky studied his cousin. He sensed that the Viking was growing ever stronger in her the closer it got to battle. Ingvar's eyes were aflame, but from fear or mad courage he had not yet been able to ask. He knew a little of what was to come, because he'd been in Bjørn at Stamford Bridge, had fought and killed as him. There was terror . . . and there was a wild abandon too! The berserker had come and taken him. And he knew the berserker was there in him still—in both him and Bjørn. He did not know how he would act when the battle began—or even *who* would act! But he knew even less how Kristin would. And when he'd tried to ask, she'd shushed him and feigned sleep.

"Kris-*Ingvar* . . ."

Perhaps she saw the question again in his eyes. "Shh," she hissed, and pointed again. "What do you think?"

Sky looked. But yet again, he had no sense of their grandfather in the army below—other than the certainty that he was there.

But looking told him something else. The last of the Normans had marched into the valley. There was some final jostling for position, some last shifting of man and horse. Then these, too, ceased, and a strange silence came while the armies of Normandy and England stared at each other.

It lasted at least ten of Sky's clear heartbeats. Those thumps and the snapping of pennants on lance heads and battle standards, the odd snort of horse and jingle of harness, were the only sounds. It ended when, from the middle of the enemy ranks, a solitary horseman rode forth. He was carrying a huge white banner, a cross of gold upon it, and in a clear voice he cried out, *"Dex Aie!"*

"Dex Aie!" the army roared as one behind him.

Neither Sky nor Bjørn spoke Norman. But he could tell, from the way the banner was shaken aloft, that the enemy were calling upon God Himself to lead them forward and guide their shining blades. But he didn't need to speak Old English to understand the reply. It was the same word in Norwegian, and close enough to the one he'd have used back in Shropshire, and it roared now from eight thousand throats.

"Ut! Ut!"

"Out! Out!" the English shouted. Command and threat both. The enemy was on their land. They would be driven back into the sea.

The cheering and jeering continued, different oaths coming from the different sides. Then, under the hubbub, Sky heard Harold call someone.

"Robert!"

Sky had talked a couple of times with the man now summoned. He was the son of a Norman knight and an English mother, for there had been many Normans at the old king's court, it was said. This one, even though he'd been raised partly in Normandy, had chosen to fight for his mother's land.

But it was for his time with the enemy that Harold wanted him now. "Tell me," the king said, pointing.

The younger man raised a hand to shelter his eyes from the morning sun. "Duke William's there, under the papal cross. I see the pennants of many of his knights around him—Hugh d'Avranches, Fulk d'Aunou, Guy de Fauchon—"

"So he keeps his countrymen tight to him at the center," interrupted Harold. "But what of his wings?"

Robert looked left, to the enemy's right flank. "I see the levies from France, from Picardy, Boulogne—"

"Mercenaries! Come for gold and pillage!" Harold leaned forward and spat between his own feet. "And the other wing?"

Robert looked to his right. "These mainly carry

the banners of Brittany, Anjou, and Maine. More scum, my lord, but even worse. Duke William cannot trust these entirely because he has placed some of his own Norman barons amongst them to steady them. I see the pennants of Homfrey de Balleroy, Henri de Barfleur, Louis de . . ."

Sky didn't need his cousin's grip upon his forearm. "Henri de Barfleur," he whispered, looking to the left wing of the Norman army, seeking there. "Sigurd!"

Robert had gone on with names, but Harold had ceased to listen and then cut him off with a raised hand. "So it is as we thought. The duke will charge his most loyal troops at us here, in the center. But his other wings will press, too, seeking glory. So, my brothers, each to your end of the ridge. Gyrth to my right, Leofwine to my left. Hold hard, and William will be forced to come for me here and watch his men die upon my shield wall." He smiled. "With God's favor, we will meet for a victory feast before sunset."

The amens came then, and further prayers, led by the abbot moving among them, making the sign of the cross. Sky knelt with the rest, although all knew Bjørn's pagan faith. But it gave him a moment to bend his head and try to think.

Sigurd *was* there! On the left wing of William's army. The harm he was planning would begin there. So Sky and Kristin had to be there to meet him. But how? Harold had kept them close. How could Sky—Bjørn!—ask to be sent where he needed to go?

And then someone else asked for him.

"Brother King!" It was Gyrth who spoke, rising from his knees at prayer's end. "My end of the ridge. I have walked it. It would be hard to ride round it . . . except for one track that skirts the wood's edge and curls around the back. Horsemen could do it, single file. But bowmen could stop them."

Harold thought for a moment. Nodded. "Take them, brother. And go with God."

The small band of archers rose, gathering bowstaves and arrow sheaves. Sky and Kristin rose too . . . and Harold saw them.

"But leave me my two Norsemen, eh?"

Sky looked up into Harold's eyes. There was a question there still, the one left from the night before. The king did not, could not, suspect anything of their true intent. But he did know that Sky was a reader of wyrd, and perhaps that theirs was somehow bound together.

Sky took a deep breath. "Let me go where my bow can be useful, King." He gestured to the men of Harold's bodyguard, the housecarls, who stood in the front rank. To a man they were enormous. "I would have to jump to shoot over your shield wall, and it would not make my arrows fly true."

A few men laughed: for a moment, the king looked like he would still deny him. But then he nodded. "You will return at battle's end and tell me how the threads of wyrd have woven this day?"

"If I return, my lord, we will both know our wyrd well enough by then."

Harold smiled. "Then return for the tale I will have for you, skald. It will be a good one, I think. Better even than Ragnarók."

Sky felt Bjørn's throat tighten. "I look forward to its telling."

"Come!" Gyrth was already moving back through the ranks to the rear of the hill. Sky and Kristin fell into the line of bowmen and followed. But he found it hard to look away from Harold, standing between his banners of the Fighting Man and the Dragon of Wessex. For the briefest moment, the king held his gaze. Then a servant brought him his helmet and he turned away.

"You all right?" asked Kristin next to him. "Are you . . . crying?"

"No!" muttered Sky, reaching up, wiping his eyes. "This bloody cold!"

They emerged from the ranks at the back, and immediately Gyrth began to run along the hill's rear slope, his men following. Sky clutched the leather pouch at his hip to stop the runestones there clattering together. For now they sounded like dead men's teeth, chattering the whispers of wyrd.

"Come on," said Kristin, speeding up, "at least we can know our enemy."

Running a few men ahead of them was Robert, the warrior who'd identified the Normans. They caught up.

"Sir, can you tell us," panted Kristin, "this Henri de Barfleur . . ."

The man glanced at them. "You know him?"

"We think he may be our grand—" Kristin bit off the word. "A distant cousin."

Robert nodded. "There's a lot of good Viking blood in the Normans. It's the French blood that's ruined them." He laughed. "What do you wish to know of him?"

"You recognized his pennant. What sign does he ride under?"

They had reached the end of the hill. Gyrth began to push through, his men following him into the gap. "His sign is—" The man halted, and not just because he needed to thrust aside a large militiaman who had stepped into the path. "You know, it's strange. When I lived in Normandy as a child, the Barfleur family were near neighbors." The wedge of men was gradually nearing the shield wall at the front. "And Henri always rode to war under the banner of the Rearing Black Horse. Then, on a visit last year, I discovered he had changed it."

"To what?" Sky asked. They had reached near the front rank now. Gyrth's housecarls were big men, too, but not as big as Harold's. Sky and Kristin could see quite clearly over them.

"To"—Robert was also gazing over the shield wall—"that!"

They looked, followed his pointing finger. It

should have been hard, amidst all the pennants down there, the many symbols moving with the shifting of horse and man. But it wasn't. They both saw it straightaway, as you would see a lightning bolt stabbing down from an autumn sky, and it swept away any doubt about who awaited them down the hill.

It was the jagged "S."

"Sowilo," they both breathed—and looked at the man who rode beneath it. The distance was less than three hundred paces and they could see him, the conical helmet, the gleaming mail coat, the sword at his side, the kite-shaped shield that bore the same insignia on one arm, the lance couched in the other. He looked like most of the men around him . . . and utterly different. Because they knew him.

"Sigurd."

"Yes."

He couldn't have known they were watching. Yet, even as they stared, he lifted his lance high into the air. And as it lowered, the enemy, with a great cry, began to move up the slopes.

Kristin shrugged off the huge shield strapped to Ingvar's back, laid it down. With shaking fingers she notched an arrow onto the bowstring. "Any advice?" she whispered, staring in horror at the men running toward them.

"Same as before," muttered Sky, pulling his helmet lower down over his eyes, notching his bow. "Try not to kill anyone, unless you have to. And don't get killed yourself."

"Norsemen!" Gyrth was beckoning them to the end of the English line. They went to him, saw that the slope dropped away sharply there, too steep for men in armor to run up, death if they tried. "There!" He pointed at the stand of oak at the hill's bottom, a narrow deer trail through its edge that led behind the English line. "Keep half an eye on that path. One man at a time could thread it," the king's brother said. "You two stop them if they try."

"My lord."

He moved away. Sky looked at Kristin. Ingvar's body was convulsing, as if he was about to vomit. "You OK?" he whispered, in modern English.

Somehow she swallowed what wanted to come up. "I don't know. I—"

"Arrows!"

The roar interrupted her, together with men suddenly ducking low. As he ducked, too, a quick glance showed Sky that the advancing enemy had halted, that archers had run before them and were loosing their first flight . . . which came like a chattering of starlings, flying high, dropping fast . . . into shields raised against them, metal biting into wood, burying harmlessly into earth, soaring over to lose power in the air behind the hill. With Bjørn's archer's eye, Sky saw the problem—shoot up the steep slope, and hit a wall of wooden shields that arrowheads could not penetrate. Shoot higher and the arrows vanished over the hill. Flight after flight came, and rarely was an unlucky soul hit, those usually to the very rear of the tight press of men. Abruptly, the iron rain halted. Sky risked looking up . . . and saw the archers running back into the ranks of their own infantry—to the jeers of the men on the hilltop, to more roars of *"Ut! Ut!"*

Then the foot soldiers closed ranks, their kite-shaped shields overlapping before them, their javelins raised high. *"Dex Aie!"* they cried, marching up the hill.

"Bowmen!" called Gyrth, and the small band of archers stepped forward, Sky and Kristin among them. Shield men shifted to give them room; arrows were notched, strings pulled back. Bjørn in him sought the vulnerable spot—the glimpse of flesh at the face, the unarmored foot. Sky shifted his sight, and when the cry came to "Loose!" he drove his arrow straight into the center of a shield.

Again and again they shot. Others found targets; men fell silently or with shrieks, the ranks opened, closed again. Soldiers stepped over their dying comrades and came on. Fifty paces. Forty.

"Bowmen . . . back!"

It was someone else's turn. They stepped away, other men came forward. Sky raised his eyebrows at Kristin, who was wiping slick hands upon Ingvar's jerkin. A shrug came. She had tried to miss like him. Maybe she'd succeeded.

Then a familiar sound turned him.

Voo, voo, voo.

It was like the hum of bees around a hive, and it built, built until a grunt ended it, a whoosh. And he recognized this not as Sky, not as Bjørn. As another of the ancestors within him—Tza! Slingshots were being used, and the Corsican shepherdess he'd once been was deadly in that art.

Sky could not help raising his head to watch the leather cups whirring above the English heads, see them build to their fastest. He watched one slinger release, marked the stone that flew and crashed harmlessly into a shield below. Sky licked his lips, something in him wanting this weapon. No, not something, he realized. Someone. Tza.

That image came again, that feeling, of Russian dolls, one within the other, within the next. Layers of ancestors, of spirits, all inside of him. He shook his head, trying to clear it. But the feelings that gripped him were lower down and everywhere. The killers in his bloodline, warriors and murderers both. All of them surging now, at battle cry, at the approach of enemies. Sky could choose whether to kill or not. Soon, though, he knew . . . others might not give him that choice.

He raised his head . . . to see the Norman line halt and men hoist javelins for the throw. Some managed to—before the storm was flung down upon them from the ranks above. All around him, Englishmen were hurling weapons: axes, hammers, spears, and anything else that came to hand—rocks, lumps of wood, water pails. The enemy quailed; men fell silently or screaming. But the rest came on now, shrugging into the storm as if it was rain and not death pouring onto them.

Then the lines crashed together . . . and all became battle-blur. Shrieks of fury, of agony, swords thrust in, axes slicing down, shields split, helms crushed. The archers had been shoved back by the blade men pushing forward. But the scene before Sky was beginning to tinge blood-red. With a grunt, he drew Bjørn's short dagger. How well the grip fitted his hand! He was moving toward a gap . . . when Kristin yanked him to the side.

"Here, Sky. Sky! Our job's here, remember?"

She whispered it in modern English; that, and the plea in her eyes, brought him back, Bjørn receding just enough. They moved to the edge of the hill . . . and saw a line of horsemen, a half dozen, obviously sent to probe the path around the English flank. The *Sowilo* pennant was not amongst them—Sky would not have known what to do if it had been—but Bjørn knew what to do now.

"Together?"

Kristin nodded. No, it was Ingvar who nodded, and Sky remembered the competition Bjørn had had with his brother, how he had needed to beat him at archery to get his father to take him on Harald Hardrada's invasion. "The oak before the front rider?" he challenged, saw a half smile come.

"Done."

Each turned, drew, shot. Two arrows sprouted in the tree, the lead horse rearing instantly, the rider fighting for control. "Shield," Kristin called, and they reached to their quivers as one, notched, drew, shot. The rider had only just regained control of his horse. Now he lost it completely as the impact of arrows tore the shield from his grip. He fell; his horse bolted, spooking the others. The man on the ground got up and began to run, ducking and weaving through the trees as if he felt winged death reaching for his back. As one, the other five turned their horses' heads and followed.

"Good shooting, brother," Kristin said, in Norse again. But their smiles were ripped away by the cry that came now from scores of throats, challenge in some, terror in others.

"Horsemen!"

They craned around the edge of the shield wall. Columns of mounted men were moving up the hill, and as they looked, trot changed to gallop. Norman infantry, those who had survived the carnage at the shield wall and had retreated, now re-formed behind and came again.

"Do you see Sigurd?" Kristin breathed.

Sky sought the "S" pennant and shield. "No!"

"Perhaps he doesn't want to kill either."

Sky grunted. "I don't think he'd care about that. He's going to wipe out millions of lives if he changes history. He just doesn't want to get killed before he does it. Whatever it is. He . . ."

His words were lost as Norman cavalry hurled themselves onto English shields. They came like the arrowheads that had preceded them, a wedge behind the pennant of their leader, his *conroi* of followers, the first of them throwing javelins, wheeling away, those that followed bearing swords, seeking any gaps that the javelins had opened. They threw, turned, wheeled, came again and again and yet again. Englishmen fell, but others stepped forward. The line held.

Sky lost count of how many times the enemy charged. How many arrows he fired. How many times he forgot he was Sky, while Bjørn drew and aimed and killed. They charged again . . . and Sky watched a huge Englishman, mail-coated and helmed, step out beyond the shield wall. Sky knew what he was doing—for like Thorkell, Bjørn's father, he needed room to swing his long, wide-bladed ax.

"Ut! Ut!" he roared. An arrowhead of horses swept toward him, he twisted to avoid the lance thrust at him . . . and leaning far back, he brought the weapon in a high arc up, over, down. And whoever was the Norman lord who led that *conroi,* he died then, died instantly, cut in half by an ax that went through him and on into the horse he rode.

It was a moment, one that many had seen. Enough

on the Norman side anyway, already despairing, to turn despair to terror.

The howl came from a hundred mouths, more, and those who were engaged withdrew their weapons abruptly, turned, and ran back down the hill.

A shout of triumph rose from the English ranks. "Hold! Hold!" yelled Gyrth. But most did not hear his command in the uproar. The enemy were fleeing—and backs were easier to strike at than shields!

Half the English on top of the hill began to run down it. "Come on!" yelled Sky.

Kristin grabbed him. "No! Bjørn! Sky! Stay here! Calm down! We don't want to kill, remember?"

"I know!" He turned her, pointed downhill, where the first fleeing knights had already crashed into their reserves below. "But we want him!"

She followed his finger, saw as clearly as he. "Sigurd!" she said, watching the "S" pennant jerk about as the man fought to control his horse. Bending to snatch up her shield, she shouted, "Let's go!"

They ran into mayhem. Of those who chased, most were not soldiers of the first rank. They were members of the Fyrd, the militia, some in stout leather coats, most just in the tunics they wore on the farm, wielding scythes from those farms, axes forged for wood chopping. Still, they were cutting at men's backs—and those men were dying.

Sky and Kristin dodged through the fight. A dismounted knight spotted them, raised his sword. . . .

Sky drove Bjørn's shoulder into his mail-clad chest, knocking him back. They ran on, looking for one shield amongst the many.

Someone was rallying the enemy. Experienced soldiers had seen the mistake. Armored men had begun to turn to those with little protection, or none. They could not crack the English shield wall. But they could slaughter those who came beyond it.

The cousins, the brothers, ran between the falling, blood-soaked blades, through the dying, over the dead, seeking. And then they came upon him quite abruptly, their eyes drawn by a terrible scream. A lance was being repeatedly plunged into the body of a slinger who had no more protection than the rope and leather he would never use again. The youth fell . . . and they saw that the lance, just beneath its spattered steel head, bore the pennant with the jagged "S."

"Sigurd!" they cried as one.

He turned at their cry. He wore a helmet with a nose guard, a strip of steel that ran down the front. On either side of it his eyes gleamed, and Sky could see that for the moment of slaying, he was not their grandfather but Henri de Barfleur killing for his lord, just as Bjørn had killed for his. Then Sky saw the eyes change, saw recognition come. And it was as if the battle roar slackened around them, as if the words were spoken in a whisper, in all their heads.

"You . . . came!"

Sky stared at his grandfather. Sigurd stared back.

And all that had ever been between them flashed through Sky now. The delight of those early secrets in his blood. The betrayal when he discovered what his knowledge was to be used for. The stealing of his cousin's soul, and his rescue of her. How his grandfather had cut Sky's Fetch off from his body, tried to kill him, tried to kill so many. *Had* killed so many, the poor farm boy now jerking on the ground merely the latest.

All this, in a moment that held for maybe three heartbeats, less . . . until the shrieking chased it away. Others were turning to the enemy at their stirrups . . . and then Kristin was yelling, "This way," grabbing his arm, tugging hard. He let her pull him, resisting for just the moment it took to bend and scoop up a dead youth's slingshot.

They ran fast—but not back up the hill with the rest of the fleeing English. She led him straight to the side, under the muzzles of the Norman horses, as their riders readied them to charge. Some men noticed, swatting at them with swords, jabbing at them with lances. But they were almost too close to be seen, and Kristin used the shield to deflect any blows that came too near.

They were close to the edge of the battle line to begin with. In a short sprint, they had cleared it. But Kristin didn't slow, pulled Sky on—and Ingvar was a big man. The ground became softer underfoot, water oozing up. There was a small stream, which they leapt.

"Kristin," Sky gasped. "Wait! Sigurd . . ."

Looking over his shoulder as he stumbled forward, Sky saw the battle still, the massacre of the fleeing English—though some were making a stand on a slight rise of ground. A party of knights swept toward them—and it was like a screen was pulled aside, to reveal the single horseman behind it. His lance was vertical, the jagged "S" on his pennant flapping in the breeze. As Sky watched, the horseman started toward them, away from the battlefield.

"Quickly!" Kristin was still pulling him. Stumbling together beyond the stream, they found a narrow path and ran into the first of the trees.

Behind them, the horseman came on.

CHAPTER TWENTY-FIVE

RAGNARÓK

The path wound downhill through a wood. They crossed another small stream, and the ground leveled. A few paces more and they stumbled into a clearing.

It was a narrow oval, a hundred paces long, half that across at its widest. They ran to the far end of it, where another trail began. They could have darted down it, vanished into the gloom under leaf and needle. But that was not why they were there.

No words were spoken. They just halted, turned, listened. The hill and the forest had cut out all sight of the battle and shrunk the sounds. They could still make out the clashing of metal, the cries of men and animals in terror, pain, and fury. But it was like the tide hitting a beach a distance away. Not as close, not nearly as loud, as the fall of hoof upon the path.

He came slowly into the glade, bending under a last branch, halting when he saw them, straightening in the saddle. The butt end of his lance rested on his stirrup, the pennant below its tip lifted almost immediately by a gust of breeze, flashing that jagged "S." For the longest moment, it was the only thing moving in the glade. Then the horse jerked its head up and down, a snort forming steam in the morning air. Sigurd stared at them over the lip of his shield, his insignia also upon it, this "S" unmoving. He had taken off his helmet, pulled down the hooded mail top, and they could see the strange cut of his short iron-gray hair, thick at the front, razored up the back to the crown. He was clean-shaven, and Sky was immediately struck by the contrast between them. Ingvar had a full beard, Bjørn the beginnings of one; both had fair hair, long to their shoulders. They were dressed as befitted Norsemen, in their tough hide coats, blue and green tunics underneath, while the man before them was encased in metal, the rings of his mail coat spiraling down to below the knee. In another time, Sky would have said he looked like some spaceman, an alien come to wreak havoc on humanity. Which, in a way, he was.

They stared . . . until Sigurd tapped his spurs into the horse's flanks, walked it forward, halted twenty paces from them. When he did, the silence ended.

"So, Sky and Kristin. Bjørn and Ingvar. You are here. Welcome to 1066."

He spoke in modern English. Sky answered in the same. "You don't seem surprised to see us."

"Why should I be? It was I who brought you here."

"Brought?" Kristin took a step forward. "We hunted you down. There's a difference."

"Not when the quarry wishes to be found." Sigurd smiled. "And not when he's left such a clear road map."

"Clear?" Sky shook his head. "Do you know what we've been through to get here?"

"I know exactly." The smug smile widened.

"Oh, no," murmured Kristin.

Sigurd looked at her, chuckled. "Oh, yes, Granddaughter. You see it now, don't you? You were always so quick—one of the things I loved about being you."

"What's he talking about?" Sky demanded.

She winced. "The family tree we've been following . . ."

"I don't see—"

She groaned. "I told you, I went to study and hike near Lom last summer. Sigurd was still in me. . . ."

Then Sky saw it too. "And while you slept, he stole someone's body, went up to the hut," he whispered, "and planted the paper."

The whisper hadn't been too quiet. "That's exactly what I did, Sky. It was a police officer, actually. A very fit young man," said Sigurd. "I knew how much our beloved Kristin craved travel, you see. It was time for her to join us fully, didn't you think? I knew you'd look at Meg and Matthew and *have* to go to them. Especially after I told you about learning from an English witch. So as I planned, you learned her skills . . . and the extraordinary link between her and Bjørn." He laughed. "The secrets that whisper in our blood, eh?

Our amazing ancestors, what they have taught us! So all I had to do was return here once more, into our other ancestor"—he raised the *Sowilo* shield high—"recite the runes of awakening as I came, and wait for you to follow."

The knowledge that he'd been manipulated so completely—again—made his knees sag. "But why?" he said weakly.

Sigurd smiled. "What you would call 'Plan B.' I told you, just before I killed Dirk, that even though you thwarted me at my conference—congratulations on that, by the way!—the Church of the Freed Spirit was only *one* way to achieve my goal."

Sky couldn't speak. But Kristin did. "OK," she said angrily. "You have plans A, B, and C. Bravo! But I still don't see why you need *us* here, if you're so supersmart."

"Oh, child! For *Ragnarók,* of course." He shouted the word. "You know the end of that tale. From the dead roots of the One Tree, two children emerge. Lif and Lifthrasir." He waved the lance over them. "You! It is what I promised, Grandson, that very first time I came to you."

"What?" Sky croaked.

"You two—blood of my blood—will fulfill our family's destiny."

"Which is?" Kristin asked softly.

He smiled, a terrible, triumphant smile. "Nothing less than to rule all Time."

And there it was—the end of all the journeys Sky had taken . . . but only as Sigurd saw it. Sky saw something else—his grandfather's absolute madness. His journeying, his possessing of all those souls, the price he'd paid for each one, the craving he felt for more . . . it had all tipped him over the edge. And Sky knew how he felt—because a part of him felt the same way. Yearned for more possession, the rush of living another human's life, the power it gave him.

But he was not Sigurd yet. Not by a long shot. He was not mad enough to want to destroy the world. But he was angry enough to try to stop the man who did.

"No, Sigurd!" he shouted. "You may have decided your destiny. But only I decide mine. And mine is what it's always been: to fight you. Here, at the last, it ends."

The smile vanished. Something made Sigurd's horse skitter under him. He won easy control, and when he spoke again, there was wonder in his voice. "Even here, even now, after you have heard of the glory I am offering you . . . you would oppose me still?"

"Yes!" For the first time in a while, Sky smiled. "I'll write my own wyrd, if it's all the same to you."

"How?"

"Oh," said Sky, "the usual way." And on his words, Sky reached back and pulled Death Claw from its sling.

Sigurd bellowed, "Then step aside, Granddaughter, and let he and I finish this forever."

"No, Sigurd." Like Sky-Bjørn had done, Kristin

reached over Ingvar's shoulders. But instead of a weapon, she brought down the great round shield. "I'm with him."

For a long moment, Sigurd just glared down at them. Then he spoke. "So. Even here, even now, you make a teenager's predictable choice. You dismiss my wisdom, challenge my authority, oppose my will. Well . . . so be it!"

Jerking the reins hard, he turned the horse. In a few seconds he'd reached the end of the glade. There he jabbed the lance's butt into the ground, then pulled the metal hood over his head. Finally, he reached behind to his saddle, grabbed his helmet, pulled it on. Even at that distance, from either side of the metal nose bar, they could see the fierce gleam in his eyes. He snatched up the lance and drove cruel spurs into the horse's flanks as the maddened beast leapt forward, and a great cry burst from him.

"It ends here!"

It amazed Sky how fast a trained stallion could cover the ground. One moment, the lance was lowered; only the next, it seemed, was it hurled into the hastily thrown-up shield, with all the force of a charging horse and a strong man's arm behind it. Kristin hadn't had time to even brace Ingvar's body. His big frame was thrown back, into his brother's. They fell in a pile of limbs. There were two distinct cracks. Sprawled on the ground, each looked at the other in horror as Sigurd galloped away again to the far end of the clearing. Then both saw immediately what had happened.

"Dammit!" Sky was on his feet first, pulling the two broken halves of the bow and the string over his head. Kristin did the same. They had time to set themselves, at least. Because at the far end of the clearing, Sigurd reined in, reached . . . and pulled his great war sword from its sheath. There was something so assured about the way he swung it through the air that Sky knew immediately—this was Henri de Barfleur's favorite weapon.

And this is mine, he thought, stepping behind the shield, cousins and brothers peering over its rim, readying themselves for the charge. But though Sigurd came fast again, he didn't drive through as before. There was a sharp stop, a horse up on its hind legs, hooves flailing in the air, striking down. The shield was pummeled, driven down by the blows.

Clutching his ax tight to him, Sky dropped to the ground, rolled from beneath the shield's shelter, a moment before a flurry of hooves and sword blows smashed it from Ingvar's grip. Sky saw his brother-cousin freeze, staring at the sword blade rising up again, both knowing where it was going to fall. And Sky leapt, his own weapon going high, falling first. It was not a stroke to cut a man in half. He had not had the time to bring it all the way up from the ground. But the axhead fell fast enough to drive into Sigurd's kite-shaped shield and split *Sowilo* in half.

"Yahh!" yelled Sky, his hands rising up the axshaft, readying to jerk the weapon from the wood. But that brought him close to the Norman knight, whose favorite weapon was a sword and who turned it now in midstroke, away from the one brother he'd been going to strike, to strike the other.

The sword sliced down. Sky-Bjørn, hands desperately pulling on the axshaft, saw it coming . . . too late. He moved, a hair beyond the full edge of the rushing blade. Not beyond its tip. It was as honed as the sharpest razor and it sliced an inch deep into Bjørn's neck.

Sky had been wounded before, within Bjørn, at his other battle. But this was a death cut. He knew it instantly. It didn't take the blood spraying onto the horse's flank to tell him so.

He staggered, slipped to his knees. His hand, raised to his throat, did nothing to halt the red flood.

Then Ingvar was beside him, arms around him, a hand thrusting to cover his, help him stem what could not be stemmed. His brother was speaking, but something had taken away Sky's hearing. Through Bjørn's misting eyes, everything was moving slower—Henri de Barfleur, riding to the far end of the glade, halting, turning; steam rising from the stallion's flanks, breath from its nostrils.

And then he did hear something. A word. One. His name.

"Sky!"

But it was not Ingvar who spoke it. It was Bjørn.

It was the name that did it. Pulled Sky out of dying Bjørn. It was as easy as breathing out . . . and he'd never had a quieter moment than the one just before death.

"Sky!" Bjørn's voice came again, weaker, thick with blood.

"I am here, Bjørn," he replied, marveling at it. Before, when he'd died in an ancestor or lost consciousness, he'd always returned to his own body, his own time. But he could not leave now. For it was not Bjørn's wyrd to die here, so young, in an English meadow. Sky could not let that happen. Not when it was his Fetch standing there. His Fetch that had learned . . . other skills.

He was looking down at one ancestor . . . but feeling another. "Tza," he said simply, in his head. And as he said it, he reached into the pouch of runestones at his waist.

No choice was required. Need, as ever, chose for him. And it was Need he chose, or necessity. The runestone that had healed one girl in the mountains of Corsica and another in the Cloisters of Trinity College.

As then, so now. Sky bent and touched the runestone *Naudhiz* to the blood-pumping cut in Bjørn's throat. As then, so now. "Peace," Sky whispered.

And under the pressure of a stone held in the

fingers of a Mazzeri Salvatore, the blood ceased to flow, the wound's edges knitted together.

Bjørn's eyes struggled to open. When they did, Bjørn and Sky looked at each other for a long moment. Sky saw that his ancestor would live . . . but he had lost a lot of blood. "Peace," said Sky again. And something came into Bjørn's eyes. A look, an acknowledgment. It was almost like that first time they'd seen each other, on a Viking longship, reflected in the polished metal of a shield boss. Then the eyes slowly shut.

Sky looked at Ingvar, at his cousin within him, and smiled. Then they heard the cry from the other end of the glade. They both turned to look, all slowness gone.

Sigurd, roaring his fury, brought the stallion up onto his rear legs again.

Sky rose. But he didn't rise alone. Tza was still strong within him. And his ancestor had another skill. It required a stone too.

Not the healing kind.

For the moment that Sigurd reared his stallion again upon his hind legs and Ingvar picked up the shield, Sky wasn't there—wasn't Sky, or Bjørn, facing death in an English wood. He was on a plain in Corsica, the sweet scent of the Maquis filling his nostrils, a waxing moon high above him, turning granite cliffs to silver. And he wasn't he. *She* was Tza! While the caress of rope, and the hunger, told him something else.

Tza was hunting.

Hooves dropped onto the turf. The horse began to come. But slowly now, though Sky-Tza could see by the way its four hooves all left the ground at once that it was already galloping. Still, there was time; fingers knew their work. They lifted rope from around the neck, found the knot at one end, found the loop at the other. A leather pouch filled with stones hung at the waist. A stone was placed, the sling beginning to whirl as Sky-Tza stepped around the shield, with the horse still fifty paces away. In three pulls of his shoulders, the weapon was whirling above his head.

Voo, voo, voo.

A boar had charged them once. Sky had wanted to shoot, let slip the stone . . . *now,* at forty paces! . . . *now,* at thirty! But Tza had waited, and she waited now. Only at twenty was the knot flung forward, aimed between the eyes. Not of beast. Of man.

It was sound that brought Sky back, the sudden *plink* of stone striking metal. Henri de Barfleur left his saddle as if plucked out by a giant's two fingers. In two more strides, the horse was on top of them, barely swerving before plunging down the path behind them. There was some crashing through undergrowth, then silence, save only for Kristin's hard breathing and his own.

Then they were running to the fallen knight, Kristin there first, placing two of Ingvar's fingers against the throat.

"Is he dead?"

"I think so." A moment. "Yeah, no pulse."

"Crap!"

"Why? He was trying to kill us, wasn't he?"

"Yeah, but . . ." Sky shook his head. "We've killed an ancestor. How's *that* going to affect the future?"

Kristin looked at him, shrugged. "Better him than us. Besides, he may have been meant to die in this battle."

"But I've killed . . . Sigurd." The shock of those words, of all he'd been through, made his knees give, and he sank down to the ground.

"And healed Bjørn." She grinned. "It's been a full day."

And they were laughing, laughing hard, Ingvar and Sky, clutching each other's shoulders. Then, as suddenly as it had come, the laughter went. "I can't believe it's over," Sky said, stepping back. There was no triumph in his voice. He was too weary to be triumphant.

"Believe it." She gestured down. "This was the last body he could occupy. He's killed Dirk back . . . then, remember?"

Sky laid his head upon his knees. Something was wrong. "Don't you think it seems too easy?"

"Easy? After what we've been through? Are you nuts?" She reached down for the nose guard, which had been smashed back into the face. It took an effort to pry the runestone from the steel that had bent around it. Finally she succeeded. She wiped it on her tunic, leaving a smear of blood there. Looked. "Oh!"

"Which one is it?"

"*Raidho.*" She held it out to show him the "R" carved into the stone. "Why did you choose that one?"

He shook his head. "I didn't. It just came to hand."

"It's perfect, isn't it?"

"How so?"

"It's the rune of the journey. Especially the journey to death." She tossed the stone to him and he caught it. "Thus . . . perfect!"

He looked at what he'd carved. He'd been unable to find dyes or make them on the march from York. But the cut lines *were* stained now—with the red of an ancestor's blood. And in them he saw . . . something else. "But it's not just death, is it?" he murmured, turning the stone over and over in his hand. "It's also the summoning of the dead. Raising them."

"So?"

"So he's not dead . . . entirely."

"Yes he is." She pointed at the body.

"No," Sky said softly. "Henri's dead, but—"

And then he heard it.

"What?"

"Shh!"

They listened. In the distance, the battle continued. But closer to, there came the crack of sticks underfoot. Something was approaching through the trees.

"Sky, it's the horse coming back, that's all!" Ingvar's voice was strong, assertive.

"No, Kristin," he said wearily, starting to rise,

needing to be on his feet for what was to come. "It's Sigurd."

"It can't b—" The word died as she turned with Sky toward the sound. As they both saw what came walking out of the woods.

It was a wild boar, a black and silver monster near the size of a bull, with tusks like scimitars. In all its enormity, the only small things were its red eyes; but even these were large enough for them to see the hatred gleaming in them. Pausing for the briefest of moments, it lowered its head and charged.

At this, the narrowest part of the glade, there was no time for rope and stone. "Split!" yelled Sky, acting on his words, sprinting fast toward the closest fringe of forest. He didn't look back, didn't need to. The beast was so heavy he could feel its weight pummeling the earth behind him, gaining fast.

It was the matter of one moment. Just as razored ivory slashed at his leg, Sky jerked it away, his running leap taking him just past one pain to others—hands scraping bark, head crashing through smaller branches that whipped and stung—to a bigger one that drove the air from his lungs with the force of his arrival.

Somehow he wrapped his arms around a branch and clung, somehow swung his legs once more beyond the reach of the slashing tusks. Then he was up, on the branch, with no clear idea of how he'd gotten there.

He looked down . . . at the beast that had jerked to

a stop and now seemed about to make the same leap Sky had. It even came up on its hind legs, its snout so close Sky could feel the hot breath on the leg he snatched away. Then, with a grunt of fury, it dropped down, turned . . . and emitted a low squeal that could only have been delight. Sky looked . . . and saw that Kristin hadn't made it into the trees, though she'd had the time. Ingvar was standing right at the forest's fringe at the far end of the field, arms at his sides, eyes closed. Within the Viking's beard, Sky could see his lips moving.

"Kristin!" he yelled. But Ingvar did not stir. With a grunt, the boar trotted forward.

What was she doing? Then, shocked, he realized—she was trying to bring out another Fetch! But she had never done it before without the use of runes and sacrifice. He had tried to teach her, as Pascaline had taught him, to just . . . step out. But they'd never seemed to find enough time, a quiet enough moment.

This was not it! "Kristin!" he screamed again. The boar was halfway there. Any moment it could break into a charge, smash into Ingvar's helpless body. Sky knew how fast these beasts moved, and he was no match.

But he had something within that moved faster. And he *had* done this before, many times. It was a place within him—like Bjørn, like Tza. The sun was still in the sky—but not far away, a full moon was making its way over the lip of the world. Perhaps it was close enough. Perhaps here, at the end of all journeys, he didn't need moonlight anyway.

He fell. But it was not two feet that took the impact but four paws, and the moment they hit the ground they powered him forward.

In ten strides, the wolf came level with the boar, just now beginning to charge. Ahead, Sky could see Kristin-Ingvar. She still hadn't moved, hadn't opened the Norseman's eyes. There was nothing else Sky could do. "Hey, Sigurd," he called.

Once, in Corsica, under a full moon, a wolf had killed a man. And it was so easy! But when, under another moon, he had tried to tackle a boar . . . well, even a werewolf had its limitations.

But now he had no choice—he leapt. Wolf teeth sank into the boar's neck; it gave a squeal, turned sharply aside. With his eyes buried in thick bristle, Sky felt, but could not see, the boar's flank sideswipe Ingvar. Then he was oblivious to everything but the fight, trying to use his weight, his wolf cunning, to pull the beast down. But the boar was strong and jerked harshly, first to one side, then the other. Finally, with a mighty shrug of its shoulders, the boar whipped Sky away, over, legs flailing. He tried to twist, to land upright. But he was too close to the ground and a foreleg smashed into it. He heard something snap, felt it a moment later, until all feeling was lost in the tumbling.

The boar stood square to him, its piggy eyes

narrowed. Then, with another snort, it began to move slowly toward the wolf. Sky got onto three feet, dragged himself a few paces, stopped.

So did the boar. Jaws opened . . . and Sigurd's voice emerged between the two cruel teeth. Sky had seen him talk as several animals, but it was not something he'd ever get used to. "Well, Grandson," Sigurd said. "At last, we reach the end. And it could have been so different. What a pity!"

There was nothing Sky could say. Both knew it. With what could almost have been a sigh, Sigurd took a step forward, lowered his head. . . .

The scream surprised them both, preceding the leap by a second. And though a wolf's claws couldn't grip a boar's pelt, a lynx's could. Did, judging by Sigurd's shriek of pain, the boar's violent twisting to shake off the wildcat on his back. Then teeth joined claw, and the lynx had the agility to hold that a wolf did not.

The bodies thrashed this way and that, the ground churning beneath them. They were on the very ground where Bjørn and Ingvar had made their first stand, and the bows that had been broken before were now smashed to kindling. Sky managed to drag himself a few paces farther away, just avoiding being crushed by the two raging beasts. There was little else he could do but watch and hope.

Kristin's lynx had power . . . but it was one-quarter the size of the boar. The larger animal ran forward, then jerked to a stop, too sharply for the lynx, whose claws at last ripped clear. The momentum hurled the wildcat forward, over the boar's uplifted tusks but downward, hard into the hard ground. The lynx crumpled . . . and then it wasn't a lynx anymore. Kristin herself lay there. Beside her, a mere arm's reach away, lay Ingvar, where the boar's sideswipe must have thrown his body a moment before Kristin's Fetch left it.

Slowly, the boar began to walk toward them.

It was Kristin—the real Kristin, or her Fetch at least, not her animal spirit, not Ingvar—that did it for Sky; that and the sight of Sigurd, saliva dripping from his huge jaws, tusks gleaming. Wolf eyes closed, he took a deep breath . . . and fur was gone, four legs, too, though the last was transformed into a hand clearly broken, fingers twisted up at ludicrous angles.

But it was his left hand. The power for his ax was mainly in the right—and Death Claw was in reach.

The boar was nearly past him. He didn't even have time to reverse the weapon to its cutting edge. He'd never have the strength of Bjørn. But he had enough to bring the weapon over in a high arc and smash its blunt back down onto the boar's crested spine.

CHAPTER TWENTY-SIX

RUNESTONES

Six bodies lay there. One, Henri de Barfleur, was dead. Five were alive. Two were Vikings—Bjørn, on his back; Ingvar, beneath the tree he'd been flung against in the struggle between wolf and boar. Both seemed to be breathing easily. Easier certainly than their descendants, all three taking in huge, ragged gulps of air.

Three human bodies, or their Fetches anyway—Kristin, lying facedown; Sky, clutching his ax; and Sigurd. For the boar had transformed, too, become the grandfather Sky was now used to. Not the frail old man he'd first met in the mountains of Norway, but a man in his prime, hair unsilvered, eyes clear . . . and full of pain. Behind the pain, fierceness still raged, so Sky held his ax all the tighter. He wasn't sure if he could lift it again; he'd put everything he'd had into that one disabling stroke. But if his enemy came for him, Sky knew he'd have to try.

Then Sigurd gave a strange kind of smile. "Grandson," he murmured, "I think you may have broken my back."

Sky dragged himself up to a sitting position, shakily stood. Wordless, he moved past Sigurd to Kristin and turned her over. Sky could see the bruise of impact spreading in red over her forehead. She must have smashed headfirst into the ground. But she was starting to breathe more normally, at least. He turned her onto her side, untwisted her limbs, then picked up the ax again and looked back.

If his back *was* broken, at least Sigurd was moving, using his hands to pull himself across the ground, his legs leaving a trail in the grass of the meadow. He was making for the stump of an old tree a few feet away, and when he reached it he pulled himself up, leaned his back against it. The effort had brought sweat to his face, made the skin white. But his eyes still had that mysterious smile in them, and Sky, his hand held before him like a broken wing, his cousin's unconscious body at his feet, was suddenly infuriated by it.

"Why are you smiling like that?" he spat. "You've just lost!"

"Have I?" The smile spread, the mouth widening. "Do you think so, Sky?"

"Yes." He took a step toward the prone man. "You're the one on the ground with the broken back.

And that," he said, gesturing with Death Claw, "is the sound of a battle taking its natural course."

They both listened for a moment to the distant sea-roar of conflict. "No," Sigurd replied. "That is the sound of a battle yet to be decided." He bent forward, the movement paining him. "Do you remember how the history books say it ended?"

"Duke William and the Normans won—"

"Yes, but more than that. . . ." Sigurd closed his eyes. "They fought all day, a terrible day of wounds and blood and death. In the end, victory hinged on a moment, one small moment. It is said that Harold looked up—and took an arrow in the eye. The world turned at that moment. Without that moment it would have turned . . . differently."

Despite himself, Sky couldn't help the question. "How do you mean 'without'?"

"Henri de Barfleur is one of Duke William's closest friends. He has ridden stirrup to stirrup with him into a dozen battles. Before that arrow flies, in the chaos of a charge, all he'd have to do is reach over, slip his sword under William's armor . . . and the Norman leader would fall first. His men would break and flee. Harold and all he believes in will triumph. The runes. A land where the Fetch lives." The smile grew. "The world turns."

A huge part of Sky wished it could be true. It made him look now to the center of the field, to where the Norman knight, Henri de Barfleur, lay. "But he's dead."

"He is. He died at the battle." Sigurd nodded. "But Bjørn lives."

"Bjørn?" Sky looked beyond the dead ancestor, to a living one.

"Henri's coat of mail would fit. His helmet too. Bjørn knows how to ride a horse, knows how to use a sword. Behind the Barfleur shield, the 'S' upon it, he could ride up next to William and . . . do what must be done." Sigurd pointed. "Bjørn loves King Harold. He'll want this."

Sky looked again at the younger Viking, saw his ice-white face. "You nearly killed Bjørn," he said. "I saved him. But he has lost a lot of blood. He'll be putting on no armor for a while. So you can't use him in your plans."

Sigurd waved his hand impatiently. "Ingvar then. Look, he stirs. It is not even midday yet, and the battle goes on till sunset. He'll revive."

Sky shook his head. It was as if a mist filled it, stopped him thinking. There was something here that he didn't understand. "But why would Ingvar do that?"

"He wouldn't," Sigurd said softly. "But you would."

"What?"

Sigurd leaned forward, his voice still low. "Come, Sky. Possess Ingvar! You know you want to. Hunger to! He's older than Bjørn, a man, a warrior. Feel his strength. Live his life. Take him! Ride to save your king!"

The mist cleared—and Sky actually laughed. "You . . . you *think,* after all I've been through, everything I've had to do . . . to learn, in order to stop you, that I will now . . . *help* you in your madness?"

"No, Grandson." Sigurd closed his eyes again. "You'll help yourself to become a god."

It was such an absurd word, it took all other words away. All Sky could do was stare at his grandfather, lying there with his eyes closed and that smile on his face.

"Do you remember, Sky, how I told you once of the first time I ever saw you? How I knew you were the one born to finish what I had started?"

Sky found his voice. "That was just another lie, to get me on your side. Get me to help you to kill, so you could move your spirit on."

"It was no lie. I needed to move on, yes. But not for me. For you! I needed to be there, to guide you, teach you. And then, the most important role I had to play—to lay obstacles in your path and watch you climb over them, one by one. Till you were strong enough, wise enough, to make the decision you will make today."

Sky stepped closer. "You're saying that all the ordeals I went through, they were all to—to—"

"To prepare you for your moment of destiny. This one, here now—when you choose to become a god. Yes, Sky. That's exactly what I am saying."

"I can't choose!" he snapped. "Gods are . . . well, *divine.*"

Sigurd nodded. "The Norse gods were divine . . . but they arose from man. Made from the earth, grown in the soil, forged in the fires of Ordeal. Odin hung himself on Yggdrasil, the world tree, for nine days. Sacrificed himself to himself, the poem says. Suffered. Gave an eye for a drink of wisdom, his whole being for the runes with which he could reshape the wyrd of the world. That's when he truly became a god! And you have suffered, like him. You have learned to kill. To heal. You have lived other lives, as men, as women, as beasts. You have transformed the forces of the world into shapes cut into stone."

"Are you claiming"—the thought nearly choked the words in Sky's throat—"that you *let* me win?"

"Oh no, blood of my blood," Sigurd replied, ferocity in his voice. "I did everything I could to defeat you. I would have killed you, or possessed you, if I had been able. I wanted to be the one to change history and become a god! But no matter what I tried, my wyrd was unalterable. It was set down the very first time I carved and cast the runestones." His voice faded. "Clearly I was only ever destined to lead you to this point. You are the one destined to move beyond it. Your triumph over me proves it."

"You're lying." He pointed at Bjørn. "You just tried to kill him. Our ancestor. If I hadn't healed him—"

"Ah, but, Sky," Sigurd said softly, "you did."

"No!" Sky yelled. "I don't believe you. It's just more lies. You're just trying to manipulate me again—"

"No. I am only trying to guide you to what you most desire. As I always have." He nodded, eyes glowing. "Think, Sky! Would you truly not have wanted to do everything you have done? Lived the lives you have? Would you rather still be a lonely, yearning schoolboy? Or a god?"

Sky stumbled forward. His knees felt weak. But within him, some certainty was fading as he recognized the truth of those words. What he'd lived had been extraordinary. Even with the prices he'd paid, and the terrible hunger he felt even now, he wouldn't wish to go back. Yet . . . "You can't just become a god. It's not like a . . . a club you apply to join."

Sigurd opened his eyes. "Shall I tell you the only thing left to do? You just have to *choose* to do it. To stretch out your hand, as Odin stretched for the first runes, and snatch up your destiny."

Sky stared back. The shock, the absurdity of the words, had faded. Something in them was pulling at him, beyond his conscious mind. A desire he knew had been there from the very beginning, that he'd tried to suppress. He'd fought it for so long. Fought it now. "But why would I want to be a god?" he said.

"Why? Ask why the sun must rise. Because it is inevitable. It *is* your wyrd. Your ultimate destiny." He studied Sky for a long moment. "You still doubt? What will convince you?" He smiled. "I know . . . something you truly believe in, that you are a master of. Come, Sky! Let us read your destiny one last time in the runestones."

Sky felt the pull in the word. "Runestones?"

"Yes." Sigurd shifted up, though it obviously pained him to do so, pointed. "There is a bag, around Henri's neck, under his armor. Fetch it here."

Unable to resist, not wanting to, Sky walked to the center of the field and the dead knight lying there. This other ancestor's eyes were open, staring from either side of the havoc that Tza's stone had wreaked on his forehead. Sky brushed his fingers across the lids, closing them, before he dug beneath the mail shirt, found a leather strap, pulled it. The bag emerged, the stones within clinking.

He was about to turn back when he realized what was in his hands. Runestones, carved by Sigurd, like the first set he'd ever held, which had set him upon the path. No, which had shoved him onto the path. The thought sent him on . . . to Bjørn. This other ancestor—his other self—was looking a little less pale. He did not disturb him, just awkwardly untied the leather pouch from his belt with his one good hand.

"Good, Sky," Sigurd said on his return. "Give them—" He paused, seeing that Sky held two bags. "What's that?"

Sky lobbed one bag across. It fell with a clink onto Sigurd's chest. Then he lifted the other. "They are my stones, Sigurd. I carved them on the march down from the North. I cannot let a runecast of yours dictate my future again. Nor the world's. I choose my own runes."

Sigurd stared at him for a long moment, then nodded. "I wouldn't have it any other way."

With his teeth, Sky loosened the leather tie at the bag's neck, tipped the stones out. Opposite him, Sigurd did the same. Swiftly, both turned them until only their granite backs showed. Finally, Sky reached inside his pocket, dug the last rune out, the one that had killed Henri de Barfleur. *Raidho,* the journey to, and of, the Dead. Ancestor's blood still stained it, lining the cuts. He didn't even try to rub it off, just set it down.

Hands dropped, swirled. Two voices spoke the invocation as one.

"Odin. All-Father. Guide me now."

Then each withdrew three stones. There was no hesitation. Three came unbidden, were laid in a row before them. They pressed their palms upon them. Sky looked across at his grandfather, then down at the back of his hand, and closed his eyes.

In the end, wasn't it always going to come down to the runestones?

All sounds were gone. The distant battle, the breathing of those around them—Kristin sprawled on the ground, Ingvar close beside her, Bjørn nearby. The sight of them gone, too, when Sky finally opened his eyes. A mist had risen, shrouding them in gray. They were in Time, and out of it. Within this world, and beyond it.

There was no grandfather and grandson now. All boundaries had dissolved—time, place, family. They were simply two rune readers. And one way or another they were going to shape the wyrd of the world.

Each lifted his hands. "I will begin," said Sigurd. And he turned his first rune over.

It didn't surprise Sky that it was the "M" of *Ehwaz,* the horse. The rune of the Fetch, too, the rune Sigurd had burned into his disciples' minds before he tried to kill most of them. And it was the two of them, their Fetches, sitting there.

"Ehhhhwaaaaz!" chanted Sigurd, his voice deep, using the sound of it, which was a part of its power. His hand moved before him, carving the rune into the air, as Kristin had carved them in the mountains. Power forming there like smoke, gathered, sent to Sky. He could feel that power sink into his chest, the hum of it resonating within him.

"Ehwaz," Sigurd said. "Fetch and Man. What wonders has your Fetch seen! What adventures have you lived! A gift of the gods to all humanity that so few can see. Your gift." His voice softened. "And remember what you thought was the price? Your love of possession? It is not price. It is reward, payment for all your suffering. Think of what awaits you! What lives you have yet to live!"

"Kristin would say that's not living, that's stealing. I'd be feasting on other people's lives."

"Kristin!" Sigurd smiled. "She said that before she experienced the wonder of possession. She wouldn't say that now." He gestured beyond the mist. "Sometimes I think she's even more like me than you are. She'd recognize all the good one can do. Think, Sky! All these people, all these great minds and talents. People who would have labored alone can labor together . . . because of you! Think of the results of that! In a world you create by one simple act here today."

I could do nothing but good. I would have that power.

The thought nearly had him rising, the desire to begin, the hunger to possess. He could feel it in his chest, where Sigurd's rune still hovered in smoke. But then he looked down, saw his own runestones. His own choices. He reached, turned. . . .

"Aaaalgiiiz!" he intoned as soon as he saw it, the sound vibrating deep within him, scattering Sigurd's rune there, its hold on him. "This speaks of protection, of blocking an attack. It is the elk's horns raised against you." He leaned forward. "It tells me that what you are offering with *Ehwaz* comes at too great a price. Even for me. I have felt it, that addiction. That desire! And of course I want more. But"—he took a deep breath—"if I gave in to it, it wouldn't be part of my life. It would be my whole life."

Sigurd shrugged. "*Algiz* could tell you that. Yet

runes are never read in isolation, are they? Let's see." As he spoke he reached to his second stone; but before he lifted it, he looked up and smiled. "For are there not many kinds of desire?"

He turned the stone over.

"Feeehuuu!"

They both recognized it. That kind of desire.

"Fehu," Sigurd said, in a normal voice. "Cattle, of course, the raising of them being the way our ancestors grew and prospered. But it's more than that, isn't it? It's growth by coming together. Cattle breeding with cattle to produce more of their kind." His voice sank to a whisper. "It's the joining together. Not of man and spirit. Man and flesh. Man and woman."

"It's love," Sky said softly.

"Yes, Sky. Love. You've always been so alone—I felt your terrible, deep loneliness for those few seconds I was inside you." The voice was soft, so gentle. "There have been your parents, of course. They love you. But you always needed more. All those moves—house to house, school to school. Always the stranger, rarely the friend. Yet in all that time, there has been one constant, hasn't there? One who knows you, one who you know."

"Kristin," Sky murmured.

"Kristin." Sigurd leaned forward. "But she has become something more than a cousin, hasn't she? More than a friend?" The voice dropped to a whisper. "I know what happened between you in the mountains."

"Know?" Sky said weakly. "How can you know? We don't know ourselves."

"You do. It seems easier to deny it, safer. But you are denying yourself your greatest desire—an end to your aloneness." He smiled. "In the tale of Ragnarók, there are two who survive: Lif and Lifthrasir." He reached out, though Sky could see the pain the movement caused him. Grabbing Sky's shoulder, he pulled him closer in, whispered, "Remember! Just as Odin had Freya . . . every god must have a goddess."

He released him, and Sky sank back. The mist that was around them seemed to invade him, fill his every pore. Yet it wasn't cold now, it was warmth *after* cold, the greatest kind, the warmth he'd felt in the mountains when the storm had chilled them, blinded them, sent them back to the tent, he and Kristin falling into each other, through each other, on, back . . .

What *had* happened between them? Whatever it was, didn't he want it again . . . and more? And yet, something lingered, some question. . . .

He reached down, turned his second rune. . . .

If it was sung, it was sung in his head. If a part of him had hoped for denial, as *Algiz* had denied, he was disappointed. And yet how could he be? Because the rune before him now confirmed Sigurd's rune, amplified it with its . . . Glory!

That's what it was. *Wunjo.* Glory itself! And joy, too, the boundless joy of a split soul rejoined. It transformed *Algiz,* no longer needed for protection. The two spoke of reunion. Fetch and man. Kin to kin. Cousin to cousin.

Man to woman.

He was on his feet, with no memory of standing. He tried to peer through the walls of the mist cave that surrounded them. Wanted to break through them, to run to Kristin, wake her, hold her, love her, tell her that the loving was right. It was sanctioned by the gods. The runestones had just told him so.

"Sky!"

It was Sigurd's voice, still within the gray cave. He looked down, saw his grandfather reach and turn his final stone. . . .

"Othaaaalaaaa!"

And there it was. The rune that had begun it all, that had stuck to his fingers in the attic when he'd first discovered his grandfather's legacy. Rune of ancestors, of the summoning of them. It had brought him to Sigurd, Sigurd to him.

"Yes, Grandson. Son. Father. *Othala* is all this and more. It is your ancestors no longer whispering their secrets in your blood. It's the secrets . . . revealed!" His voice rose. "This is the beginning. This is the end. This is all our destinies, throughout Time, you the inheritor of us all. Because . . . don't you see? You have worked your way through every single runestone now! Every one! Used the power of each to arrive at this moment—when you will take up one ancestor's sword, ride with the courage of another, thrust deep with the skill of a third"—his voice soared to a mighty shout—"and remake the world!"

"Yes!"

The mist was fraying. He could see that he was standing again in a clearing in a forest. Around him were his kin. Bjørn and Ingvar. Dead Henri. Kristin, his beloved. Sigurd, on the ground. His teacher. His grandfather who he was so like. The one who had set him onto the path that led . . . here! "Ingvar waits. Your destiny waits," his teacher whispered. "Seize it!"

The mist was almost gone, taking doubt with it. Sky took a step, another. The sound of battle grew loud again. And how he loved a battle! He came to Ingvar, whose eyes were fluttering behind his lids. Sky bent over him and felt his spirits bending with him, all those who would accompany him to glory. Bjørn would bring his berserker rage; Tza, her murderous skills and the courage of a wolf. And Meg! Mad Meg was with him most now. He could hear her laugh as he reached, just as she had reached to another man's chest, to press hands through, down. . . .

"*What* did you say?"

Was it even him who had spoken? It didn't sound like his voice, any of his voices. But it made him turn back. Something Sigurd had just said had slipped into his mind, like a sword slipped under a chain-mail coat. What was it?

He stood there, swaying, trying to think. Sigurd

shouted, "Go! Go! The battle calls!" But he couldn't move. Not until he remembered . . .

Then he did, and he walked back, step by stumbling step. Passing Death Claw, half hidden in the long grass, he bent to pick it up.

"Why are you here still?" Sigurd was trying to raise himself from the ground. "The battle is reaching its climax. Your moment calls."

Sky stopped, swayed. "You just said . . . said I'd worked through every runestone."

"Yes," replied Sigurd impatiently. "And you have returned again to the beginning, to *Othala*. Rune of ancestors. And all of us tell you now to *go*!"

Sigurd shouted it. Sky's voice was a soft contrast.

"But I haven't. In attics, in graveyards and caves, on floors and fields, wood and stone I have carved and cast. Yet there's one rune that has never featured in any of my seeking."

"It doesn't matter. . . ."

Sigurd's hand had moved forward, toward Sky's runecast, to the one granite back that remained. With a swift motion, Sky lifted the ax and jabbed one curving tip between Sigurd's hand and the rock. Then he bent, till his head was only a hand's breadth from his grandfather's.

"Is this it? The stone that's truly the end of the journey?"

Sigurd stared up at him. Something in his eyes. Placing the ax tip under the runestone, Sky flicked.

It was just a stone amongst stones, lines cut into it like all the others. Two triangles, points touching, an hourglass on its side. And yet it almost blinded Sky, as the sunrise can do. He closed his eyes, but the imprint of the symbol was etched inside his lids, flashing on and off, rising into his skull, lodging there, spreading over his mind.

"You know what it is, Sigurd?"

"It is *Dagaz*. The day. And it means—"

"I know what it means!" Sky didn't need to shout, didn't even need to open his eyes. Not when he held the sunrise within them. "It is the return of light. It is the banishing of the dark. Your darkness, Sigurd. What you were trying to bring down upon the world."

"No!"

"Yes. I can see again, by its light. See Kristin, who I love more than anyone . . . but not in that way." He smiled. "Really, not in that way. I can see Bjørn, who has his own life to live. Lives, perhaps, for he is a traveler too. See Ingvar. See myself, as I have become: Sky March. Rune-reader. Wyrd-shaper. Man and Fetch. But a god?" He shook his head. "No. Never a god."

At last, he opened his eyes, blinked against the brightness of the runestone and the day, watched as the last fingers of mist were pulled back into the ground . . . pulling Sigurd with them. His solidity was fraying, his edges turning to light. He knew it, too; Sky could see that on his fading face.

"You are killing me," he gasped.

"No, I'm not . . . *Grandfather,*" Sky said. It was the first time he had called him that in an age. "How could I be?" He turned away. "You're already dead."

He thought he heard a last whisper then . . . though it might have been the breeze shifting the grass blades in the meadow. Or maybe it was just the final exhalation that we all must make. Even Sigurd.

He glanced back . . . to nothing. The breeze rose up into the branches, shaking loose the last of the leaves there. He caught one, the red and gold of a chestnut, as he walked toward Kristin.

CHAPTER TWENTY-SEVEN

THE DATE

As he passed Ingvar Sky glanced down . . . and saw that the Viking's eyes were now doing more than just moving behind his lids. They were beginning to open.

Sky hurried past him. He went behind Kristin, grabbed her by her jacket collar. It was tough one-handed, but, fortunately, his cousin had fallen right where meadow turned again to forest. Breathing hard, he was able to drag her about ten feet through the fallen leaves and collapse behind a tree.

He peered around it. Watched Ingvar sit up, lift a hand to his head. The Norseman rubbed it, groaned, then began to look wildly around. Sky saw him spot Bjørn, get up fast and run to his brother, kneeling to check him. Then he stood again, tipping an ear to the battle sounds, relentless in the distance.

"Take him," Sky breathed. "Take him away!"

Ingvar bent again. This time, though, he lifted Bjørn

onto one shoulder. With a grunt, he walked to the forest path and headed down it—away from the fight. He passed within a few feet of Sky. But Bjørn's body was between them, and anyway, the big Viking was concentrating on where he put his feet.

Sky watched them until the trees took them from his sight. "Go well," he whispered. He felt an emptiness where Bjørn had been. But his ancestor had been returned to his destiny, as Sky had gone to his. He doubted he'd ever see him again. But he knew he would always be there.

Kristin moaned, caught between sleep and consciousness. He thought she would wake soon and decided to let her do it by herself. After all he'd been through, it was good to just sit there, wait, and listen to the battle. Think of Harold making his last stand, his housecarls around his dying body. Sky would have liked to have seen that. He'd have liked it even more if somehow history *had* been different, and he could go as Bjørn to the fireside tonight and tell the tale of Harold's great victory. But he couldn't. All he could do was close his eyes, cradle his broken hand in his lap, and wait for his cousin to wake up.

And then she did. Sat up quite suddenly, her arms flailing around. He leaned back to avoid them, called gently, "Kristin! Kristin!"

Her eyes opened, searched around, unable to focus. Finally they settled on him. "Sky," she mumbled.

"How are you?"

"Terrible." She raised a hand to her forehead. "Ouch," she said, fingering the bruise. "My head!" She squinted at him, one eye closed. "How are you?"

He showed her his swollen hand, the fingers bent at odd angles. "Ow," she said again, reaching toward it, stopping halfway, whipping her head around. Then she was up and staggering back into the clearing. He followed. "Where are the Norsemen?" she demanded.

"Gone." Sky jerked his thumb over his shoulder. "Getting away. I don't know where to." He chewed on his lip. "I hope they'll be all right."

"Bjørn and Ingvar?" she mumbled. "Those are two boys who can take care of themselves." Then her eyes went wide. "Henri's there. But where's Sigurd?"

"Gone too."

"Gone as in . . . gone to the battle? Gone to sleep?"

"No. This time I think he's finally . . ." He shrugged. "Gone."

Her eyes focused on him completely. "What happened?"

"Nothing much. Aside from Sigurd offering to turn me into a god."

"What?"

"Don't worry—I said no."

"Am I dreaming this?" She shook her head to clear it. "You had better tell me everything. Now." She sat down and looked hard at him.

He sat, too, and told her. Not everything; he wanted to spare himself some blushes. The gist, and quickly.

"So you're saying it's over? Finally? Totally?"

"Yes."

"But—"

He held up the unbroken hand against her horde of questions. "More later. That battle's going to end soon, and I suspect there'll be a lot of people running through these woods. They might think we are a bit strange." He gestured to the modern clothes their Fetches wore. "And strange in 1066 could get us a sword thrust." He stood, stuck out his good hand to help her up. On their feet, they leaned against each other for a moment, breathing hard. Neither was in great shape.

"Where are we going?" she asked.

Standing up had seemed pretty ambitious. Now he had no clue. "Uh . . . I suppose we . . . try to return to our lives?"

"To the car crash? Not appealing."

"We have to sometime, Kristin." He wasn't sure he liked the look in her eye. "Unless you've got a better idea?"

Under the bruise, her eyes sparkled. "Yes, actually, I do. Let's go back."

"You're delirious. That's what I just said."

"No . . . *back*!" She jerked a thumb over her shoulder, and he even looked. "No, fool!" she said. "Back in *time.* Keep going."

"What—"

"Listen! We don't know what happened to us back there . . . then. The car crash, yeah?" She pointed to her head, his hand. "These could be the least of our worries. Do you want to return and face all that?"

"Uh, not really, but—"

"Forget 'but.' We will go back then sometime, sure. Back to that exact moment. Probably we'll have no choice. But while we do have a choice, why don't we just, you know . . . put it off for a while? There are lots of other ancestors to explore, right?"

Her eyes were shining so much he laughed. "Yeah, but—sorry. *But* now we really don't know who we'll go into. Or when. Sigurd's family tree only went back as far as 1066."

"Good! So we're off his plan." She raised a hand. "I, for one, am pleased. We can do our own stuff."

Sky scratched his head. "Chances are, though, we won't go back aware." A thought came, with a shiver. "Unless we recite the runes of awakening as we go."

"Why would we want to do that?" Kristin snorted. "And have all that responsibility about altering Time? No way. I want to live an ancestor's life as them, not me." She grinned. "And kill whoever I feel like."

He knew she was joking. Well, *thought* she was.

"We'd be lost in Time. And"—he spoke louder to stop her interrupting—"we're always drawn to need, right? Mine might be different than yours. We might get separated."

She slapped his arm, the one his broken hand was attached to. He yelped. "Idiot! If we aren't aware back there, together or not, we won't know the difference."

He rubbed his arm, studied her, the wild excitement on her face. "But, Kristin," he said, "you're forgetting something."

"What?"

"The price. There's always a price to be paid. You want to have another experience like . . . like you had in Matthew?"

"N-no!" The smile barely left her face. "Matthew was horrible. But what price did I pay, apart from the bad memories? None that I can see," she laughed. "And Ingvar? It was so cool being in him. I want more of those."

"Yeah, but there's no guarantee that you'd get them." Sky shook his head. "And what need would you be drawn to now? None that's obvious. You'd be like . . . a tourist!" Suddenly something their grandfather had said came into his mind: She's even more like me than you are. "Kristin," Sky said, putting a hand on her arm, "this is the sort of thing Sigurd would do."

"Sky, come on!" She shrugged his grip off. "Look, I can see why you wouldn't want to go—"

"Part of me does, of course—"

"But the other part is wary. Understandably so, after all you've experienced, all you've taken in. Plus, you think of it as an addiction, right? That if you feed it, you'll increase its hold on you?" He nodded. "Well, I don't feel that way. I've hardly begun. I learned to free my Fetch here today, unaided." She smiled. "Did you see me? Split-second timing, too, just before you and the boar sideswiped Ingvar. Cool or what? And now I just want a chance to, you know . . . explore some more! Get more experience under my belt before . . . I go back, to a car crash, a lot of pain . . . and your very angry mother!" She laughed. "She'll blame me, you know."

Sky didn't laugh. He just looked at his cousin, whom he loved. How could he deny what made her *her*? Wasn't she the one who'd led him down all those walls? "Kristin . . . ," he murmured.

"Look!" It was she who reached for his arm now. "Let's make a deal. You go . . . home. Look after us both, back there. Presumably, I'll be unconscious while my Fetch is a-traveling. So don't let them turn off my life support, 'kay!" She shook his arm. "Plus . . . well, the time you've spent back then has no relation to time in the present. I could spend a week, a month . . . then I'll probably wake up a few hours after you have. Something always sends you back to the present, right? To yourself."

"Sure, but . . . the something that sends you back could be horrible."

She overrode him. "I'll take my chances. I'll have a life and be back before you know it."

"And if you don't?" He frowned. "What if you do come *aware* back there somehow and decide not to return?"

"Well, then I'd be a very, very bad girl . . . and you'll just have to come and get me, won't you?" She frowned. "Tell you what, let's fix a rendezvous!"

Her sudden seriousness made him laugh. "But where? When? Er, both?"

She raised her bruised head, studied a cloud in the sky. From far away they heard a great shout. She tipped her head toward it. "What we need is another really famous date and place, like this one." She snapped her fingers. "Got it. One even you will be able to remember, Sky. *March*." She beamed. "The Ides of March."

"The what?"

"The Ides of March. Fifteenth of March to you. It was the day Julius Caesar was assassinated at the Capitol—in Rome. 55 BC."

"Oh, yeah. I saw the film." He nodded. "I think I'll remember that—if I get the chance."

"Plenty of Italian in your Corsican blood . . . *Marcaggi*! And my dad's Sicilian-American, so . . . should be some ancestors around. I'll see you there. Steps of the Capitol anytime from noon till three." She put the back of her hand to her forehead, struck a pose. "I'll be the one in the ravishing green toga."

"Are you asking me out on a date?"

She laughed. "We may already be married."

"I hope not! That didn't work out so well the last time."

They were both silent a moment, looking at each other.

"So," she said finally, stepping closer. "Are we agreed?"

What could he say? He knew he couldn't go, no matter how much a part of him wanted to. He couldn't handle many more ancestors moving inside him. But how could he deny Kristin what had, for a time, been such a wild and wonderful ride? "Agreed," he sighed.

"Hurray!" She hugged him, stepped back. "But how do we go?"

"The runes, of course." He led her over to the tree stump, where he and Sigurd had cast their destinies. And stopped. "That's weird," he said.

"Which spelling?"

"Just plain old strange." He pointed. "Sigurd's runestones? They're gone."

"So?" Kristin was shaking with impatience. "Maybe he's a draug now. So all he had is vapor. Serves him right." She pulled him down to the ground. "Come on."

He looked at the runecast he'd made. *Algiz. Wunjo. Dagaz.* It had helped him recognize Sigurd's trickery, helped him defeat his grandfather in the end. But it was a wonderfully optimistic cast in its own right. One to guide him in life perhaps? *Algiz,* protected . . . and protecting! Maybe there was a way he could protect people in the future. *Wunjo* spoke to that, to the glory of that.

He turned the two over, then lifted the last one, held it tight in his hand, closed his eyes.

Dagaz. It meant the whole day. So if it had been sunrise before, it was also sunset. An end and a beginning. He smiled. Suddenly, going back to his own life didn't seem such a bad thing to do. Not with runes like this to guide him. The car crash? He'd deal with it. School? Well, anyone who'd been offered, and turned down, godship could probably manage to graduate!

He opened his eyes again—to sunlight and his cousin's excited face. "Come on, Sky." She pressed her palm down into the runestones. "Are we walking or are we talking?"

He laid the last rune facedown, began to swirl them all. "Walking."

He stopped swirling, left his hand there beside hers. Then they said it together. "Odin. All-Father. Guide us now."

Each of them picked up a runestone. For a few seconds, both studied the simple lines carved into rock. Then, together, they leaned forward and placed their destiny before them on the ground.

To Steve McKie

AUTHOR'S NOTE

When I was five years old, I decided I was a god.

Well, near enough. I believed I could not be hurt, that I was invulnerable. To prove it, I encouraged several of the neighborhood kids to sit on a fence and throw rocks at me. I was about twenty feet away, and as they were five, too, most of their attempts were pretty feeble. If the odd stone hit me, it had no force. "See!" I called. "I am a god."

Then a slightly bigger girl had a rethink. Instead of throwing straight, she took a larger stone . . . and lobbed it. I watched its arc through the air. I felt it smash onto my skull. I ran home crying, blood between my fingers.

It has been so wonderful, all these years later, to take my main character, Sky, from boy to the brink of god-dom!

And speaking of gods . . . originally, this novel was to be called *Ragnarók,* which those of you who have just read it will know was the last battle of the Aesir and the destruction of the world. But my editor thought the title might make people think the book was *about* Norse gods, which it is, but only a little. It's much more about possession, how it is achieved, at what cost. As ever, she was right, and I was happy to take her suggestion for the new title.

I can hardly believe we are at the end of this

journey. Three years ago I hadn't even begun to imagine Sky, Kristin, Sigurd, Bjørn, Tza, the Brakespeares, and all the rest. But, it is said, even the longest journey begins with a single step. I put one foot in front of the other, stumbled often, picked myself up, had the flashes, made the connections . . . and here we are! I know some authors plot ahead in great detail, but I don't. When I began writing *The Fetch,* I had only the vaguest idea of how the whole trilogy would end, beyond its location (the Battle of Hastings) and some high stakes—apocalypse!

My theory to keep me at my desk is quite simple—write what fascinates, amuses, or frightens me. The whole Runestone Saga has kept me intrigued—and sometimes terrified!—from the beginning. That's partly because it's such a personal story (if a tale about time-traveling killers, draugs, and Dream Hunters *can* be personal!). As I have written before, I am aware of some of the secrets that whisper in my blood—and not aware at all of others that affect the way I live. It was wonderful to journey with Sky and watch him figure out who he is. Writing him has helped me figure out some different parts of myself too. (Though I have tried to reassure my wife that "the berserker" is unlikely to appear at dinner parties!)

Writing what fascinates! *Possession* is full of my passions. A book that I loved as a ten-year-old was *Hounds of the King* by Henry Treece, all about Harold's housecarls and their last stand on Senlac Hill. I wept then, I smile now—because now I get to write about the battle! (There is also an old family tree somewhere that says I am descended from Harold, but I am not sure I believe it.) And what a battle it was. A true turning point in English history. I used various sources—*Hastings 1066* by Christopher Gravett from the Osprey series, *1066* by David Howarth. And I had to include one particular thing I read. When the English on the hill answered the Norman battle cry with their own: *"Ut! Ut!"* ("Out! Out!"), they were telling the invader, "Get out of my country!" Don't know why, but it makes my eyes water. Especially given the battle's result and consequences.

All through the saga I have been able to explore fascinating periods of history and myth. The Viking gods are beautifully described—and drawn—in *D'Aulaires' Book of Norse Myths.* In *Possession,* I also got to study the whole seventeenth-century witch thing, with Craig Cabell's book *Witchfinder General* a marvellous—and chilling!—guide to the Prickers. Yuck!

But it's not all creepy. I also play jokes on myself—Sky discovers the computer password to be the nickname of the soccer team I have supported all my life, Leicester City (who are usually dreadful!); Baron Homfrey, mentioned briefly on the Norman side, is another supposed ancestor, my surname descending from him.

Speaking of history, I should mention this book's main "eureka" moment. There are often several in a novel, when research and thought collide and fuse. This one happened in the British Library in London, when I was reading a Victorian book on runic inscriptions. One was found in a churchyard in Northern England, carved into a sundial sometime around—drumroll!—1066! They became the runes of awakening. For Meg. For Bjørn and Sky. For me!

I should also mention a couple of times I somewhat bent the history. Though knights were already adopting symbols to paint on their shields and pennants, heraldry was in its infancy in 1066—so the naming of knights by Robert is a little premature! Also, the news of William's invasion actually reached King Harold while he was at a victory feast about a week after Stamford Bridge, not the next day.

Also, the very acute observer of these books will notice there has been a small change of heart about runes. On deeper study, I agree with those rune masters who have guided me, especially Kveldulf Gundarsson in *Teutonic Magic* and D. Jason Cooper in *Using the Runes,* who say that runes cannot be reversed, that their meanings remain the same whether or not they're upside down. I wasn't sure about that to begin with, hence the effect of a reversed rune in *The Fetch.* I am now convinced that reversal is a hangover from tarot card readings, where upside-downness does affect meaning. Runes are irreversible.

Writing is a solitary business. All that sitting alone,

conjuring the spirits. Fortunately, it becomes more of a team game when you need it to be. And I am blessed with a brilliant team (if only Leicester City could say the same!). On the business side, there are my agents at ICM: Kate Jones, in London, who suggested this area of fiction to write in and shepherded me through it; her colleague in New York who helped sell it, Liz Farrell; and Margaret Halton, Liz Iveson, and Daisy Meyrick, who are spreading *The Fetch* throughout the world. I'd also like to mention the great Lawrence Tejada, who ensures I get paid efficiently and on time, so I can focus on books, not bank statements. Closer to home there's my ever-supportive wife, Aletha, always an early reader and acute commentator. And my son, Reith, three now, whose growth has paralleled *The Fetch*'s and who thinks that working is sitting down at the computer making up stories. So that's the brain-surgeon plan gone, then! I should again thank all at the brilliant Kidsbooks, Vancouver. And Jill, Scott, and Dean at the Granville Island Hotel, who sheltered and looked after me when I needed quiet to finish the first draft. (The latter two making it into the novel, not very gloriously!)

And then there's Nancy Siscoe. I know I praised her in the Author's Note to *Vendetta,* dedicating that book to her. But the debt that the whole saga owes her is enormous. When I went through her notes for *Possession,* there were many times I harrumphed, wrote an irritated comment on her comment, tried to move on. Inevitably, I looked back, scratched out my reaction, and implemented her note. This book was especially complex with all the ins and outs of spirits, the tying up of three books' worth of loose ends. She helped me render the complex clear. Always with humor, grace, and a clear message that she loves what I write and she just wants to help me make it a little better! I hope we continue to work together often.

Finally, this book is dedicated to my friend and brother-in-law, Steve McKie. I hadn't even begun to write *The Fetch* when, over a beer, I told him about my fears of trying to tell a story aimed at teens. Could I figure out what they'd want? Steve is a great reader but not in the writing trade at all—he's a welder. But he marked my path clearly for me. "Freak the little fellows out," he said. "Make them cry themselves to sleep."

I wrote it down and kept it above my desk. (Except he didn't say "fellows.")

I hope many of you have cried in terror, been freaked out, amused, and excited by this saga. And who knows? Perhaps there will be more to come. I said before that all journeys begin with a single step. They end with one as well, and in some ways, all endings are a little false, just the point chosen to stop at. Sky and Kristin, Bjørn and Ingvar, Tza and her child, the Brakespeares' children, even Sigurd? They all go on after I stop typing. And I know there are other characters out there whose Fetches may invade my dreams, with their own ideas about where they should go, what they should do . . . whose soul they should steal! Perhaps *Possession is* just one more step along the path.

As is written on a certain gravestone in Norway—*NON OMNIS MORIAR*.

And if it applies to people, why not to sagas?

Chris Humphreys
Vancouver, August 2008

A GUIDE TO THE RUNES

rune: a mark of mysterious or magical significance
(The Oxford English Dictionary)

Runa: secret, whisper *(Old German)*

Just as the word *alphabet* is taken from the first two letters of the ancient Greek alphabet *(alpha, beta),* so the Elder Futhark is named after the first six letters of the Old German alphabet: *F(ehu) U(ruz) Th(urisaz) A(nsuz) R(aidho) K(enaz).*

There are variations on each rune name, depending on whether it is from the Germanic, Old English, or Scandinavian Futharks. I use the Germanic (though even this has some variations)—the oldest, with the most runes, twenty-four. The order of the runes is consistent in this Futhark, except for the last two, *Othala* and *Dagaz,* which are often switched.

Runes have both literal and symbolic meanings. The symbolic meanings of each rune can change depending on the other runes in a particular cast—how they work together, for weal or woe.

Rune		Some Literal Meanings	Some Symbolic Meanings
Fehu	ᚠ	Cattle	Prosperity / Fertility
Uruz	ᚢ	Wild ox	Risky gain / Transition
Thurisaz	ᚦ	Thorn / Ice demon	Test / Berserker's rune
Ansuz	ᚨ	Mouth / Questions	Seeking advice / Answers
Raidho	ᚱ	Journey	Travel / Visiting one's dead
Kenaz	ᚲ	Torch	Initiation / Purification
Gebo	ᚷ	Gift	Sacrificing / Receiving
Wunjo	ᚹ	Glory / Joy	Untapped power / Thrust to destiny
Hagalaz	ᚺ	Hailstorm	Random, uncontrolled events
Naudhiz	ᚾ	Need / Necessity	Sudden power / Success
Isa	ᛁ	Ice / Spear / Staff	Freezing action / Challenge
Jera	ᛃ	Harvest	Rewarded effort

Eihwaz	ᛇ	Yew tree	Solutions/ Strengthening the will
Pertho	ᛈ	Dice cup	Chance
Algiz	ᛉ	Elk	Defense/Protection
Sowilo	ᛊ	Sun	Returning life/ Salvation
Tiwaz	ᛏ	Spear	Victory/Justice
Berkana	ᛒ	Birch tree	Purging/Atoning
Ehwaz	ᛖ	Horse	Fetch/Out-of-body travel
Mannaz	ᛗ	Man/Humanity	Perfected being/ Reason/Intuition
Laguz	ᛚ	All liquids	Essential life
Ingwaz	ᛜ	The people	Fascination/ Stored power
Othala	ᛟ	Inheritance	Blood secrets/ Summoning ancestors
Dagaz	ᛞ	Return of day	Moment of blinding truth/Banished dark

THIS IS A BORZOI BOOK PUBLISHED BY ALFRED A. KNOPF

Visit us on the Web! www.randomhouse.com/teens

Educators and librarians, for a variety of teaching tools, visit us at
www.randomhouse.com/teachers

Library of Congress Cataloging-in-Publication Data
Humphreys, Chris.
Possession / Chris Humphreys. — 1st ed.
p. cm. — (Runestone saga ; bk. 3)
Summary: Sky and Kristin travel to the seventeenth century to learn secrets from their ancestor, the witch Meg, then to the Battle of Hastings to use that knowledge to prevent their evil grandfather Sigurd from ever possessing another person.
ISBN 978-0-375-83294-9 (trade) — ISBN 978-0-375-93294-6 (lib. bdg.)
[1. Spirit possession—Fiction. 2. Supernatural—Fiction. 3. Time travel—Fiction. 4. Cousins—Fiction. 5. Grandfathers—Fiction. 6. Adventure and adventurers—Fiction.]
I. Title.
PZ7.H89737Pos 2008
[Fic]—dc22
2008004162

Printed in the United States of America
August 2008
10 9 8 7 6 5 4 3 2 1

First Edition